HARLEQUI[N]
Celebrates [...]

*Two decades of bringing you the very best
in romance reading.*

*To recognize this important milestone,
we've invited six very
special authors—whose names you're sure to recognize—
to tell us how they feel about Superromance.
Each title this month has a letter
from one of these authors.*

Although critically acclaimed author Anne Mather—
whose foreword appears in this book—has never
written for Superromance, she has been reading the
line since it began. "It is not difficult to see why
Superromances have become so successful," she
writes. "I'd recommend that anyone who is looking
for a longer, exciting read give them a try. I did, and
I've never regretted it."

The Newcomer by Margot Dalton is a worthy addition
to our anniversary lineup. Margot began writing
for Superromance in 1990 and has written 22 titles
for the line. In addition, she was written five
mainstream novels and has contributed to several
continuing series and anthologies.

In *The Newcomer*, readers are taken back to the
town of Crystal Creek, Texas. Margot wrote seven of
the original CRYSTAL CREEK series titles,
and Superromance is proud to present her newest
book about that friendly ranching community.

Dear Reader,

Almost ten years ago, Harlequin approached a number of authors with an exciting new idea. We were given the challenge of helping to create a central Texas town and ranching community, along with a host of exciting, heartwarming characters to populate this setting. The result was the 24-book CRYSTAL CREEK series, which has remained popular with readers since publication of the very first book in 1993.

As an author, I loved everything about writing the CRYSTAL CREEK books. So you can imagine my excitement when the Superromance editors suggested I might want to return to Crystal Creek with a new series of books. I could hardly wait! *The Newcomer*, the third book in this trilogy, shows what kind of tension can arise when a close-knit town is divided by the arrival of strangers. It also wraps up the stories of Bella, who appeared in the first book, and her sister Lucia, who was trying hard to save the Crystal Creek middle school in the second book of the trilogy. And it introduces Douglas Evans, a handsome, kilt-wearing Scotsman who has somehow become the mayor of a small town in Texas!

I loved making this nostalgic return to Crystal Creek. I hope you're enjoying it as much as I did.

Warmest regards,

Margot Dalton

Other Crystal Creek titles by Margot Dalton

Harlequin Superromance
#914—IN PLAIN SIGHT
#928—CONSEQUENCES

FOREWORD BY ANNE MATHER

The Newcomer

Margot Dalton

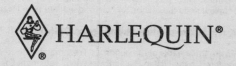

HARLEQUIN®

TORONTO • NEW YORK • LONDON
AMSTERDAM • PARIS • SYDNEY • HAMBURG
STOCKHOLM • ATHENS • TOKYO • MILAN • MADRID
PRAGUE • WARSAW • BUDAPEST • AUCKLAND

ISBN 0-373-70940-4

THE NEWCOMER

Copyright © 2000 by Margot Dalton.

This edition published by arrangement with Harlequin Books S.A.

® and TM are trademarks of the publisher. Trademarks indicated with ® are registered in the United States Patent and Trademark Office, the Canadian Trade Marks Office and in other countries.

Visit us at www.eHarlequin.com

Printed in U.S.A.

FOREWORD BY ANNE MATHER

I've been asked to write a brief foreword to celebrate the 20th anniversary of Harlequin Superromance, and I have to tell you, I was very flattered by the request. I have never written for Superromance myself, but I'm an enthusiastic book buyer, as well as a writer, and I have read many of the books over the years.

It's not difficult to see why Superromances have become so successful. Harlequin has always kept a close eye on what its readers want, and when Superromances were first published, they were much longer than they are today. But, as with all new ventures, there have been obvious refinements and the line has gone from strength to strength.

I started reading Superromances at their inception, and naturally, I had my favorites. Many writers who started out with Superromance are household names today—authors like Stella Cameron, Sandra Canfield, Janice Kaiser, to name a few—and you may still be lucky enough to find their early books. I'm fortunate enough to have a collection of many of these novels, and they bear favorable comparison to what is being written today.

Of course, these days a whole new batch of authors is making their mark with Superromances. It's a very fertile breeding ground, and I'm sure many of these writers will go on to become the household names of tomorrow. Whatever happens, I know Harlequin will support and encourage them in every way.

Because of their length, Superromances can explore character development in greater detail, and the stories reflect the lives of ordinary people—often in extraordinary situations. I'd recommend that anyone who is looking for a longer, exciting read give them a try. I did, and I've never regretted it.

Anne Mather

Anne Mather is a renowned and much-published author of romance and women's fiction—one of the world's most popular. She's particularly well-known for her work in the Harlequin Presents series. Her distinctive stories offer intense passion and high drama—an unbeatable combination!

CHAPTER ONE

THE CAROUSEL HORSES stood frozen in the misty chill of the February afternoon. Silver hooves pawed silently at the floorboards, dark eyes rolled wildly, while manes and tails streamed as if blown by the wind. A fitful sun broke through dark clouds above the hills, sparked fire from gold-mounted saddles and jeweled breastplates.

Lovingly, Douglas Evans caressed the blond mane of a fiery sorrel with bared yellow teeth, then knelt to examine a splintered board on the floor near the big tiger, whose jaws were drawn back in a menacing snarl.

The tiger had been discovered wrapped under layers of oilcloth in June Pollock's cellar, more than sixty years after the dismantling of the Crystal Creek carousel. Unlike many of the other animals, this one had hardly needed any restoration. Its broad striped back was worn smooth from the thousands of tiny riders who'd sat on him, wide-eyed and awed at their own daring, as the tiger paced slowly around the carousel platform.

"Unca Dougie," a small voice called from somewhere outside the carousel enclosure. "I'm cold."

"Put your brush down, Robin, and come up here," Doug said.

His rich Scottish brogue sounded loud and a little intrusive, even to his own ears, on this silent winter afternoon in the Hill Country of central Texas.

He smiled as his niece plodded up the carousel steps and tumbled at his feet in a bright plaid jacket and hood. She lay on her back and waved her green running shoes in the air.

Robin was four years old, a plump, happy little girl with golden curls, red cheeks and an irrepressible personality, as different from her older sister Moira as two children could possibly be. Doug loved his young nieces as if they were his own children, and spent a good deal of time worrying about them.

Especially nowadays...

Hiding his frown of concern, he bent and lifted Robin into his arms. Then he sat on the bench next to the tiger and cuddled the child, making a great show of putting his big hands over her ears and rubbing her cold cheeks.

She squirmed and giggled, forgetting her complaints, then settled contentedly against his denim jacket and looked around at the carousel. With a surreptitious glance at her uncle, Robin jammed her thumb in her mouth and began sucking it thoughtfully.

Doug gently removed the thumb and kissed her bright hair. She made no objection, just nestled more cozily in his arms.

"Tell me again about all the horses and stuff," she commanded.

Doug settled back and extended his long legs in blue jeans and heavy work boots.

"Well, this carousel is the most wonderful thing,"

he told the little girl, his burr becoming more pronounced, as it always did when he told stories to his nieces. "And the animals are verra, verra old."

"How old?"

"Almost a hundred years."

"Older than Mummy, then."

Doug chuckled. "Yes, my sweetheart, much older than Mummy. These fifty-four horses, and the lion and tiger and giraffe were hand-carved, every single one of them, by a man called Franz Koning who lived in Germany. For many years the carousel was one of this town's proudest possessions. But in the Great Depression, Crystal Creek lost its carousel," he said sadly.

Robin frowned with anxiety, which she always did at this point in her uncle's story.

"What happened?"

Doug cuddled the child, and reached over to stroke the tiger's glossy head. "It was broken up and sold, piece by piece, to the highest bidders. The horses and all these other animals were scattered all over the world."

"How did they get back here, Unca?"

"A very rich, very kind man found all the parts of the carousel, and paid a lot of money to have them restored to their former glory. Then he presented them as a gift to the town of Crystal Creek. This carousel is a symbol, my chickie."

Doug nuzzled her hair again. Robin was warm and heavy in his arms; he could tell she was getting sleepy.

"Symbol?" she asked, her eyelids fluttering drowsily.

"It stands for the pride of the town." Doug looked with satisfaction at the bright carousel in its enclosure on the lawn in front of the courthouse. "This is the jewel in our lapel, my darling. It shows that Crystal Creek has pride in itself and its history, and will always be a fine town to live in."

But Robin was asleep by now, slumping against his chest.

Carefully Doug made a nest for her on the bench, using his jacket to wrap her against the chill and taking care to cover her little shoes with the sheepskin-lined denim.

He bent to kiss her again, then went down the steps and around a corner to find his older niece working doggedly, applying a coat of green stain to the lower portion of the carousel enclosure beneath tall Plexiglas windows.

Doug looked with fondness at the child.

Moira was nine years old, a timid, serious little girl with big gray eyes, straight blond hair cut in a Dutch bob and a thin body in blue jeans and a parka.

The girl had a quaintly old-fashioned air about her, as if she should be sitting in some Victorian nursery, dressed in a pinafore and buttoned boots, doing her sums and letters on a slate. Moira was always quiet and self-contained, with little of the pushing or shouting common to most children her age, and none of her younger sister's cheerful ebullience.

Poor Moira carried the weight of the world on her shoulders, Doug thought with sympathy, picking up a brush to join her. And narrow, fragile shoulders they were, too.

"Robin fell asleep," he reported.

"Where is she?" Moira looked around in concern. Taking care of her impulsive younger sister was one of her responsibilities.

He gestured over his shoulder. "She's curled up on the bench next to the tiger."

"Is she warm enough?" Frowning, Moira dipped her brush carefully and squeezed excess stain onto the edge of the bucket.

Doug chuckled and reached out to touch his niece's shining cap of hair.

"Nine years old, but going on twenty-nine, you are," he said teasingly. "Take care of us all, don't you, Pumpkin?"

She smiled a little, then drew back tactfully from his hand. Unlike her sister, Moira disliked being touched or cuddled.

They worked in silence for a while. Doug, always sensitive to her moods, could tell something was bothering the child.

"So, Moira." He carried the pail of stain around on the grass and knelt to paint a new section. "What is it, then?"

She looked away from him, biting her lip. Doug studied the vulnerable line of his niece's neck, the pale curve of her little freckled cheek.

"Mummy cried last night," she said at last, her face still averted.

Doug's heart sank but he kept his voice deliberately casual. "Did she, now?"

Moira nodded, concentrating on painting a lower row of boards with extreme care.

"Well," Doug said with false heartiness, "as I

understand it, ladies cry quite often. When they're upset, it makes them feel better.''

Moira cast her uncle a skeptical glance. "How do you know about ladies? You've never even been married, and you're older than Mummy."

He threw back his head and laughed. "Indeed I am. In fact, I'm thirty-five years old and no wife anywhere in sight. But I've known a few ladies in my time, Moira dear, and they all seem to cry sooner or later."

She kept her face turned away, but he could see her lower lip quivering. "Mummy cries a lot, Uncle Doug. She's really worried."

Doug set the brush down. For the second time that afternoon, he picked up a child in his arms. He sat on the steps of the carousel, cradling this older niece who almost never allowed herself to be held.

"Yes, Mummy has some problems," he whispered into Moira's silky hair. "But you mustn't worry, dear. They'll get worked out."

Thoughtfully he gazed across the quiet streets, the church steeple and withered grass, the rolling hills that turned from blue to mauve to pale gray in the distance.

"Everything will work out," he said.

Moira twisted on his lap to give him a tearful, questioning glance.

"How do you know for sure? Just because you're the mayor?"

Doug laughed. "Oh, my sweetheart, I wish being the mayor of Crystal Creek gave me enough power to wave a magic wand and fix everybody's troubles."

"Maybe the magic lady will fix everything," Moira suggested.

"What magic lady?"

"You know." Moira glared at him impatiently. "The magic lady who drives around in her big car and looks at everything."

"Oh, no. Not that again," Doug said with a mock groan.

"Tell me about her, right from the start," Moira commanded.

Her uncle sighed. By now he was weary of the story he'd made up to entertain his nieces, but the children still loved to hear it.

"Well, I saw her again this past week, lovey," he said, squinting at the horizon.

"What did she look like?" Moira asked. "What was she doing?"

"She was a woman as lovely as a picture, Moira, in a big yellow Mercedes with California license plates. Doing the very same thing she's been doing for months—driving around very slowly and looking at our town."

"And from the very first time you saw her, you knew…" Moira prompted.

"I knew that huge changes were coming for Crystal Creek," he said obediently.

"But will the changes make Mummy stop crying at night?"

Doug's smile faded, and he hugged the child closer. "Your mother's problems are separate from the troubles of our town, my darling. But perhaps the magic lady will work everything out at the same time."

Moira wriggled from his grasp and stood erect, staring at the carousel with narrowed eyes. "I don't believe in the magic lady anymore," she said. "Nobody's seen her except you. I think you just made her up to have a story for Robin and me."

Doug thought about the big yellow car he'd first seen a few months ago, gliding silently past the hotel in the autumn sunlight.

And the beautiful dark-haired woman who sat at the wheel of the Mercedes, piloting her golden vehicle through the streets and avenues of Crystal Creek.

She'd looked around at his town with such intent, concentrated interest. And when she turned away, her profile was as finely sculpted as Waterford crystal.

"No," he told the child, falling into a soft brogue as he remembered. "I didna imagine her, my lassie."

"And she'll make everything better?"

"Ah, yes," Doug said with a hearty optimism he didn't feel. "One day soon our princess will reveal her plan, and we will all be verra, verra glad to hear it."

"You're crazy, Uncle Doug." Moira scrambled from his embrace and picked up her brush again. But she seemed a little reassured, and her face wasn't quite as tense.

Doug grinned and followed her down the steps to replace the lid on his bucket of stain.

"Let's go back for our scones and tea," he said. "You bring the paint cans and brush, and I'll carry that lumping great sister of yours."

While Moira collected the supplies, Doug lifted the sleeping Robin into his arms, still warmly wrapped in the denim jacket. They started up the street toward the Crystal Creek Hotel, a bright little procession in the silent winter afternoon, Doug making a conscious effort to slow his long strides so Moira could keep up.

"Do you like it better here than in Scotland?" she asked, trotting along at his side.

"Much better," Doug said briefly, glancing down at the child. "And how about you?"

"It rains all the time in Scotland. And the cities aren't clean like this."

"Exactly right, my pet." Doug grinned at his niece. "The weather is generally a lot better in Texas, even if it does get far too hot in the summer for any sane man to enjoy."

"But do you ever get homesick for Scotland?" Moira asked.

He thought it over. "Sometimes, but not for long. And you know what? As soon as I go back for a visit, I remember why I'm so fond of Texas."

"Mummy and Robin and I have never gone back there for a visit," Moira said.

"You girls and your mother only arrived a year ago," Doug said. "And Mummy's afraid that if you went home—" He fell abruptly silent, but Moira picked up on what he'd been about to say.

"She's afraid they wouldn't let us come back," the child said. "That's why Mummy cries at night, isn't it? Because we might have to leave Texas."

"Citizenship issues are too big a problem for a wee girl like you to worry about," Doug said. "You mustn't let it bother you, Moira."

"But why won't they let us stay?"

"The immigration laws are very strict," he said. "Even more strict than when I moved here six years ago. Your mother brought you over to visit me, and then decided she wanted to stay. But the government still thinks you're all just visiting."

Moira's small face grew pale. "So Mummy and Robin and I will have to leave here and go back to Scotland?"

"Not if we can help it," Doug said. "I'm still trying to get things fixed up."

"I don't want to go back there," Moira said gloomily.

Doug gave her a thoughtful glance. "But in Scotland you lived in a fine big house, and here your Mummy just has a little cottage."

"I hated that big house," Moira said with passion. "Every one of us hated it. The bedrooms were cold all the time."

"I suppose they were." Doug thought about the stately old home that his sister, Rose, had inherited from their mother. "A lovely place, that house, but not exactly cozy."

"So what do you like the best about Texas?" Moira asked.

He thought it over. "The fact that Rory McLeod's not here." he said at last.

"Do you hate him, Uncle Doug?"

Doug shook his head, thinking about his mother's second husband.

Stephen Evans, his father, had been a cultured, soft-spoken man, and much loved. But Stephen had died when Doug was nine and Rose was little more than a baby, leaving their mother a valuable whiskey distillery in the Scottish Lowlands.

A few years later she'd married McLeod, a hulking, overbearing foreman at the plant who'd soon insinuated himself into his wife's inheritance. After college Doug had also gone to work in the family business, mostly to protect his mother's property.

But his stepfather had always been a hard man to endure...

"No," he said at last. "I don't hate anybody, Pumpkin. But I'm just as happy to have an ocean between me and Rory McLeod."

In fact, Doug had come to Texas six years earlier to set up a distributorship in the Hill Country for the family business. But his heart had no longer been in the work. The spring before his trip to America, their gentle mother had succumbed to breast cancer, and except for Rose and the girls, Doug had nothing holding him to Scotland anymore.

Something about the town of Crystal Creek had drawn him with passionate, irresistible force. Doug stayed a whole month longer than necessary, and afterward he went home only long enough to sell his share of the business, pack his belongings and begin the long battle to obtain a green card.

Now Doug owned the Crystal Creek Hotel, was mayor of the town, ran the real estate office and served as a stockbroker for local investors. Sometimes he felt as if his roots had already grown deeper into Texas soil than they'd ever been in the home of his ancestors.

"But why do you like it here so much?" Moira persisted with characteristic doggedness.

"Texas is almost ten times bigger than Scotland." Doug shifted the burden of the sleeping child in his arms. "But it has only twice the population. And the sunshine warms me clear to the bones, Moira. I love this place."

He gazed off at the rolling hills with their scattering of trees and rimrock outcroppings that sometimes reminded him of his homeland, especially on these blue, misty winter days.

"You know Mr. Wall, in the drugstore?" Moira gave her uncle a worried glance. "Mr. Wall says Crystal Creek is dying."

"Does he now?" Doug said grimly.

"Yesterday Robin and I were in the store buying Gummi Bears, and he said I should tell you that half the people in the town will pack up and leave this year if they can't get their taxes lowered."

Doug, who was normally an easygoing man, felt a surge of real anger when he thought about the fat, gossipy druggist using children to carry his messages.

"Well, if Mr. Wall says something like that to you in future," he told the girl, trying to keep his voice casual, "maybe you could suggest, my darling, that he might want to bring his concerns to me instead of telling them to a nine-year-old child."

"I don't like him." Moira grimaced and scuffed her toe on the sidewalk. "Mr. Wall smiles all the time, but I think he's mean."

"Never trust a man who smiles too much," Doug said. "Often they're—"

He stopped abruptly, clutching Robin tightly in his arms.

"What's the matter?" Moira asked, squinting up at her uncle.

Doug stared at the sandstone bulk of the Crystal Creek Hotel, a building on which he'd lavished a great deal of money and hard work since his arrival. The hotel's facade glistened in the afternoon sunlight, its windows flaring gold against the darkening sky to the east. The freshly painted sign above the lobby entrance was as bright as a new coin, and all the windows shone.

A sleek yellow Mercedes was parked on the street in front of the hotel.

"Is it her?" Moira breathed, standing tensely at his side and staring along with him. "Do you think it's the magic lady?"

"I believe it is." Doug knew the reaction was absurd, but he felt his heart beginning to pound with excitement against his rib cage. "You know, sweetie, I do believe it is."

"What does she want?"

He began to walk again, forgetting all about adjusting his pace to Moira's. She puffed along at his side, looking up at him anxiously.

"Why is she here, Uncle Doug?"

"We'll soon know, won't we, Pumpkin?" Doug mounted the wide brick steps of the hotel and entered the lobby with the little girls, pausing to let his eyes adjust to the lack of sunlight.

Since her arrival the previous spring, Rose had worked along with Doug to redecorate the hotel's interior. Now the old brasses shone, the woodwork gleamed with a satiny finish and chintz brightened the windows and the lobby furniture. The place had

a rustic charm that drew guests from all over the Hill
Country and beyond, making the Crystal Creek Hotel
one of the few really thriving businesses in town.

On the back of a chintz sofa near the window, a
big tabby cat drowsed lazily in the sun. She belonged
to Doug and was named Dundee. Though he'd acquired her from June Pollock just a few years earlier,
this plump female continued a long line of ''Dun-
dees'' that stretched all the way back to his boyhood
in Scotland.

But nothing in the lobby registered on its owner's
mind at this moment. Doug's eyes were fixed on the
scene at the reception desk, where Rose perched on
a high stool behind the polished wooden counter, appearing so worried that Doug felt a stirring of protective concern.

Rose looked exactly like their mother, and a lot
like little Moira. His sister was a small, dainty
woman with fine blond hair and big blue eyes that
often seemed anxious and frightened. She wore a
blue sweater over a plaid shirt, and chewed the end
of a pencil, gazing in distraught fashion at the hotel
register.

Two people stood in front of Rose at the desk,
surrounded by a small mountain of expensive-
looking luggage. One of them was a handsome
young blond man in khakis and a battered leather
jacket. The other was Moira's ''magic lady''—the
dark-haired driver of the yellow car.

The sight of them was confusing to Doug, render-
ing him temporarily speechless. Every time he'd seen
the mysterious young woman she'd been alone.
Somehow he'd never associated her with a man. He

felt a sharp pang which he realized was disappointment.

But of course, that was ridiculous...

"They want a two-bedroom suite for an extended period of time." Rose turned to her brother with obvious relief. "But they need all kinds of telephone outlets, too. I told them we only have the..."

Doug placed Robin carefully on one of the sofas by the old rock fireplace, then turned to face the group at the desk.

"We can give them the gold rooms on the second floor," he said to Rose.

Rose smiled and handed him a key.

"It's not exactly a suite," Doug told the guests, "but the two adjoining bedrooms have doors that lead to a common sitting room."

"Sounds perfect." The young man gave Rose an engaging smile. "Don't worry, ma'am, adjoining rooms will suit us just fine."

Rose's shy, delicate face turned an even deeper shade of pink. "This is my brother," she said, her Scottish burr very pronounced. "He's Douglas Evans, the proprietor of the hotel. Dougie, this is Margaret and Terence Embree, from Los Angeles."

"Terry," the young man said, coming forward to shake Doug's hand. "Nobody ever calls me Terence."

Doug pocketed the key and shook the man's hand, liking the firm grasp, then turned to greet the woman who approached.

In spite of himself, she took his breath away. Up close she seemed even lovelier than all those times he'd seen her behind the wheel of her car.

She was tall and graceful, wearing leather boots and a long woolen skirt and matching jacket in pale taupe. Her face was finely sculpted, with high cheekbones and big dark eyes. A golden drift of freckles across the bridge of her nose added a touch of boyishness, an appealing contrast that seemed to heighten rather than diminish her elegance.

Her hair was long and dark, carelessly swept up and held at the back of her head by a big tortoiseshell clip. Doug studied the clip when she turned to glance at the sleeping child on the couch.

So tempting, he thought. A man would only have to reach out and unfasten that clip, and her hair would tumble down onto her shoulders in a rich, glistening mass...

He drew himself up with a guilty start.

What thoughts to be having about a woman whose husband was standing not ten feet away, he chided himself.

"Mr. Evans," she said. Her voice was like honey warmed in the sun, sweet and husky. "I'm glad to meet you. Terry and I are planning to stay for quite some time in your hotel. We'll need to make immediate arrangements to get a computer modem and fax machine installed in our room."

She extended her hand and Doug took it, his whole body thrilling at the touch.

What was there about a woman that could make her very skin seem electric? Her hand was firm and slender, and he could have held it forever.

"A fax machine?" he repeated, still a little dazed. "Computer modems? That's going to require some thought, Ms. Embree. Our rooms don't even have phones.''

Her eyes weren't as dark as he'd first thought, but heavily shaded by dense eyelashes. Her irises were exactly the color of those sunny backwaters in the Claro River where the water ran brown and cool over mossy stones. They gleamed with intelligence, and Doug could happily have drowned in them.

''Call me Maggie,'' she said, then smiled down at Moira who stood watching her with awestruck solemnity.

As he shook Margaret Embree's hand and gazed into that lovely face, Douglas Evans wondered if maybe the little girls were right after all.

Maybe this woman *was* magic.

CHAPTER TWO

MAGGIE DISENGAGED her hand from the big man's grasp and stepped back to examine him.

Definitely a fine specimen, she decided. Tall and broad-shouldered, with an appealing rough-hewn look and a dancing light of humor in his green eyes. His hair was very black and crisp, with a lock that fell over one eyebrow in engaging fashion.

And she loved the gentle way he'd placed the sleeping child onto that couch, then covered her so tenderly.

The soft rich brogue of his speech was also attractive, although the incongruity of his accent, here in the heart of Texas, puzzled her a little.

Maggie tried to remember what she'd recorded in her notes about Douglas Evans. To the best of her recollection he was actually the mayor, though that title probably held little significance in a place like Crystal Creek.

And he also…

"Welcome to our town, Maggie Embree," he said softly, looking into her eyes.

Ridiculous as it was, she felt her knees turning weak. A little thrill shivered all through her body, warm and moist.

The same thing had happened when he'd taken her hand.

Maggie gave him a smile that she hoped was cool and remote, then turned away to pick up a couple of pieces of luggage. Terry shouldered some duffel bags and the tall innkeeper took the rest, except for one he offered to the solemn golden-haired child at his side who seemed anxious to help.

Obviously sensing something going on, the tabby cat leaped down from the back of the couch. She yawned and stretched, rump in the air, forelegs extended, then joined the group.

They trudged up the wide staircase, and followed the big Scotsman and his cat down the hall. "You're very lucky," the proprietor said over his shoulder. "We've just finished some renovating, and this is our slowest time so you're the only guests at the moment. You'll find it very quiet. Although," he added, "the pub still does a lively business." He paused by a polished wooden door with a high transom, took out an old-fashioned skeleton key to unlock the door and led them into a charming room furnished with floral couches, matching drapes and a television set concealed in a mahogany armoire.

"There are bedrooms on either side, each with its own bath," the man said to Terry, gesturing toward a pair of doors. "But if you and your wife should prefer to—"

"My wife!" Terry laughed, a warm, infectious sound in the quiet room. Even the little girl smiled. "Maggie and I are brother and sister, Mr. Evans."

"Are you now?" The tall man glanced at Maggie,

and she caught a surprising flare of light in his green eyes that made her tingle again.

All these wayward reactions were beginning to upset her.

Maggie turned away nervously and tried one of the doors, which opened into a bedroom with a wooden four-poster bed and a deep padded seat at a window enshrouded in clouds of airy white muslin. Hooked rugs covered the shining hardwood floor.

For a moment she forgot everything else in her delight at the beautiful room. It was like something out of the storybooks her mother had read to her and Terry when they were children.

The cat entered with her. Clearly familiar with the room, it sniffed daintily at a floorboard near the window, tail stiffly extended. Maggie, who loved cats, smiled and bent to scratch behind the furry ears. The cat purred loudly and rubbed against Maggie's leather boot.

"You're brother and sister," Doug Evans was saying behind her in the sitting room. His deep voice sounded warm and thoughtful.

"It's really funny, that you thought we were married," Terry told the man.

"Why?" Doug asked.

"Well, I don't know what kind of man would ever win my sister's hand," Terry said, "but he'd have to be a lot different guy than I am. A billionaire industrialist or a Texas land baron, maybe."

"Indeed?" the host said. His voice was still solemn, but Maggie could now detect a note of teasing. "So your sister prefers wealthy men?"

Alarmed by this turn of conversation, she returned

to the sitting room and gave her brother a stern glance. But Terry was clearly enjoying himself and, as usual, paid her no attention.

"No, I don't think Maggie's particularly attracted to money," he told the Scotsman, "but she's fond of strength." He gestured at the coat of arms above the small fireplace, topped by a bit of tartan and a pair of ornamental crossed swords. "You know, maybe she'd even go for some kind of warrior chieftain," he suggested with a grin.

"Do ye really think so, then?" the man asked, his burr deepening. He cast Maggie another glance, his green eyes dancing.

"That's quite enough," Maggie said firmly. "Terry, I'm sure Mr. Evans has no interest in speculation about my love life, or lack thereof."

Nervous and confused under those sparkling eyes, she rummaged through her shoulder bag and withdrew five dollars, offering the bill to the dark-haired man by the door.

"Thank you for helping with the bags," she said politely.

He glanced at the money, then looked down at her again, his jaw tightening a little.

Maggie realized, too late, that she'd made a mistake, but she was too rattled to back down.

"Please," she said, holding the bill while the little girl and the cat pressed up against the man's legs. All three stood watching Maggie solemnly. "You carried all those bags upstairs for us."

"You and your brother are very welcome here, Maggie," the man said quietly, making her feel even more ridiculous, almost like a child being scolded.

"But it's not our policy to accept payment for assisting our guests."

He turned with quiet dignity and left the room with Moira and Dundee at his heels.

Maggie went to the doorway and watched as he strode along the hallway. His shoulders looked wide and strong, and his hips were lean and hard under the faded denim jeans.

"Well, that's great." She came back into the room and closed the door. "A Scottish cowboy with lofty moral principles. Just what we need to complicate things even more than they already are."

Her brother watched her with interest. "The guy really gets to you. Doesn't he, Maggie?"

She shrugged and took off her jacket, then massaged her shoulders wearily. "I'm a little worried about that lord-of-the-manor attitude. This man's going to be trouble for us, Terry. I can just feel it."

"Trouble for you, maybe." Terry removed his shoes and reclined on one of the couches, stretching contentedly. "I have nothing to do with this whole crackbrained scheme, remember? I'm just along to drive the car and provide technical support."

"And to escape the paint fumes and sawdust in your apartment." Maggie sprawled opposite him in a big overstuffed chair and tugged off her leather boots. "Are you sorry you came?"

"Somebody has to look after you, kid. Especially when Natasha's being so irrational."

"Look after *me!*" She smiled at him. "When you're this deep into a book, you hardly even know where you're living, even when your place is being renovated. I'll bet a houseful of carpenters would hardly have bothered you."

"I have two hundred pages left to write, Maggie," he said, suddenly serious. "I need peace and quiet to finish the book. And this town certainly looks peaceful enough."

"But you really don't approve of what Natasha's doing here, do you?" Maggie continued to watch her brother thoughtfully.

"Approve? You've got to be kidding. I think it's the craziest thing I ever heard of. And so do you," he added shrewdly.

"It's what Natasha wants." Maggie sighed and stretched her feet, wiggling her toes in relief.

"Well," Terry said with a grin, "that would explain the craziness."

"Look, what can I do, tell her she's being completely irrational?"

"I think that's a major part of Natasha's problem." Terry's pleasant face turned thoughtful. "Nobody's ever refused her anything in her whole life. Imagine what it must be like to have a hundred million dollars and everybody in the world falling all over themselves to fulfill your smallest whim. Anybody's view of life would get a little distorted."

Maggie watched him for a moment, then shook her head and dug into a leather briefcase. She took out a bulky file folder and sat back to leaf through it.

"Here it is," she said at last.

"What?" He rolled his head on the chintz cushion to glance at her.

"Douglas Evans," she said, reading aloud from a

sheet of paper. "Hotel proprietor, mayor, real estate salesman and stockbroker. Thirty-five years old, bachelor, lives in a suite of rooms on the main floor of the hotel. Arrived in Texas more than six years ago from his native Scotland and immediately applied for a green card, became a naturalized citizen two years later. Rumored to be independently wealthy, and a passionate booster of Crystal Creek. More in love with the town, it appears, than many of the natives."

"He sounds like a very nice guy," Terry commented. "I like him."

Maggie stared at the paper, feeling a rising concern when she thought about the stern look on Doug Evans's handsome face after she'd offered him that money.

The man had seemed almost disappointed in her. But of course, that was ridiculous. He didn't even know her.

"I knew he was going to be trouble," she said again. "He's the mayor, Terry, I wonder how much influence he has around here. Maybe I should..."

"It makes me nervous when you get that look in your eye," her brother commented, smiling at her. "Keep reading the file, Maggie. What does it say about those two kids, and the sister?"

Maggie consulted the paper again. "Sarah Rose Murdoch, arrived from Scotland almost a year ago on a visitor's visa, which apparently is near expiry. Rose helps in the hotel and rents a little cottage down near the river. She's divorced and has two children. Moira, aged nine, and Robin, who's four."

"So those two kids belong to Rose," he mused,

staring at the stamped tiles on the ceiling. "Cute little things, aren't they?"

"Very cute." Maggie smiled fondly, thinking about Robin's plump sleeping face and Moira's solemn gaze. Then she began consulting other pages in her files.

"And their mother is cute, too," Terry was saying. He shifted his long legs to a more comfortable position on the couch. "Did you notice how Rose got all flustered and pink when she was worried about finding rooms for us? Not many women actually blush anymore, did you know that, Mags?"

"It's a lost art," Maggie agreed, jotting down some reminders to herself on a sheet of paper. "Terry, how soon do you think he'll be able to get us set up in here? Because I really don't see how we can manage if—"

She was interrupted by a knock on the door. Maggie tensed and closed the file abruptly.

"Come in," Terry called. He swung his feet to the floor and sat erect.

The door was opened by the smaller of the two girls, the one who'd been sleeping earlier on the couch in the lobby. She was wide awake now, her golden curls standing out all around her head, blue eyes sparkling with excitement.

"Mummy's bringing you tea," she announced, waving her hand at the hallway. "And oatmeal scones. They're yummy. Moira and I always..."

"Now, don't bother the lady and gentleman with your chatter, Robin." The child's mother entered the room and deposited a large silver tray on the table, laden with oatcakes, pots of butter and jam, a brown teapot and a pair of cups.

Moira followed, carefully bearing a small platter with cream, sugar and napkins. The cat came with her, striding along in lordly fashion.

"Rose, this is a lovely surprise." Maggie beamed at the smaller woman, who still looked painfully shy. "How thoughtful of you."

Rose Murdoch stood awkwardly by the door in her blue jeans and sweater, hugging her arms, with the two children close to her.

"We always have tea at this time of day," she said in her appealing soft brogue. "And if you've driven a long way, I'm sure you could use a wee bite."

Robin edged back across the room in her little green running shoes. She stood cautiously next to Terry, who was looking with appreciation at the contents of the bigger tray.

"Taste them," the little girl whispered, pointing a finger at the steaming oatmeal scones. "Uncle Dougie says our mummy makes the best scones in all the world."

"Well," Terry said solemnly to the child, "your uncle Doug strikes me as a very smart man, so I'll bet he's right."

He gave Rose a sunny smile and a wink, and the woman looked away quickly, appearing flustered.

"Rose, I love this cat," Maggie said, mostly to set the shy woman at ease. "What's her name?"

"She's my brother's cat," Rose said, with a smile that made her face light up. "Her name is Dundee."

"Uncle Doug always has a cat called Dundee," Moira said. "But this is the best one ever."

"Yes, she's a beautiful cat." Maggie smiled again at Rose, who ducked her blond head, murmured something to the two girls and hastened from the room, closing the door quickly behind her.

After they were gone, Terry bit into one of the scones and sighed in bliss, then reached for the teapot.

"Robin's right, this is just delicious." He gave Maggie a bright glance. "I'm glad to see you're capable of learning, kiddo."

"What do you mean?"

Terry spread strawberry jam on a bit of scone. "I was afraid you might offer the poor woman a tip."

Maggie looked over at him, stung by the implied criticism. "Come on, Terry," she said. "If this was a big-city hotel and I hadn't offered a tip, the man would have been mortally offended."

Terry poured a cup of tea and offered it to her. "But we're not in the big city, Maggie. This is small-town America. That's what you and Natasha don't seem to realize."

"The setting may be different," Maggie said. "But don't you think human nature is the same all over the world? Natasha's so certain that when these people learn what we're offering…"

She paused and took a sip of tea.

Her brother gave her a measuring glance over the rim of his cup. "Go on, say it. How will these people react when they find out a rich, famous movie star wants to buy their town, and turf them all out of here?"

"Natasha has no intention of turfing anybody out," Maggie said wearily. "You know I'd never be part of something like that."

"Of course you wouldn't. You're a nice, good-hearted girl, Maggie, underneath all that sophisticated big-city veneer."

Maggie frowned, staring out the window.

"Natasha just wants to buy all the houses and businesses," he said, "and then rent them back to the folks. What a great deal."

"Oh, God, they're going to hate it, aren't they?" Maggie said in despair. "Even though most of these businesses are in financial trouble, and the houses are burdened with high property taxes. You know, Natasha truly believes her project will provide an infusion of cash that's badly needed in Crystal Creek."

"And in return, she'll own the whole town. It'll be Natasha's private playground, to do with exactly as she pleases. She'll get to be the undisputed queen of Crystal Creek."

"I doubt if that's what she wants, Terry."

"How do you know what she wants?" he asked bluntly.

Maggie thought about Natasha Dunne, her baffling and enigmatic employer.

"I'm not sure anybody knows what Natasha really wants, or how she thinks about things," she confessed. "But the way she explained it to me, this is entirely a sentimental project. Crystal Creek has always meant a lot to her."

Terry helped himself to another scone and munched it with pleasure.

"Yeah, I know all about the sentiment," he said.

"How touching it is. Natasha films a movie here thirty years ago while her brand-new husband is fighting valiantly in Vietnam…"

"He was killed over there, Terry." Maggie gave her brother a reproving glance.

Terry ignored her. "And only the warmth and support of the Crystal Creek townspeople helps our poor little Natasha to pull through and go on living. The whole story's become a national legend."

"So why do you sound sarcastic whenever you talk about it?"

He shrugged. "I just wonder about things sometimes. Sentiment doesn't seem to me like sufficient motivation to buy a whole town. For God's sake, who buys a town, Maggie?"

"Natasha does," she said dryly.

"Hell, no. She sends her loyal administrative assistant to scout the area and buy the town, while she lounges on a cruise ship in the Mediterranean."

"She's recovering from surgery, Terry. You know that. Natasha's in a great deal of pain."

He chuckled. "You make it sound like a heart transplant. The woman had a face-lift, for God's sake."

"It's still very painful," Maggie said. "And she needs to recover in privacy."

Terry looked at her curiously. "Why are you always so loyal to the woman, Mags? Even when she's being completely bizarre and irrational. I know how much this stuff drives you crazy, but you hardly ever let me say a word against her."

"I'm closer to her than you are," Maggie said. "And you know what? I really like her. Underneath all the glitz and nonsense, there's a core of goodness in Natasha. I think she's a vulnerable person.''

Terry grinned and buttered a bit of scone. ''I can't say I've noticed the vulnerability all that much.''

''She helped us all those years before Mom died,'' Maggie said.

''I guess so. But we were no more to her than names on a page, Maggie. Our family was Natasha's designated charity—her tax deduction.''

''Aren't you even a little bit grateful to her?'' Maggie asked, sipping her tea.

''Sure I'm grateful. But I still don't believe charity gives Natasha the right to own you, and make you do anything she wants you to.''

''Terry, eight years ago I chose to work for Natasha, and it's been a damn good job. Certainly not some kind of indentured servitude, the way you're implying.''

Her brother watched her thoughtfully. ''So how much are you allowed to spend, buying this nice little place? What do towns sell for nowadays?''

''Natasha's prepared to invest up to thirty million dollars. She'd like to acquire all of the business area, and a good portion of the private residences.''

''And what's she going to do with them?''

Maggie shrugged wearily. ''I told you, nobody really knows. Maybe she'll change the name of the town to Dunne Creek, or have her picture on the postmark.''

''Maybe she'll build a theme park, and call it Natasha Land.''

Maggie laughed at this. ''You're right, Terry. Who knows what she might do? Maybe after the cruise,'' she added hopefully, ''Natasha will change her mind altogether.''

''Well, if she doesn't,' he said with an answering grin, his good humor apparently restored, ''I sure don't envy you the task of trying to buy this hotel from Doug Evans.''

Maggie's laughter faded. She set down her teacup, staring at the window.

''I know there'll be lots of opposition,'' she said. ''If Natasha insists on going ahead with this, the only hope would be to find one or two people who are willing to sell, and approach them first with offers to purchase. Once we've already acquired even a small block of local property, others might be tempted by the cash.''

''But?'' he prompted.

''But I'm really hoping she'll just forget the whole project,'' Maggie confessed.

Terry got up and wandered across the room to look down at the quiet street. Maggie watched his casual, lounging figure, wondering what he was thinking.

''How old do you suppose Rose Murdoch is?'' he asked without turning around.

Maggie looked at her notes again. ''It doesn't say, but I'd guess she's about my age.''

''And you'll be thirty-one in March, right?''

''How nice of you to remember,'' Maggie said dryly. ''I'm really touched.''

Terry ignored her, still gazing at the street. ''Rose is probably closer to my age,'' he said at last. ''Late twenties, don't you think?''

''If that's true, she must have been married very

young,'' Maggie said, ''because the older girl is nine years old.''

''Do your notes say why she got divorced?''

Maggie looked with sudden interest at her brother's blond head, glistening in the late-afternoon light from the window.

''Terry, what's this all about? Why the big concern about Rose Murdoch?''

''I just like the look of her,'' he said, coming back to sprawl on the couch again.

''Yes, I noticed that.'' Maggie gave him a teasing smile.

''She seems like a nice person,'' he said with studied casualness. ''Is it so strange that I'd notice a good-looking woman?''

''When you're in the middle of working on that book, you never seem to notice anybody.''

''Well,'' he said, ''I'm not working at the moment. I haven't written a word in the past week, since we decided to come out here on this crazy project.''

''You should have rented that apartment down on the beach while they were working on your place.''

''I didn't want you out here all alone, dealing with Natasha when she's on one of her tangents. And I don't care where I live as long as I can work. But I won't be working anytime soon,'' he added restlessly, ''unless your big Scotsman gets some computer equipment installed up here.''

''He's not my Scotsman!'' Maggie said hotly.

Her brother arched an eyebrow, his face sparkling with amusement. ''Why, Maggie,'' he said, raising a cup in her direction. ''If I hadn't seen it with my own eyes, I wouldn't believe it.''

"What?" she said.

"You're actually blushing. You've turned as pink as Rose Murdoch."

Maggie frowned and swatted her younger brother with the file folder while he ducked aside, laughing. Then she began hauling her luggage into the bedroom with its snowy-white curtains and four-poster bed.

CHAPTER THREE

MAGGIE AND HER BROTHER unpacked and rested for a couple of hours in their separate rooms. By the time they went downstairs, it was about seven o'clock in the evening.

Doug Evans was behind the reception desk, on one of the tall stools occupied by his sister earlier in the day. He pored over an open ledger and punched numbers onto a computer keyboard, looking annoyed. Invoices and receipts littered the desk. Dundee lay partly upon the stack of papers, occasionally swatting playfully at the keyboard.

"Can't make head nor tail of this damn stuff," Doug muttered, giving them a distracted glance. "I really should take a computer course to update my skills."

Maggie, who was a certified accountant in addition to holding an advanced degree in business, looked with interest at the masses of paper.

Though her job with Natasha Dunne had involved all kinds of strange and exotic duties over the years, Maggie Embree's first love would always be computers and bookkeeping.

"Why don't you hire somebody?" she asked.

"Who would I find in this town? Anybody who's

remotely qualified has a job already. The hotel books were in a mess when I bought the place, and computer software seems to change every ten minutes.''

''What would you say is your most immediate problem?'' Maggie asked.

''Hell, who knows?'' He glared at the screen. ''We need somebody to work here for a few days, at least, and design a profit-and-loss statement, cost projections and decent spreadsheets, some kind of a plan for our future computer development...''

''Maggie could sort that out for you in ten minutes,'' Terry said. ''Give her a set of books and a good computer, and this girl's a marvel.''

Doug gave her a quick thoughtful glance that made her feel awkward again. She forced herself to meet his eyes casually.

''Is there by any chance a dining room in the hotel, Doug?'' she asked.

For a moment he seemed both startled and a little unsettled by her casual use of his first name. Then he shook his dark head and leafed though a messy pile of invoices.

''We serve burgers and snacks in the hotel pub, but that's about all. Most of our guests eat their meals down the street at the Longhorn. Nora makes the best home fries in the state.''

''The Longhorn,'' Terry said, grinning. ''Now, that sounds interesting. You'll love it, Maggie.''

She gave him a warning glance.

''My sister's a big-city girl,'' Terry told the man behind the desk. ''Maggie eats alfalfa sprouts and sushi. I'll bet she's never had a plate of home fries in her life.''

"Is that so?" Doug laughed. "Well then, she's got a terrific experience ahead of her.''

Maggie headed for the lobby door, with Terry ambling behind her.

"Look, quit talking to that man about me as if I'm not even there,'' she muttered to her brother when they were outside on the darkened street.

"He seems interested," Terry said innocently as they made their way toward the restaurant. "Don't you think?''

"I couldn't care less if he's interested." A few minutes later they reached the Longhorn. Maggie pushed open the door of the restaurant, relieved to step into the smoky warmth after the chill of the street.

"You don't find our laird Douglas Evans just a tiny bit attractive?" Terry followed her to a booth near the window.

"Not a bit," Maggie lied, sliding onto the vinyl seat. "But even if I did, I'd have to ignore those feelings," she added.

"You would?" Terry smiled at a waitress in a checked apron who arrived to hand them a couple of gingham-patterned menus. "Why?''

"Because feelings like that would complicate the job I've come here to do.''

"Mags, you have no intention of doing that job. Unlike our Natasha, you're not entirely crazy." His eyes sparkled. "Just a wee bit smitten," he said in a mock brogue.

Maggie ignored her brother's teasing and frowned at the menu. "Do you suppose they have something like a salad? It seems this is all meat and potatoes."

"You'd better get used to some dietary changes if you want to make any friends here," Terry said mildly. "Look at this place, Maggie. It's terrific."

She glanced around at the restaurant, which could have been lifted directly from a fifties movie. But the effect wasn't cutesy and artificial like similar establishments in Los Angeles. The Longhorn had a look of authenticity, as if thousands of people had sat in these booths over the years, ordered from the same menus, studied their reflections in the polished chrome napkin holders and played selections on the individual jukeboxes above each table.

"Isn't it great?" Terry said.

"Yes," she said. "The place has a wonderful ambience. And," she added with sudden inexplicable sadness, "I'm afraid it soon could belong to Natasha Dunne, along with everything else in this town."

Terry gave her a quick glance but didn't respond. They ordered mushroom burgers and home fries, and Maggie ate the rich food with guilty pleasure.

"Oh, this is so good." she sighed, wiping a trickle of mayonnaise from her chin.

"Welcome to the real world." Terry grinned, saluting her with a forkful of coleslaw. "Maybe this new assignment of yours is going to be a valuable experience for you, kiddo."

"In what way?"

His face was suddenly grave. "I'm hoping by the

time you're done, this town will own you, instead of the other way around.''

''Terry, what do you mean?'' Maggie asked, genuinely puzzled.

But he refused to elaborate. Half an hour later, he paused outside the restaurant with his hands deep in his pockets.

''You can find your way back to the hotel, can't you?'' He glanced at her. ''It's only a couple of blocks away, and I want to go for a walk.''

''Where?'' she asked.

He turned, looking a little evasive. ''Just down there by the river,'' he said, then headed off into a darkness lit in ghostly fashion by street lamps circled with frost.

Maggie watched her younger brother, troubled by conflicting emotions.

Her research file had stated that Rose Murdoch and her two daughters lived down by the river...

But Terry was an adult, and his personal life was none of her business.

Maggie turned up her jacket collar against the chill and wandered back toward the hotel, pausing briefly outside Wall's Drugstore, which appeared to be open for business.

A fat, swarthy man worked behind the counter, and a slim blond woman stood nearby. Muffled in a long coat and damask scarf, she leaned wearily against a tall cowboy in a sheepskin coat and Stetson. The woman held some toiletries, which she placed on the counter.

When the customer stepped back and her coat

swung open, Maggie realized the woman was pregnant. The man at her side, a smiling, handsome fellow with curly auburn hair, hugged his wife and whispered something to her, with a look of tenderness that made Maggie feel lonely and excluded.

The couple gathered up their purchases and left. As they passed by and the two women glanced at each other, Maggie was stunned by the tall blonde's effortless grace and style. This woman could have been the president of some major corporation in the city, or even one of Natasha's glamorous friends.

Not exactly the kind of woman Maggie had expected to find here in Crystal Creek, shopping with a cowboy in the local drugstore...

"That's Jim and Lucia Whitley," the druggist said cozily, following her gaze. "They just got married at Christmastime. And not a minute too soon," he added with a leer, "judging by the looks of her. Lucia's got a bun in the oven."

Maggie felt a sharp distaste for this overweight man with his narrow eyes and shiny red face. But he was clearly disposed to talk, and she needed information, so she forced herself to smile casually.

"Mrs. Whitley is a very lovely woman," she said, examining a rack of grocery and food items that stood near the front desk.

"She's the principal of the middle school, and her husband is one of the teachers on staff," her informant said, as if this was a bit of juicy gossip.

Maggie glanced around at the drugstore, which looked and smelled like some vanished bit of childhood. She breathed in the scent of polished wooden

floors, soap and lemon oil, dust and perfume and
warmth. The place itself seemed ageless and comforting, even though its proprietor made her uneasy.

She found a couple of cans of ruinously expensive
cat food and took them to the counter, rummaging
in her bag. "So that woman's the school principal,"
she said, still thinking about the graceful blonde in
the scarf. "I'd really like to meet her sometime."

"Well, you better hurry, then, because Lucia
won't be around long," he said with a wink. "The
school's probably shutting down."

"Really?" Maggie offered a bill and stood looking at the man. "Why?"

He shrugged his fat shoulders and rang up the purchase. "Taxes are too high. Folks know we can't
afford that school anymore, and they want it closed.
We're voting on it next month."

"Where will the students go?"

"On a bus," the druggist said carelessly, "to the
middle school over in the next town."

"Is this common knowledge in town?" Maggie
asked. "About the school closure?"

"Oh, sure. Everybody's talking about it." He
leaned across the counter with a confiding look. "But
me...well, I got kind of an inside track on things,
you might say."

"Why's that?"

"Well, because my wife is the chair of the school
board."

Maggie searched her memory, trying again to recall the careful notes she'd made.

Gloria Wall, she remembered. Chair of the Crystal Creek School Board, and wife of...

"So you would be Ralph Wall?" she asked with a polite smile.

"That's right, I sure would." The druggist gave her a gratified smile and squared his shoulders a little. "And your name is...?"

"Margaret Embree. I'm here in town for a while on business."

"Movie business?" he suggested with an avid expression.

"I beg your pardon?" Maggie said, startled.

"We've all seen that big Mercedes you drive around in, with the California plates. Folks reckon you're planning to shoot a movie here in Crystal Creek, the same way they did over in Wimberley last year, and make us all into big stars."

Maggie considered his words, and decided that for the moment this was as good a cover as any.

"So would you like to be a movie star, Mr. Wall?" she asked.

"If it pays good enough." His grin faded. He began to arrange the bright rows of gum and chocolate bars under the glass counter. "God knows, we could use some money around here."

"How would you feel," Maggie asked carefully, "if somebody who was making a movie in town should want to buy your drugstore?"

His close-set eyes sharpened with interest. "Why would he need to buy my store?"

"Well," Maggie said, improvising rapidly, "you know, a lot of big production companies like to own the properties where they're shooting, just to avoid possible legal complications.''

"But what would they do with my store after the movie was over?''

Maggie took a deep breath, a little appalled at herself for even broaching the topic. Hopefully the man would scoff at her suggestion, and then she could report to Natasha that the whole idea was impossible.

"I suppose,'' she said with deliberate casualness, "the producer would buy out your property for cash. Then if you chose, he'd just hold on to it and rent it back to you. I think that's how it works.''

His face took on a startled, cunning look. "You mean he'd give me cash for this place? Full market value? And then afterward he'd let me keep running my business like nothing ever happened?''

Maggie nodded. "And of course the new owner would be responsible for taxes and improvements to the property. Your only requirement would be the payment of a nominal rent.''

Ralph Wall's cheeks glistened with excitement. Maggie could almost smell the scent of greed exuding from him, and had to force herself not to back away from the counter.

"So how many businesses would your movie producer want to be buying this way?'' he asked. "Just my drugstore, or what?''

"I think it's possible he might be interested in the entire downtown area,'' Maggie said. "Possibly even a number of the residential properties.''

"But…'' Ralph Wall stared at her, his hands gripping the edge of the counter. "But something like that…it'd have to cost thousands of dollars. Maybe…" His voice was hushed. "Maybe millions."

"These days, even the smallest movies have multi-million-dollar budgets, Mr. Wall."

She turned to go, but he reached out and clutched her arm.

Maggie paused, hating the feeling of his hand against her jacket.

"Look, Ms. Embree, is this on the level? This movie producer might really give me cash value for my drugstore, and then let me stay here and run it?"

"Does that really appeal to you?" Maggie asked with genuine curiosity. "I thought people always dream of owning their business themselves."

"Not when they're so strapped for cash they can hardly turn around, like most of us are in this town," he said with a dark, bitter look. "Working for somebody else and having him take over the money worries sounds pretty damn good to me."

There was no doubting his eagerness. If other people in Crystal Creek turned out to be this anxious to sell, Natasha's ludicrous plan might actually be feasible.

"It's not something I'm free to discuss at the moment, Mr. Wall." Maggie dropped her voice, shook her arm free of his grasp and glanced toward the door. "And I'll also have to ask you not to talk with anybody else about this, please."

The fat man licked his lips, staring at her. "Not a

word," he breathed in a hoarse whisper. "I won't say a word."

"Thank you."

Maggie headed for the door with her sack of cat food, glancing over her shoulder. The druggist already had his back to her and was dialing the phone, his body trembling with excitement.

Frowning, she strolled down the moonlit street toward the hotel, brooding over her first testing of the waters in Crystal Creek.

Ralph Wall had the look of an incorrigible gossip. Within a day or two, the story of the rich movie producer buying up real estate was probably going to be all over Crystal Creek, and then the discussion and argument would begin.

And judging by what Maggie now knew about the financial state of this town, maybe she wouldn't even have to seek people out.

They would be coming to her, she thought, her stomach tightening with concern. All she had to do was wait a while, and begin signing checks. Unless she could somehow talk Natasha out of this whole grotesque plan.

Not that she hadn't tried, of course. In recent months Maggie had spent long hours arguing with her famous employer, battling to convince Natasha that she could earn the love and loyalty of these townspeople simply by making a substantial donation to the small Texas community.

But Natasha wasn't interested in being the town's patron. She wanted to own Crystal Creek. And nothing, it seemed, was going to stop her.

DOUG WAS STILL WORKING over his snarl of invoices and computer printouts when Maggie came back into the hotel lobby. Apparently the younger brother had gone off somewhere on his own because she was alone now, carrying a sack from Wall's Drugstore and looking preoccupied.

She seemed more approachable, too, dressed in pleated khakis, a cable-knit sweater and a duffel coat with hood. The enticing hair clip had been replaced by a long casual braid.

Again he thought about unfastening that braid, letting her hair fall free across her shoulders.

Doug loved the look of a woman with long hair. Especially when it was dark and glossy like Maggie's, with chestnut highlights...

"Hi." She paused by the counter. "How's it going?"

"Not well," he said, catching a whiff of the tantalizing perfume she wore. It smelled more woodsy than sweet, like the forest after a rain.

A lovely, elusive fragrance...

"So how much would I have to pay you to sort this all out for me?" he asked, gesturing at the computer and the messy stack of papers.

She stared, and again he was conscious of her classic features, the fine dark eyes and high cheekbones. "You're kidding."

"On the contrary, I'm deadly serious. How long would it take to bring my bookkeeping system into the new millennium?"

"A good accountant could analyze your needs and set up a couple of decent spreadsheets within..."

Maggie glanced at her watch. "Oh, I'd say…a few hours. But it might take a day or two if the problems are widespread."

Doug was almost dizzied by her nearness, to say nothing of this incredible statement. "If you could do that for me," he told her, "I'd give you a week of rent-free accommodation."

"Don't be ridiculous."

Her darkly lashed eyes were so beautiful. He couldn't stop gazing at them. And her body under the casual clothes was so enticing, slim and richly curved, with long legs and high, sweet breasts…

"Ridiculous?" he asked.

She hesitated, then tossed her package and duffel coat onto a couch, opened the little gate and came around behind the desk, perching next to him on another stool.

"Let me have the computer," she said. "I don't want to look at your books, but I'll download a useful spreadsheet for you right now, and you can pay me back by giving me a drink of Irish cream in the pub later on."

In the midst of his enchantment, Doug felt a sharp twinge of suspicion. This offer was too good to be true, and so was the lovely woman at his side.

"What's the catch?" he asked.

She gave him one of the enchanting, luminous smiles that made his heart beat faster. "Are Scotsmen always so suspicious of ordinary human kindness?"

"We Scots have discovered over the years," he

said, "that a healthy dose of suspicion helps us to get along with our neighbors."

"It does?"

"Well," he amended after brief consideration, "suspicion and a bloody great wall."

She chuckled, and he was undone. He would have given anything just to hear her laugh again. When she pressed closer to him, punching numbers on the keyboard, one of her breasts touched his arm and it was all he could not to sweep her into his arms.

"So you wouldn't worry about a stranger looking at your business affairs?" she asked, dragging him back to reality.

"Why should I be? There's nothing to hide in my books. The temps I hire to come up from Austin and wade through this mess, are all strangers."

By now, Maggie was all business, entering instructions, pulling down packages of software he'd never seen before. Her fingers flew over the screen, and as she concentrated, she bit her full lower lip between perfect white teeth.

Her only pause came when Dundee edged closer and rested a furry chin on her arm, begging to be scratched. Maggie stopped and stroked the cat's ears, then bent to whisper something to her.

Doug watched, moved by the tenderness of her gesture, feeling irrationally envious of his own cat.

"Do you like animals?" he asked.

"I really love cats, but I travel too much to have one of my own." Maggie looked wistful. "Dundee is just such a beauty."

She watched in obvious regret when the tabby

leaped down from the reception desk and padded off in the direction of the hotel pub. When the animal was gone, Maggie sighed and returned to the books.

"Okay," she muttered after a while. "That's all you need for now. Look, you start with your ledger entries in this column..."

She demonstrated the use of the spreadsheet she'd established. Doug watched with interest.

"Could you go over that last bit again?" he said, frowning. "Like I told you, computers really aren't my strong point."

"I'll tell you what, Doug." Maggie glanced at him. "You're right, a drink in the bar isn't nearly enough payment for teaching you how to use this accounting software."

"You greedy woman," he teased. "I already offered you a week of rent-free accommodation."

"And I said that's ridiculous, though teaching you this would probably take me the better part of a week in my free time." Maggie frowned at the screen. "Still, it's an interesting challenge."

"So how shall I repay you?"

As she looked over at him, a strand of hair worked itself free of the braid and fell across her cheek. He longed to reach up to smooth it back behind her ear.

"Hire a technician to put some phone jacks in our sitting room and our bedrooms," she said. "I'll consider that a wonderful repayment."

Doug watched her curiously. "Nobody's ever wanted a phone in their room before," he said.

"Oh, come on. Whoever heard of a hotel without phones in the rooms?"

"This isn't the big city, Maggie. Our guests always use the phone at the end of the hall, or down here in the lobby."

"But my brother and I will be using two computers, a laptop and fax machine," Maggie told him. "We need at least four phone jacks and two dedicated lines for e-mail and Internet access, or we can't stay here."

"And if I install them, you'll teach me how to computerize my bookkeeping?"

"My brother's a novelist." She looked fully at him, her eyes grave and thoughtful. "He's at an important point in the book he's working on, and he needs to be able to write every day."

"Is he published?"

"His first book comes out in late spring. He's working on the sequel."

"And what about you?" Doug asked. "Are you just along to nurse the creative genius, Maggie?"

Her cheeks turned faintly pink, a reaction that he found intriguing.

"Hardly." She looked back at the screen. "I have work of my own to do."

"In Crystal Creek?"

"You've never heard of networking?" she asked a little evasively. "With a computer modem and a good-quality fax, I could conduct my business from a mountaintop or a desert island."

"Ah yes, 'tis a brave new world indeed," he said in a soulful brogue, earning a suspicious glance from his companion.

When she frowned, a tiny vertical line appeared

between her delicate eyebrows. Doug wanted to kiss it.

"So," he asked, getting a firm grip on himself, "why have you and your brother chosen Crystal Creek as your desert island?"

She smiled, causing a dimple to flash briefly in her right cheek. He was even more enchanted.

"Maybe," she suggested, "I've decided to learn the fine art of Texas cuisine."

"And maybe not," he said.

But she refused to rise to the bait, and before long they were fully involved again in the business of input commands and program files.

CHAPTER FOUR

DOUG EVANS WAS amazingly quick-witted, with an incisive grasp of new concepts that left her breathless.

"Let's start putting some of this into practice," she said at last, trying not to show how impressed she was with him. "Which part of your business would you choose to enter on the main ledger?"

"The pub," he said without hesitation. "It makes more money than the hotel. It's a real godsend during slow times like this."

"And what do you consider the main areas of difficulty in your accounting?"

"Wage deductions and capital cost depreciation," Doug said. "I'm afraid this old software has cost me a fair amount in taxes over the past few years."

"You're probably right." Maggie frowned at the computer. "Now, if I can just remember where to find the Web site, I'll be able to download the neatest program for calculating your capital depreciation. It works like magic...."

While she worked, Doug sat nearby and answered her questions until she had all the programs running in different windows. Then he got up and roamed around the lobby, sat for a while on one of the

couches and leafed through a magazine, strolled into
the back to lock the outside door.

"Come on," he said at last, pausing by the desk.
"You've been at it almost two hours, Maggie. Call
it a night and have that drink with me."

"Two hours?" she looked up at him, blinking in
surprise. "Really, it's been that long?"

He chuckled. "You love this, don't you? I was
watching you at that computer and your face was
completely absorbed, like someone watching a good
movie."

She smiled and leaned back on the stool, stretching
her arms. "You know, it's really fun. Looking for
the right software is like solving a mystery, or going
on a treasure hunt."

"So, are you going to find a treasure for me?"

"Well…" Maggie hesitated. "No promises,
now," she warned, "but I think you might be able
to save quite a lot in taxes."

"How?"

"Things like capital cost allowances, wage deductions and writing off some of the hotel expenses
against the profit you make on the bar. This new
software will help you with all that."

He brightened. "If that's true, I'll have to raise
your wages."

Maggie laughed and switched off the computer.
With his help she stacked the files neatly, then
climbed down from the stool and followed him in
the direction of the pub, which was called the Tartan
Lounge.

Doug Evans had obviously been aiming for an old-
world atmosphere in this part of his business, and

judging by his casual statement about profits, his neighbors appreciated the effort.

The bar with its rows of colorful, gleaming bottles was topped by a crest that matched the one up in their sitting room. Bright swathes of tartan and crossed swords adorned the other walls, and a fire burned low in the big stone hearth, where Dundee drowsed in the warmth on a folded blanket.

Three young cowboys and their girlfriends were engaged in a lively game of darts, while a group of older couples chatted over cribbage boards in a corner.

The place was warm and welcoming, rich with quiet companionship, a cozy refuge from the winter night.

Doug settled Maggie near the fireplace, then went to the bar and came back with a martini, and a glass of whiskey-and-cream liqueur on ice for her. She looked at it, surprised to find he'd remembered the brief mention of her drink of choice.

Most of the men she encountered these days would have missed that comment, Maggie realized. They were usually too wrapped up in themselves and the impression they were making to pay much attention to a woman's conversation, even when they found her attractive.

But Doug Evans seemed to be a supremely confident man. He was quiet and considerate, but gave no evidence of being worried about the impression he was making on her.

"You were joking about wages a while ago." Maggie sipped the excellent liqueur. "And it made me wonder about something."

"What's that?" His hard face was highlighted softly by the flames.

Maggie could picture him as a Highland chieftain sitting near a turf fire, with his horses nearby and his warriors gathered around him.

She shivered in the grip of sudden sexual arousal, and forced her mind back to the topic.

"Do you have any full-time employees besides Rose?" she asked. "If not, the wage deductions won't amount to very much."

"I don't even get a deduction for Rose," he admitted. "She just works here to help out."

"Why?"

"Because she's on a visitor's visa—not a work permit."

"You mean she and the children are in the country illegally?" Maggie asked.

"Not exactly. But her visa is on the point of expiry, and she hasn't been able to get it renewed." He sighed. "It's easier to find the Hope Diamond than get a green card."

"Why are you telling me this?" Maggie asked curiously. "You don't even know who I am, Doug. What if Terry and I were immigration agents, coming here to investigate your sister?"

He met her eyes steadily, with a gaze so probing that she was forced to look down at the table.

"That's not who you are, Maggie," he said gently. "I'm still not sure what you're doing here, but I do know you're not at all interested in my sister and her citizenship."

Maggie traced the damp circle left by her glass on

the shining wooden surface of the table. "You're right," she said. "I'm no threat to Rose."

"So do you think I'm daft, Maggie?" he asked casually. "Opening my books to you?"

Maggie shook her head. "I never saw your numbers, not even one entry. I just offered a bit of computer software, that's all. But I'd say your business seems pretty well managed."

He chuckled, a pleasant sound in the cozy firelit pub. "Oh, I'm a good manager, all right. I'm just not much of a computer technician."

She smiled at him. Their eyes met and held for a long moment, and again she was the first to turn away. "So Rose doesn't want to go back to Scotland?"

"Not at all. Her ex-husband is a harsh, cruel bastard. He's been abusive to Rose and a terrible influence on the girls. For the sake of the kids, she'd much prefer to keep an ocean between them."

Maggie thought about the gentle blond woman and her two little girls. "Oh, I'm so sorry," she said. "Do you have any family there who could help her if she's forced to go back?"

"Our father died when we were small and our mother remarried not long after. She's dead now, too. There's nobody left but a stepfather. And he's not a man who'd help either of us, not unless there might be some profit in it for him."

"How sad." Maggie thought about the meaning of his words, and what his childhood must have been like. "So did you come to Texas to escape all that?"

"Not at the time. I was still working in the family business then. It was soon after my mother died, and

I came here in the line of duty. But once I was here, I couldn't seem to leave.''

''It's a long way from Scotland.''

Doug laughed. ''Moira and I were just talking about the same thing. In many ways the landscape in the Hill Country is similar to the place I grew up, you know. But there's more sunshine here.''

''It sounds like you really love Texas.''

He considered her words for a moment, sipping his drink. ''Not so much as I love the town,'' he said at last. ''This is the first place I've ever felt truly at peace with the world. Crystal Creek and my hotel…'' He waved his hand at the comfortable room, the flickering glow on the hearth. ''It's home to me, Maggie.''

She felt a sudden tug of uneasiness, and a deep, painful feeling of guilt over what she was doing in Crystal Creek.

''What is it?'' he asked, watching her intently.

She sipped her drink, avoiding his glance. ''I don't know what you mean.''

''You have a very expressive face. And just now, you look troubled.''

''Troubled?''

He reached out to touch her forehead with a gentle hand. ''Whenever you frown, you get this lovely wee line between your eyebrows.''

She ducked away from his hand and shifted awkwardly on the padded bench.

''Look, Doug,'' she said with forced casualness, ''don't keep watching me so closely, all right? I'm not used to it.''

His eyebrows arched in disbelief. ''You're not

used to a man watching you? That's hard to believe, for a woman like you."

She stared at him, genuinely surprised. "You're kidding."

"About what?"

"I'm quite an ordinary person, Doug. And when you get to know me, I'm not even all that nice," she added with another pang of remorse.

"I'll be the judge of that," he said with a gaze so warm that she felt the color rise in her cheeks again.

"Now it's your turn," he told her after an awkward silence.

"Me?"

"What's the story of your childhood? Did you grow up in California?"

She shook her head. "Terry and I were raised on a farm in Ohio. We didn't move to California until we were adults."

"I see. And what took you from Ohio to the Golden Coast?"

She thought about the question. "Well, mainly the fact that we had a patron who sponsored our college education out there. Like you, we'd lost both our parents by the time we reached our late teens."

"I'm sorry," he said with genuine sympathy. "That's a hard road, I know."

"But our situation was the opposite of yours," Maggie said. "Our mother died of ovarian cancer when I was seven and Terry was five. Our father did such a wonderful job of raising us on his own," she added with a fond, faraway smile. "He worked all day on the farm, and then at night he was a mother to us as well, doing laundry and packing school lunches.''

"I never knew what it was to have a loving father,'' Doug said. "I can't even remember mine.''

"Daddy was our hero. And then when we were in our mid-teens and his life was starting to get a little easier, he was killed in a tractor accident on the farm.'' Her eyes stung with unshed tears. "It was just a careless mistake,'' she said, swallowing hard. "He took a shortcut up an incline behind the barn, and the tractor flipped over on him. He was pinned there all alone for most of the day. By the time we got home from school and found him, it was too late.''

"I'm so sorry, Maggie.''

Doug covered her hand with his own and waited for her to compose herself.

"Do you look like him?'' he asked, clearly trying to set her at ease again. "You and your brother are not at all alike.''

Maggie hesitated, surprised by how easy it was to talk with this man. These were topics she almost never spoke about, even with people she'd known for a long time.

"Actually,'' she said, "I was adopted. My birth mother was a high-school girl from Cincinnati. She was sixteen years old, an honor student and a talented musician. When she got pregnant, her family forced her to carry the baby to term.''

"And that baby was you,'' he said, his voice rough with emotion.

"Yes, it was me.''

He released her hand, and she was almost sorry.

Again she marveled at how comfortable she felt, wrapped in this semilit intimacy with a man she barely knew, talking about the most emotional parts of her life.

"My adoptive parents wanted a baby for years before I came along," she said in a low voice. "They made me feel so loved and wanted. It was part of the family history, how they got the call about the baby and they were so excited. packing up the little clothes they'd been saving all that time, and driving to Cincinnati to get me. I was nine days old when they took me home."

Doug smiled, his face so warm and tender that Maggie had to fight the urge to reach out and lay a hand on his cheek.

"So what about your brother?" he asked. "Was he adopted, too?"

Maggie laughed and shook her head. "No, it was one of those classic cases. They'd been married ten years when they got me, and never been able to conceive. But a little over a year after I arrived, my mother got pregnant. They were so happy. Terry and I have been good pals all our lives."

"So you had a nice childhood, happy and loved on a farm in Ohio."

"Yes," she said. "I really did."

"I'm glad to hear it. I like to think about you growing up like that."

The physical attraction between them had grown almost palpable. Maggie was afraid that if she stayed with him any longer, he'd invite her to his room and she wouldn't be able to resist.

And that would be a huge mistake, something she certainly couldn't afford at this point.

"Well," she said with false brightness, "thanks for the drink and the nice conversation, Doug. It's getting late, and I'd better head upstairs."

He didn't press, though his eyes burned a deeper green as he watched her get to her feet.

"Good night," he said courteously. "I'll see you in the morning. Do you think we can do some more work on those computer programs?"

"I should be free in the morning," she said.

"That's great." He raised his glass in a quiet salute. "Until then, Maggie."

Her knees felt suddenly weak. As she headed for the door, every part of her body was conscious of him watching her leave.

MAGGIE WAS UP early the next morning, drying her hair in the bathroom. A knock sounded on the door and she padded through the sitting room in her terry-cloth robe to admit a skinny young man in blue overalls, carrying a metal tool kit and a big spool of wire.

Dundee pressed by the man's legs, then stepped daintily into the room and looked around with a proprietary air.

"Phone jacks and new lines," the young man said curtly, moving past Maggie into the room. "Doug said you could tell me where they should go."

"Phone jacks!" Terry said in delight.

He sat at the round table in the sitting room, where he squinted at the flip-up screen of his laptop.

"This is great. Maggie, your Scotsman is a man of his word."

"Hey, I'm buying this technology with hours and hours of my time." Maggie watched as the young man crawled around on the floor and tapped the wide oak baseboards with a hammer.

"And you're loving every minute of it," Terry told her. "There's nothing you enjoy better than playing with computer software. Especially," he added in a teasing undertone, "when there's information you want."

Maggie frowned at him, then turned to the phone technician. "We'll want an outlet over there," she said, pointing, "for our fax machine, and another one here by the table. And one in each bedroom under the window, if you can manage it. I think that would be the logical place, don't you?"

"Okay." The man popped a stick of gum into his mouth. "So where should I start?"

"In the other bedroom." Maggie indicated Terry's room. "I'll be dressed in a minute, and then you can work anywhere you like."

She hurried back into her own room, put on jeans, a white cotton shirt and moccasins, and dabbed on a bit of makeup.

Before she was finished she heard more arrivals in the sitting room, followed by the whir of equipment and the high-pitched voices of children.

Maggie pulled her hair back into a ponytail, pinned it on top of her head and went out to find Rose Murdoch, in khaki shorts and flowered apron, running a vacuum cleaner around the sitting room, followed by Moira, who plied a feather duster on every exposed surface.

Robin was there as well, squatting next to the

phone technician. She had apparently been given the task of helping him, because she held a screwdriver and a couple of drill bits, and looked rigid and solemn with responsibility.

Terry had given up his work to move aside heavy pieces of furniture for Rose to run her vacuum underneath.

Normally her brother hated being interrupted when he was writing, but today he seemed calm in the midst of the uproar.

After they moved the couch back in place, Rose ran a hand over her forehead and gave Terry a shy, grateful smile. He beamed down at her so warmly that Maggie was a little startled.

"Terry, do you want to work in my room?" Maggie called over the roar of the vacuum. "It's a lot quieter in here."

"That's okay." Terry gave his sister an unabashed, cheerful grin. "I've just made a deal with Rose. If I help her with the vacuuming, she'll make breakfast for me down in the bar."

"It seems the Embree and Evans clans are making a lot of deals these days," a deep voice commented from the hallway.

Doug entered, looking more handsome than ever in his jeans and shirt.

Maggie glanced around, unnerved by the way he seemed to fill the room. "My goodness," she said with an awkward laugh. "There are seven people in here now, and one cat."

"Are there really?" Doug grinned at her. "Then let's remove a couple of these bodies, shall we?"

"You and me?" Maggie asked as he paused close

by her side. His eyes were richly green in the morning sun, and so bright they were hard to look at.

"I was hoping you could give me a minute. I've run into a nasty snag in that program you installed," Doug told her. "It won't bring up any data entries prior to 1998. I need your help to unlock the thing."

"Already? What a slave driver," she said lightly, though she was excited and a little uneasy to have him so near.

"Hey, I'm already keeping my part of the bargain, right?" He indicated the technician with his small assistant.

"Doug, I haven't even had breakfast yet."

"Just as well. Nora sent a plate of her famous biscuits and some homemade jam. I'm hoping you'll have breakfast with me."

"But I..." Maggie glanced around in distracted fashion.

Rose and Terry had moved into the other bedroom with their cleaning equipment. Moira was with them, still dusting.

Maggie heard a steady hum of conversation over the noise of the appliance, accompanied by occasional bursts of laughter.

Terry, it appeared, was getting along very well with the local populace.

"Robin, I need that yellow screwdriver," the technician said, frowning at a hole he'd drilled in one of the baseboards.

Solemnly, Robin handed over the proper tool, then gave Maggie and her uncle a proud smile.

"It looks like everything's under control up here," Doug said, taking Maggie's arm. "By lunchtime you'll be able to establish a Pentagon office in this suite if you want to. For now, come downstairs and have some breakfast with me.''

"And help you with your computer problem," Maggie said dryly.

"Well, since you're going to be nearby anyhow..." He gave her a boyish grin.

She didn't resist further, mostly because it was so pleasant to feel his hand on her arm. A treacherous part of her wanted to nestle closer, and see if his long body was as hard and muscular as it looked.

Horrified at herself, Maggie suppressed the dangerous thought.

As they neared the lobby with the cat at their heels, a delicious aroma of fresh coffee and hot baking drifted up the stairs.

"Oh my," she said. "Doesn't that smell wonderful? By the time I leave here, I'm going to weigh two hundred pounds."

A phone rang behind the reception desk. Doug vanished into his office and returned a few moments later, tucking a folded piece of paper into his shirt pocket.

"And when will that be, Maggie?" he asked quietly, lifting the little gate so she could walk behind the reception desk.

"Beg your pardon?" She perched on one of the stools and looked hungrily at the carafe of hot coffee, the platter of fluffy biscuits.

Doug poured her a cup of coffee and offered the biscuits, along with napkins and utensils.

"How long will you be staying, Maggie? And

what," he asked with a sudden steely edge to his voice, "exactly are you doing here?"

Maggie tensed, but forced herself to sip coffee and butter one of the biscuits with a casual air. "Well, the fact is, at the moment I'm working on a little research project of my own," she said. "Why do you ask?"

He settled onto the stool next to her and helped himself to a biscuit.

"Because Ralph Wall's been telling everybody within a fifty-mile radius that you're working for a movie producer who's planning to buy up all the real estate and shower the place with money. I was hoping you might want to tell me what's really going on."

CHAPTER FIVE

AT HIS WORDS, Maggie almost choked on her mouthful of coffee, though she made a gallant attempt to sound cheerful.

"My goodness," she said. "You certainly have to give that man credit. I only talked to Ralph Wall about twelve hours ago, and he's already spread the word over the entire county?"

"Let me tell you, if your goal was to spread the word," Doug said grimly, "you couldn't have picked a better man. The whole town's in an uproar."

"It is?"

"Folks are arguing with each other down at the Longhorn over their coffee this morning, and talking about you at the beauty parlor and the feed store. J. T. McKinney and his wife have already organized a community meeting at their ranch tomorrow night to discuss this threat to the community. And Mary Gibson and her husband aren't speaking to each other."

"Why not?"

"Because when they were feeding their ostriches this morning, Bubba made the mistake of saying the whole plan might not be such a bad idea, and Mary whacked him with a plastic pail."

Nervously, Maggie set aside her coffee mug and

reached for the computer mouse, but he took it from her and moved it to the other side of the desk.

"If it's all the same to you, Maggie," he said quietly, "I think I'd rather talk for a little while before we get started on this again. I want to ask you a few things."

"Hey, I thought you dragged me down here so I could get straight to work," she said with another attempt at bravado. "And I may be a guest staying in your hotel, but my private concerns are really none of your business, Doug."

"They are when they arrive on my fax machine in an open message."

Maggie tensed, and her heart began to pound nervously. "What do you mean?"

He took the folded sheet of paper from his shirt pocket and handed it to her. "This came just a few minutes ago. Apparently it started out as a ship-to-shore message somewhere in the Mediterranean, then got relayed through an office in Los Angeles before it wound up here."

Maggie's uneasiness deepened. She took the sheet of fax paper and saw Natasha's code name at the top of the page, accompanied by a jumbled series of transmission encryption and relay signals. The message itself was brief, unsigned and desperate:

Maggie, please come to me at once! Darling, I can't survive this without you. I'll go mad.

"So that's from your employer?" he asked after she read the message and put it down at her elbow.

"Yes," Maggie said, avoiding his eyes. "It's from my employer."

"He seems very fond of you."

She frowned at the clear implication in his words. "Not that it's any business of yours," she said stiffly, "but my employer happens to be a woman."

He arched an eyebrow, one of his most appealing and maddening expressions.

"Look," she said, "you're getting this all wrong. She's being overly dramatic, that's all. Everybody talks that way in Hollywood."

"I wouldn't know much about Hollywood," he said curtly. "Is this woman a movie producer?"

"No," Maggie said. "She isn't."

"So who is she?"

"I can't tell you that. She's...a very famous person, actually a legend. A big part of my job is to guard her privacy."

He looked skeptical. "But you told Ralph you were working for a movie producer who wanted to buy up a lot of local real estate. So was that whole story just a lie, Maggie?"

She looked down at the computer keyboard, feeling a new flood of shame. The standard Hollywood way of doing things seemed so tacky, somehow, here in the quiet tree-lined streets of Crystal Creek.

Maggie sipped her coffee, but the delicious flavor had turned bitter.

"Just the movie-producer part was a bit exaggerated," she said at last. "But it's certainly true that my employer wants to buy a large block of real estate in Crystal Creek."

"Why?"

"I don't see how that's any concern of yours," she said.

"No concern of mine?" He stared at her in disbelief. "I'm the mayor of this town, Maggie, and a part of the business community as well as a major property owner. I also operate the local real estate office. How could it not be a concern of mine?"

He looked so outraged and disapproving that Maggie's heart was torn. She even had to fight an urge to apologize for her involvement in all this.

But her first loyalty was always to Natasha, who'd done so much for her and Terry. Until Maggie had a chance to talk with her employer, she couldn't discuss the matter with anybody else.

Not even Doug Evans...

She slipped down from the stool and headed for the staircase. "I certainly hope we have a telephone in our room by now, because I'll need to make some immediate travel arrangements."

"So you're off then?" He watched her with a cool, remote expression. "Heading for the sunny Mediterranean, where you've been summoned?"

"I'm a loyal employee. I do as I'm told."

"An admirable work ethic," he said, but there was no warmth in his voice, none of the admiration she'd sensed the night before.

Maggie was a little surprised how much she missed it.

"You know," he said as she neared the stairs, "I noticed you before, Maggie. Back in the fall when you were coming here on those scouting trips."

She paused with her hand on the carved newel post and glanced back at him cautiously. "You did?"

"Every time you came, I watched you drive slowly up and down the streets and get out to look at different buildings and chat with people. I thought you were the most beautiful woman I'd ever seen."

"Doug…"

"And I even made up a story about you for my nieces," he went on, his voice quiet and sad. "I told them you were some kind of magic princess who was coming to save our town. I didn't know who you were or what you were doing, but I had the feeling deep in my heart that you would be good for Crystal Creek. Now I'm not so sure."

The disappointment in his voice put Maggie on the defensive. "I have nothing to be ashamed of," she said, trying to meet his eyes without flinching. "We're not doing anything wrong."

"Whatever it takes to convince yourself," he told her quietly.

Before she could respond, he got up, gathered his files and disappeared into the office, closing the door without a backward glance.

Maggie fought an urge to go down and knock on the door, explain everything and beg for his understanding. Then she remembered the coldness of his voice, the look of disappointment in his eyes, and her shoulders slumped in defeat. She trudged up the stairs toward the suite of rooms.

INSIDE SHE FOUND the technician gone. Dundee slept in a furry lump on one of the sunlit couches and Terry worked in his bedroom, where he had already set up his computer and was plugging the modem into the newly installed phone jack.

Her brother couldn't work properly on a laptop, and he felt incomplete without access to the Internet, where he did most of his research. Having a proper computer up and running would be such a blessing for him.

"I feel great, Mags," he told her, beaming over his shoulder. "My head's bursting with new ideas."

Singing a few snatches of an old Scottish ballad, he switched on the computer and ran their antivirus program, then brought up a file containing the current chapter of his novel.

Maggie hovered, watching him. "Well, I see we're mostly connected with the world again."

He turned to smile at her. "Isn't it great? Thanks for wheedling this out of your Scotsman. Now that I'm up and running, I don't mind if we stay here forever."

"He's not my Scotsman," she said automatically. But as usual, Terry could tell she was upset about something.

"What's wrong?" he asked.

"Oh, various things."

She went into the sitting room and opened a can of the cat food she'd bought at the drugstore, setting it out on the floor.

Dundee woke at once and leaped down to edge nearer, examining the food with interest before squatting and beginning to gnaw at it daintily.

Terry lounged in the doorway, watching with a bemused smile. "You're stealing his cat?"

"Certainly not," Maggie said with dignity. "I'm merely being hospitable to a visitor."

"Whatever you say, Mags. So tell me about these problems you're worried about."

Maggie stroked the cat lovingly, then settled in a chair nearby and took out the big cross-stitch sampler, only about half-finished, that she'd been carrying around the world for the past year.

"Well, our Scottish hotel owner has found out a bit of what I'm doing here, and he's far from pleased. In fact, I'm pretty sure he hates me. So do most of the townspeople, it seems."

"You're just doing your job," Terry said, still watching the cat. "Doug can hardly hold that against you."

"You'd be surprised what that man thinks of me," she said dryly, though she felt on the verge of tears. "Although it might help if I could tell him what my job really is."

"So why don't you, if his opinion matters to you so much?"

"Terry, you know why I can't. I have to protect Natasha," Maggie said wearily, rummaging through her skeins of thread for the particular shade of blue she needed. "And until Natasha's ready to go public, I can hardly be using her name all over the place."

"Maybe it's time she started allowing you to mention her name sometimes," Terry said, clearly troubled by his sister's unhappiness. "Why should you have to be out there taking it on the chin all the time, while she stays safe and cozy in the background? It's not fair, the way she treats you."

Silently, Maggie took out the folded paper and handed it to him.

Terry read the piteous request, then shook his head

in disbelief. "A face-lift must be a truly agonizing experience."

"Terry, don't keep making fun of her. You know how lonely and isolated she feels when she's forced to be away from us. She always has to be so careful about her interactions with people."

He refolded the paper and tapped it on his knee. "So what are you going to do?"

Maggie set aside her needlework, lifted the big cat onto her knee and cuddled her wistfully, gazing out the window. Dundee settled heavily and began to purr, then licked Maggie's hand with a drowsy rough tongue. Obviously this was a cat who appreciated expensive bribes.

"Well, to start with," Maggie said in response to her brother's question, "I need to use one of our new phone lines to make arrangements for my trip."

"Are you leaving today?"

"I have to. She sounds so desperate. I'll get Tony to book me through from Austin to New York, then get me on the Concorde to London and find some helicopter to take me out to the cruise ship. I should get there sometime tomorrow, if I'm lucky."

He shook his head. "Poor Maggie. It all sounds so exhausting."

She put the cat down regretfully, tucked her needlework away and started toward the door.

"Natasha is an exhausting person. But all in all—" Maggie paused with her hand on the knob "—it might not be so bad if I disappear for a little while. People will have a chance to talk about what I've hinted at doing here, and get some of the initial argument out of the way. When I come back in a few days, if Natasha is still determined to buy up part of this town, maybe a few of them will be willing to sell their properties.''

"Unless your big rugged Scotsman should get to them first.''

"He's not my…'' she began again, then stopped when her brother grinned.

"Better start packing, Mags,'' he said gently. "After all, you can't ignore a direct command from the great lady herself.''

"No, I can't.'' She looked back at him. "I thought Rose was cooking breakfast for you.''

"The morning's been getting away on us so quickly that we decided to make it brunch instead.''

"Where?''

"Over at their house,'' he said casually, turning back to his computer screen. "The girls are making French toast. Apparently it's Moira's specialty.''

"Terry,'' she said, "don't you think it might be a little—''

"Okay,'' he interrupted cheerfully, waving at the computer. "Make your calls. There's a functional jack in your room, too, and after lunch the technician is going to connect the ones in the sitting room.''

"Listen to me,'' she said from the doorway, feeling wretched with sympathy. "Rose Murdoch and her little girls have visas that are about to expire. They'll probably all have to go back to Scotland soon.''

His sunny face turned pale. "How do you know that?''

"Doug told me.''

"Well,'' her brother said after a brief, tense moment, "they're here now, and Moira's making French toast for me. Not much point in worrying about what's going to happen in the future, is there?"

"It's not a bad idea to think ahead, and consider the consequences of one's actions," Maggie told him.

"I appreciate your concern," he told her. "But I'm a big boy, and I can look after myself. I've been taking care of myself for years, Maggie."

"And you think I haven't?" she said, stung by his implication.

"Don't be so touchy. You stayed with Natasha because she's your employer, not because you're getting a free ride. Neither of us has ever accepted handouts from her. Not since we were adults, anyhow."

"But it's more than just that," Maggie said.

"I know." Terry looked at his sister steadily. "You really love the woman."

"Yes, I do." Maggie smiled ruefully. "No matter how frustrating and outrageous Natasha can be, there's just something about her that...touches me."

"I know she can be endearing at times," Terry agreed. "And there's no doubt she's generous. Still, you've got a whole lot more patience than I do, Mags."

She plucked nervously at a splinter on the door frame. "I'm worried about you and Rose."

"Why?" he asked when she paused.

"Well," Maggie said, an awkward flush mounting on her cheek, "if I go ahead with Natasha's plan, and Doug remains as opposed as he is now, that's not exactly a basis for warm feelings between our two families, Terry."

He turned around on the chair to look directly at her, with a thoughtful, measuring glance.

"Then to hell with Natasha and her plan," he said at last.

She opened her mouth to protest, but Terry waved her away. "Go make your arrangements, Maggie." He stood up and switched off the computer. "Call up your travel agent in L.A. and get your bags packed. As for me, I have a brunch invitation."

TERRY'S MOOD IMPROVED as he left the hotel and started down the street toward the river. He'd already discovered that it was hard not to feel good when you were out on the streets of this little town.

The trees were still hung with shrouds of mist, and a pale sun gleamed overhead, flickering like a candle. Though the day remained cool, the cottony fog created a hidden, mystical effect. He felt as if he'd found himself in the enchanted city of Brigadoon.

The rest of the world seemed to matter so little out here. All stress drifted away, leaving him feeling cleansed and at peace.

This was a place, Terry realized instinctively, where he would really be able to write. If he could settle down here, become a part of the community and get to know his neighbors, life in Crystal Creek would function like a giant energy cell that constantly recharged his creativity.

Lately, the big, smog-ridden cities had left him increasingly drained and restless. Even his comfortable apartment in Malibu was no longer appealing, though it had seemed like a palace last year when he'd paid the lease with part of the advance on his first novel.

But here in a place like Crystal Creek, far away from…

He came back to reality with a start, recalling that if Natasha got her way, there would be no retreat in Crystal Creek. The damn woman was going to own this place just as she owned the Malibu beach house, the Rockingham town house, the sunny villa in Tuscany and the nine-room apartment in Manhattan.

Scowling, he plunged his hands in his pocket and kicked at a rock on the sidewalk, sending it up the street to land with a satisfying thud on the grass near the old carousel.

Now, that was a sight to behold. If he didn't have such a pleasant and pressing date at the moment, Terry would have liked to stop and explore the lovely antique animals.

Maybe, he thought, brightening, he could come down here after lunch with Moira and Robin, and the girls could tell him all about the carousel. That sort of thing was a job for children, after all.

And Rose could probably use a break from their constant presence. They were sweet little things, but even the nicest children could get tiring when you had the sole care of them.

He thought about Rose with her timid air and look of old-fashioned primness, her shy luminous smile and the odd air of sadness he detected in her sometimes.

So Rose and her daughters might have to go back to Scotland soon?

Terry felt a painful tug of concern.

He passed by the middle school, where Moira had told him she would be going next year. At the moment, Rose's older daughter was being home-schooled, and he realized that must have to do with the citizenship issues. Rose didn't want to enroll Moira in school and then have to take her away again, or run the risk of bringing their residence under scrutiny.

The old sandstone school was silent in the mist. Rose had told him how the place and its principal were being threatened by a new movement in Crystal Creek, backed by the school board, to have the middle school closed and the students bussed to a nearby town.

"It's all to save taxes," she'd told him in her soft brogue. "This town's in deep trouble, Terry. It can't even afford its middle school anymore."

He kicked at another rock, thinking about Natasha Dunne's absurd, grandiose plan to buy herself an entire town.

Would it really, as Maggie sometimes argued, prove to be an ultimate benefit to Crystal Creek? Was the huge infusion of cash that Natasha would offer just what these townspeople needed to save their local institutions and services?

Or was it simply a greedy, manipulative scheme by a wealthy and self-serving woman to get herself a whole lot of national attention at the expense of these people and their peaceful life-style?

In all the years he'd known her, Terry had never managed to figure out the motives of the woman who loomed so large in his life—and his sister's.

Natasha Dunne had first appeared on the scene not

long after their mother's death. The legendary movie actress maintained a charitable foundation that helped children across the nation who'd lost a parent to cancer.

As Terry often said to Maggie, it was like winning a lottery. Of all the eligible children in America, their names had somehow been the ones drawn for that year. And money had started to flow from Natasha Dunne's Hollywood foundation to the Embree farm in distant Ohio.

At first their father had refused to accept any of the money. With quiet, stubborn pride, he'd insisted that he could look after his own family.

But when Maggie and Terry were a little older, needing expensive things like orthodontic work and music training, Paul Embree had given in and taken some cash from the movie star's foundation...

A small dog, oddly blue-gray with brownish patches, appeared from nowhere and trotted along at Terry's side for a while. The dog was fat and appeared unused to exercise. He panted loudly at Terry's brisk pace, and cast a reproachful glance upward.

Terry laughed. "Hello there, boy," he said, stopping to pat the little heaving body. "Are you lost? Or are you hungry, maybe?"

Close-set brown eyes regarded him hopefully, and a ragged tail pounded against the sidewalk.

Terry grinned and took a granola bar from his pocket. The dog's eyes brightened, and his tail rotated furiously. Terry peeled back the wrapper, broke off a piece of granola and gave it to the dog, who munched on it with messy enthusiasm.

Then, clearly losing all interest in his new friend, the dog wandered back over to the feed store and climbed laboriously into the back of a dark blue pickup truck parked by the curb.

Feeling cheered by the little incident, Terry continued on his way to the row of houses along the river, and returned to his memories.

After Paul Embree's death, Maggie and Terry learned that all their father's land was heavily mortgaged. He had been keeping his farming business afloat with annual bank loans. Once the estate was settled and the property sold, Terry and Maggie were not yet out of high school and in danger of becoming wards of the state.

Until Natasha Dunne stepped in personally and took over their lives.

In retrospect, Terry thought grimly, it was almost as if the aging move star had decided to buy herself a family. She'd picked Terry and Maggie up as casually as if they were puppies in a pet store, flown them both out to California and installed them in bewildering, unimaginable luxury.

After high school, their college educations at Ivy League schools were completely paid for, as well as travel to exotic places. If Terry had wanted a Ferrari for graduation, Natasha would have bought it for him without hesitation. He often thought she was disappointed that all he wanted, ever, was a roomful of books and a quiet place to write stories.

For five long years he'd labored as a carpenter's helper to pay back every penny she'd spent on his education, often working until late into the night. Natasha stiffly refused the money at first. Finally she donated it to her foundation, but let Terry know she was hurt by his attitude.

Natasha had a much closer relationship with his sister. The famous woman trusted Maggie, confided in her, and relied more and more on the girl's youth and energy as her own strength began to wane. It had seemed natural that after her college training, Maggie would come back to California and take over the management of Natasha Dunne's complex business affairs.

By now, Terry's sister had a lot of power for such a young woman. Still, in his opinion, Maggie carried around a heavy load of guilt, indebtedness and emotional bondage to their patron, and he wasn't at all sure it was good for her....

But his worried thoughts faded into the background when he arrived at the little house occupied by Rose Murdoch and her daughters, and stood gazing up at it with pleasure.

CHAPTER SIX

TERRY HAD ONLY SEEN Rose's house before at night. In full daylight the place was like a storybook cottage, a cozy, well-tended vision of utter peace and beauty. He looked around, blinking his eyes, unsure whether the effect was a trick of the sunlight and mist.

The cottage was made of pink stone glistening in the sunlight, half covered with tattered remnants of Virginia creeper that rustled in the February breeze. The mullioned windows shone and twinkled warmly above flower beds emptied for the winter.

At one side of the house stood a white trellis that supported a climbing yellow rosebush. The flagged walk seemed to coax visitors around to the back garden where even more delights awaited.

Across the street, the Claro River lapped softly against rocks and boulders at the shoreline with a soothing, eternal sound.

Terry gazed at an upstairs dormer with a window overlooking the river. If he could get a desk and a computer into that room, he'd sit there happily for the rest of his life and produce a whole series of great novels.

He almost hesitated to go and knock on the door

of the cottage. What if the interior of the enchanted house was ugly and disappointing?

Sternly, he put all his imaginative fancies aside, walked up the path and lifted the brass knocker, which was a dragon's head with a droll smile.

Terry grinned back at it.

Robin, who was by now a good friend, answered the door and stood gazing up at him with a quizzical look. She wore a pair of blue jeans, a dinosaur-patterned shirt and her green running shoes, and carried a magnetic slate with big multicolored letters and numbers stuck to its surface.

"Hi, Terry," she said. "What are you smiling at?"

"This fellow on your door." Terry lifted her up to show her the brass knocker. "He looks like Puff the Magic Dragon. That was my favorite song when I was a boy."

"Sing it," Robin commanded, settling happily in the visitor's arms.

Terry carried her inside and shut the door, singing the first verse of the old folk song.

Rose appeared before he was finished, and listened, smiling, in the entry to the kitchen. On the chorus she joined in, her voice sweet and clear. When the adults finished singing, Robin clapped in delight and Rose laughed aloud.

Terry looked around. "It's even prettier on the inside," he said. "Rose, what a wonderful little house this is."

"I'm only renting it at the moment," she said. "But I'd dearly love to buy the place. You're right, it's truly wonderful.'

Actually, the house seemed roomier than it appeared from the outside. It was built on the square like an English cottage, with four rooms on the main floor. To his left was a comfortable living room dominated by a wide brick fireplace, and behind Rose was a bright kitchen that faced the street. In the back he could make out a dining room and a study, both with leaded glass doors.

Narrow wooden stairs carpeted by a Turkish runner led the way up toward a landing with a round stained-glass window.

The little place was probably Edwardian, he thought, with its golden-oak sliding doors, its wide moldings and wainscoting.

"Oh my. Just look at this," he murmured, stroking the hand-carved figure on a polished newel post. It was the same laughing dragon that adorned the front-door knocker.

"Is that Puff?" Robin asked at his side.

"Indeed it is." Terry caressed the shining wood. "What a beautiful work of art."

"In Scotland we have a giant big house," Robin told him solemnly. "With a gardener, and a lady who cooks and cleans."

Terry glanced at Rose, who wiped her hands on her apron and reached for her daughter.

"You mustn't bother our guest, dear," she said in her softly accented voice. "Go and help your sister set the table."

"Moira said I couldn't go back in the kitchen," Robin told her mother in a matter-of-fact tone. "She's really mad at me. Can I show Terry my room?"

"If he doesn't mind," Rose said, distracted by a shout and a wraithlike drift of smoke from the kitchen just behind her.

"Let's go," Terry said, taking the smaller girl's hand and climbing the stairs with her. "I'd love to see your room."

The four rooms on the lower floor were repeated upstairs in the same charming proportions. Each little girl had her own room facing the back garden, full of toys and colored posters.

"Moira sleeps in there, and this one's mine," Robin told him. "She gets to keep the hamster in her room, but I have the ant farm."

Through an open door Terry caught a glimpse of a third bedroom. He saw a double bed covered by a chaste white knitted spread, and a couple of good watercolors on one of the walls.

"That's Mummy's room," Robin said when he glanced in that direction.

"Does Mummy have an ant farm, too?"

"She hates the ant farm and the hamster," Robin said cheerfully. "But Hippo sleeps in her room."

"You have a hippo?" Terry asked in mock surprise, making the little girl shout with laughter.

"Of course not! Hippo's our cat."

"And you call him that because he's fat?" Terry guessed.

"He's very fat. Uncle Doug says if Hippo ate any more, he could get a job as a soccer ball."

"I'll bet he wouldn't like it much, though." Terry paused by the fourth door in the upstairs hallway. "What's in this room?"

"Nothing." Robin tugged on the doorknob and

opened it to show him an empty room with a deep window seat and a bare, gleaming hardwood floor.

Terry stepped inside, taking a deep breath. It was the same room he'd seen from the street below, the one that overlooked the river.

The one where he knew he could write the best work he'd ever done…

"I really, really like this room," he said to the little girl.

"Why?"

"I don't know. It feels like it would be a nice room to work in."

"Wait'll you see my room," Robin said smugly. "I have all the neatest toys."

Terry laughed and tousled her blond curls. "I'll just bet you do."

A few minutes later he was sitting on the floor in Robin's bedroom, wearing a fireman's hat and making siren noises while Robin chopped energetically at the bedspread with a yellow plastic ax.

Rose appeared in the doorway and stood smiling down at them.

"Well, the crisis is over and brunch is ready," she said. "All firefighters are required to wash their hands and come downstairs."

"Bang, bang!" Robin shouted, still deep in her play. "Whoosh!"

Terry lifted her in his arms and kissed her hair. "Time to eat, Firefighter Robin."

They trooped downstairs where Moira stood nervously by the kitchen table wearing a pair of blue oven mitts. Little bowls of fruit salad adorned each place setting, and a wobbly stack of French toast graced the center of the table. On the counter a few candles were burning, apparently in an attempt to dispel the lingering odor of charred toast.

"I burned the last ones," Moira admitted, her tense face coloring a little. She looked unhappy and stressed, almost on the verge of tears.

"That's okay." Terry set Robin down at the place that bore her name on a plastic cup. "We're firefighters," he told Moira gravely. "We don't mind burnt things, not one little bit."

Rose gave him a grateful smile and shyly indicated the place opposite her, and they all settled in to eat their brunch.

After taking time to praise the meal and pronounce it the most delicious food he'd ever tasted, to Moira's obvious gratitude, Terry sipped coffee and looked around with growing contentment.

He marveled at how homey the little kitchen seemed, and how comfortable he felt even though he was normally uneasy on anything resembling a date.

And children aside, in his mind this occasion was a sort of date, albeit a very odd one...

"I can't believe how nice you've made this place, Rose," he said.

"It would be much nicer," Moira told him, "if we could get all our own stuff over here from Scotland."

"Why can't you?" Terry asked.

Moira shrugged and muttered something. Her mother gave her a quick warning glance.

"What did you say, Moira?" he asked politely. "I didn't catch that."

"I said," the older girl repeated, avoiding her

mother's glance, "there's not much sense in bringing all our stuff over here if we just have to go back to Scotland anyhow."

"I don't want to go back!" Robin shouted. "I want to stay here!"

Terry took his napkin and wiped a milk mustache from the little girl's upper lip. He lifted her onto his knee and cuddled her. She hiccupped a couple of times, then settled.

"Uncle Doug's friend is a lawyer. He said there's only one way we could stay in Texas," Moira announced, "and that's if Mummy gets married."

"Moira Murdoch, that's quite enough!" Rose got to her feet swiftly and began to clear the table.

Terry saw how badly her hands were shaking.

"But Uncle Doug's friend said…"

"Never you mind what your uncle and his friends say," Rose told the child with unusual sharpness. "And don't you be discussing things that are none of your concern, young lady!"

Moira's eyes filled with unhappy tears.

"Hey," Terry said with forced cheerfulness, "may I see the hamster? I love hamsters, you know. Maggie and I always had them when we were kids."

Moira brightened and scrubbed a hand across her eyes. "He's really a nice hamster," she said. "He plays all the time on his little wheel."

"Good, let's go have a look at him."

Terry stole a cautious glance at Rose, who stood with her thin back to them, stacking piles of dishes in the sink.

"Rose?" he said from the doorway while the two children tugged at his hands.

"Yes?"

"Are you all right?" Terry said, feeling clumsy and inadequate. "Would you like me to stay and help you with the dishes?"

"No, I'm just fine," she said, her voice still muffled. "Go with them to look at the hamster while I do the washing up, and then we'll all walk back to the hotel together."

He was going to say more, but something in her tone discouraged him. At last he turned away and climbed the stairs along with the two little girls, feeling troubled.

OF ALL THE DUTIES Maggie undertook for her famous employer, trips to Europe were among her least favorite. Despite the lavish comfort of the Concorde, she got miserably jet-lagged on eastbound trips, and so weary that it often took a week to recover.

Another thing she hated, Maggie thought gloomily, was helicopters.

Many times she had to reach Natasha by helicopter in some distant corner of the world, dropping out of the sky into mountaintop chalets or remote villas or private islands. And as always, she had the same heart-stopping sense that the flight could be her last.

This time the fragile, noisy craft really would stop whirling and crash into the sea, taking her along with it…

She gripped the armrest and tried not to look down through the bubble of glass in front of her as the chopper lowered unevenly toward a gigantic cruise ship adrift on the calm waters of the Mediterranean.

But she couldn't keep herself from peering out to see how close they were getting.

She could see people sunning themselves on the lower decks, strolling the hardwood promenades, swimming in the pool at the rear of the ship and playing tennis on the topmost deck. Three elderly men jogged slowly around the track beyond the tennis players.

A helipad stood ready between the tennis court and the upper-deck salon to serve those guests who were far too important to board and leave the ship by conventional means.

A gust of wind caught the chopper, making it rock in an alarming fashion as it drifted toward the pad.

"Sorry about that," the young British pilot shouted cheerfully. "Caught a ragged bit there, but we're down and dry now."

"Thank you." Maggie forced a smile and unfastened her seat belt as she yelled back at him. "No matter how often I do this, I never get used to landing."

"Most people don't." The pilot opened his door and heaved Maggie's bag out from behind the seat, then waved. "Cheery-bye, then. Have a nice cruise, and eat a spot of caviar for me."

"Thank you, I will," she said, not bothering to tell him her reason for coming out to the ship.

Maggie climbed down from the aircraft, ducking away from its whirling blades as it lifted off and spiraled back up into the endless blue arch of sky. The tennis players and the joggers watched curiously as she shouldered her duffel bag and walked across the deck toward the stairwell.

She made her way quickly down to the veranda deck, then up front to the largest suite, where she knocked on a closed door with a lavish gold panel.

A trim, gray-haired Mexican woman in a pink uniform and white apron answered the door and smiled gratefully at her.

"Oh, Maggie," the woman said in hushed tones, "I'm so glad you're here! She's been just impossible. The poor dear is suffering so much."

"Is she really?" Maggie peered into the half light of the suite beyond the door. "I'm sorry to hear that, Carla. You know, Terry thinks she's just being whiny and melodramatic."

"Terry is too hard on Natasha," the maid said with a disapproving frown. "He doesn't take her seriously enough. And after all she's done for him, too."

"That's what I keep telling him. But you know, I think he's getting tired of all those ties to the past."

Maggie felt a pang of concern and an odd touch of envy when she thought about her brother back in the Crystal Creek Hotel.

"Can't say I blame him for that," the maid said. "We're a pretty weird houseful of women, after all, Maggie. I guess we can get a bit tedious for him."

Maggie walked into the suite and smiled wryly as her eyes adjusted to the dim light.

"Look at this," she said. "What a total waste of six thousand dollars a day. Has she ever even opened the drapes, let alone used the veranda?"

Carla shook her head, looking worried. "Maggie, she just lies in her bedroom all day long and begs me for painkillers."

"You're not giving her any?" Maggie said in alarm. "Are you?"

Natasha Dunne's addiction to prescription drugs had been luridly documented in the tabloids over the past decade. But at the same time—in real life—a heartrending battle was being waged by all the people who loved the woman.

Natasha herself had fought hardest of all, and finally beaten her addiction, to Maggie's intense relief and admiration.

"You knew about that bit of morphine they gave her in the hospital right after surgery," Carla said. "And since then..." She stood on tiptoe to whisper in Maggie's ear. "I'm just giving her aspirin and placebos."

"Placebos?" Maggie still felt a tug of worry. "But doesn't the doctor think that could just foster a new psychological dependence?"

"Not if we tell her in a few days that she's only been taking sugar pills," Carla said calmly. "The doctor feels that will even help to reinforce the fact that she doesn't need drugs at all."

Maggie nodded thoughtfully. "So if she's not really in that much pain, what's the matter with her?"

"I think she's just lonely," the maid said. "She misses you."

"So I've had to travel halfway across the planet in less than a day because Natasha misses me?" Maggie said wearily.

"Who else can she talk to, honey? She's still all wrapped in bandages, and she looks a sight. She's a prisoner up here."

"Do any of the other passengers know she's on

board?'' Maggie asked, sprawling on one of the wa-
tered-silk couches.

Carla shook her head. "The staff and crew have
been very discreet, just wonderful. I think the room
steward, at least, knows the truth. But he hasn't
breathed a word to anybody.''

"I'll leave some extra cash for his tip,'' Maggie
said, making a note. "How about food service?''

"They bring trays to the room, and I collect them
at the door.''

"Is she eating anything?''

"Not much.''

"Okay.'' Maggie made another note. "And you
haven't even had her outside on the veranda since
the cruise started?''

"Not once,'' Carla said. "She claims the light
hurts every part of her body, including her toenails.''

"Oh, what nonsense,'' Maggie said impatiently.
"The sea has always been so soothing for her. That's
why I thought this would be the ideal place for her
to hide out while she recuperates.''

"Well, I can't handle her like you can,'' the maid
said. "I wish I could.''

Maggie hugged the smaller woman and patted her
back. "Carla, sweetie. You're an angel, and probably
a saint as well. I honestly don't know how any of us
would manage without you.''

"If only you could stay until she's feeling better.
Just a week or so,'' Carla said plaintively. "She's
really a handful, Maggie.''

"I know what she's like.'' Maggie studied her
notes. "But I still have this job to do for her in

Texas. Unless,'' she added, brightening, ''maybe Natasha's lost interest in that whole plan?''

''Hardly,'' Carla said. ''She talks about it all the time. She says if she could just have a little home in Crystal Creek, her very own place, all her loneliness would be over. She makes the place sound like it's one step short of heaven.''

''Oh, what nonsense,'' Maggie said. ''It's just a small town in Texas. A nice enough place, but the folks who live there are ordinary people with real-life problems. And a lot of them are none too pleased about us being there, let me tell you.''

With shattering clarity she saw Doug Evans with his tall lean body, the crisp black hair and green eyes, that winning smile. Her palms began to moisten, and her body suddenly felt weak.

''God,'' she muttered aloud. ''I need to get over this, I really do.''

''Over what, honey?''

''Nothing. There's just a…''

''A what?'' Carla looked up curiously when Maggie paused.

''A man,'' Maggie said reluctantly. ''Back there in Crystal Creek. He runs the local hotel, and…'' Her voice trailed off once more.

''A man, is it?'' The maid's black eyes sparkled with laughter. ''Well, how nice to hear you talking about a man, Maggie Embree. I thought you never had time for that sort of thing.''

''It's not 'that sort of thing'!'' Maggie said. ''This guy is just a…I mean he's handsome enough, and he can certainly be nice if he tries, but he…'' Again she paused.

"What?"

"He hates me," Maggie said in a low, miserable tone. "Carla, he despises me for what he thinks I'm doing to his town."

"Why should he? It's Natasha's doing, not yours," Carla said.

"Explain that to the proprietor of the Crystal Creek Hotel," Maggie told her grimly. "He doesn't even know Natasha's involved at this point. All he sees is me, trying to buy up his town."

"And are they all angry with you?" the maid asked curiously. "Everybody in this town?"

"Not everybody. I'm sure a few of them will be thrilled to take the money and run. But most of the longtime residents won't be happy at all. And they don't know the half of it," Maggie added. "Not yet, at least."

Again she thought about Doug's handsome sculpted features, the way his cheeks creased when he smiled, the soft, musical burr in his voice when he spoke to her gently.

"Ah, well," Carla said. "We all have our jobs to do." She sat down on the love seat and began to organize a big leather case fitted with cosmetics.

"Is she ready for makeup?" Maggie asked, watching the slim brown fingers dart among colored tubes and glass vials.

"Not yet, but when she starts coming back to life," Carla said with a broad smile, "it'll be the first thing she asks for."

Maggie laughed, feeling a little better.

"I'll go and talk to her," she said, "and then I'm

going to crash for about twelve hours. Is there a bed where I can sleep?''

''Three bedrooms in this suite.'' Carla gestured toward a door opening into an inviting room with a view of the ocean. ''I already had the steward make that one up freshly for you.''

''And gave yourself the one without the window, I suppose,'' Maggie said.

''You can't bully me,'' Carla told her calmly, sorting out dozens of black-handled brushes. ''I'm smaller than you, so it's not fair. Now go in there and talk to her. She's still pretending to be asleep, but I know she's waiting for you.''

Maggie smiled and dropped a kiss on the other woman's cheek, then took a deep breath and headed for a closed door on the opposite side of the room.

CHAPTER SEVEN

MAGGIE OPENED the door and tiptoed inside, into a room even more darkly shrouded than the sitting room. Both the slatted blinds and damask draperies were closed to block any view of the water and distant shoreline.

The air was scented with disinfectant and furniture polish along with the unforgettable aroma of Natasha's perfume, a designer fragrance made specially for her in Paris.

Hands on hips, Maggie stood for a moment until her eyes adjusted to the dimness. Eventually she could make out the slender form in the bed, lying on a mound of silk pillows under a soft drift of blankets.

"Natasha," she said. "Wake up, it's Maggie. I just got here."

Silence from the bed, though Maggie could tell her employer was awake by the shallowness of her breathing and the general air of expectancy in the room.

Natasha Dunne, despite her wealth and power, was like a child in many ways. Maggie understood that the woman didn't want to look as if she'd been lying awake and waiting, so she pretended to be asleep. When finally coaxed "awake," she would be prettily confused for a while, and then express surprise at Maggie's arrival.

Maggie sighed, crossed the room and pulled the drapes aside, then opened the blinds as well. Light flooded into the room, eliciting a gasp from the bed, followed by a lusty curse.

She grinned, but was careful to compose her expression before she turned around.

Natasha whimpered piteously, her hands over her bandaged face.

"What a lovely view," Maggie said calmly, looking out the window. "Natasha, I think you could see all the way to Crete from here. And that light on the water...isn't it just incredible?"

"It hurts me. Close the drapes, Maggie. The doctor said I'm not supposed to be exposed to light until I've begun to heal."

"Nonsense, he said no such thing," Maggie told her briskly. "In fact, he said you could go home and resume any of your daily routine that you felt up to. But Carla tells me you don't feel up to much of anything."

"I'm afraid."

"What are you afraid of?"

"I'm positive the surgery didn't work," Natasha whispered. "I'm afraid I'll be a monster when they take the bandages off."

"You damn well better not be," Maggie said, "after the money we paid to hire the best plastic surgeon in the world. Come on, let me look."

She sat on a rose-colored velvet armchair by the bed and leaned over to study her employer, whose hands still covered her face.

"I can't."

"Look, dear, this is Maggie you're talking to. I flew here all the way from Texas just to be with you. Now, are you going to be nice," Maggie said patiently, as if she was addressing a three-year-old, "or am I going to get on that plane and go right back to America?"

Fearfully, Natasha lowered her hands and Maggie gave her a long, thoughtful examination.

Natasha Dunne was fifty-three years old, and on her first foray into plastic surgery she'd shown her usual flair and gone for the whole thing. On one of the most famous and photographed faces in the world, the eyelids, under-eyes, cheeks, upper lip, chin and neckline had all been done at once.

When she came out of the surgery, Natasha had looked like something from another planet, her eyes blackened and bruised, with blood all over her hospital gown. A gauze bandage had wrapped her face and supported her chin so only the damaged eyes and scabbed lips were visible.

Natasha's staff had rushed her out to the airport and onto the cruise ship as quickly and discreetly as money allowed, while she was still stunned with drugs and painkillers.

Maggie shuddered at the memory of that battered face. But now, only a few days later, the woman already looked much better.

"For goodness' sake, you're almost human now that the bandages are gone," she said, peering critically at the visible scars around Natasha's eyes. "And it looks like he did a lovely job, Natasha. In a few weeks you're going to be fabulous."

"Really?" The puffy, discolored eyes blurred with tears. "You're not just saying that, dear?"

"Have I ever lied to you?"

"And I don't look too hideous right now?" Natasha asked shyly. "Darling, you're not…offended by the sight of me?"

"Oh, sweetie," Maggie said at last, touching Natasha's shoulder under the blanket. "Is that why you've kept the drapes closed? You don't want Carla to look at you and feel bad?"

Natasha stared toward the window with her bruised eyes. "I was always so beautiful," she murmured. "It made people happy to look at me. I can't bear the thought I might be…giving offense."

"Carla!" Maggie called toward the open door. "Could you come in here, please?"

The maid appeared with an inquiring look. Again Natasha quailed against the pillows and covered her face with her hands.

"Look at Natasha," Maggie told the maid, dragging the thin hands away. "Don't you think she's looking a lot better?"

"Oh, she is," Carla said after a brief examination. "Natasha, you're going to be lovely. I can't believe how fast it's healing."

"She thought the sight of her would be offensive to you," Maggie said, waving a hand at the drapes. "That's why she wanted all this spooky darkness."

Carla laughed, a merry sound that dispelled the final constraint in the room.

"Oh, what a big silly," she said fondly, leaning over to kiss the bandages wrapping Natasha's hair. "Now I'll go and get a lounge ready for you on the veranda, and you can sit and watch the ocean until dinnertime.''

''And Maggie will stay out there and talk to me?'' Natasha asked.

''Maggie needs to sleep,'' Carla said firmly, taking a green velvet robe from the little closet. ''She's been traveling nonstop since Texas.''

''I'm always so selfish,'' Natasha murmured through her stiff lips. ''Just a mean, selfish woman. How's Terry?''

''I'm afraid he's feeling a bit restless.'' Maggie got to her feet and turned away. ''But we'll talk about that another day. You have a sunbath and I'll get some sleep, and tomorrow we'll talk.''

''Just tell me...'' Natasha grasped her wrist.

Maggie paused, looking down with a flood of affection at the distorted face on the pillows.

''Tell me how it's going,'' Natasha pleaded.

''In Texas?''

''Of course.''

Maggie hesitated, wondering what to say. ''We've only been there a couple of days, Nat. I've just been able to put out a few feelers, nothing more.''

''But people are reacting positively? They're excited about the idea?''

Maggie thought of Ralph Wall's fat face shining with greed, and Doug's cold, disapproving gaze, and the townspeople gathering at a local ranch to express their outrage.

''Reactions are...sort of mixed at the moment. But I haven't exactly outlined the whole idea,'' she said, sinking into the velvet chair again. ''I didn't want to get your name involved until I was more certain about how things were going to proceed.''

"But using my name is the heart of the plan," Natasha said. "I want them to know I'm buying their town. I want them all to be my friends and rejoice in the fact that I'm going to be around a great deal, and that they'll all be able to speak to me as if I were just another of their neighbors.''

In growing despair, Maggie remembered the Longhorn restaurant with its lively, laughing clientele, its vigorous sense of community and history.

"I'm not sure how much that's really going to matter to these people, Natasha," she said cautiously.

"Of course it matters!'' the older woman said, her voice strengthening. "When I was there in the late sixties, the people in Crystal Creek treated me like a princess. They couldn't do enough for me, from the oldest residents down to the little children who brought flowers and scattered them at my feet wherever I went.''

"But dear, you have to remember it was a different time back then," Maggie said gently. "I think people in those days were more thrilled about the movie-star idea. Now they're much more cynical. They mostly just care about their own lives. And," she added, "some of them care a lot about money.''

"They love me in that town," Natasha said stubbornly. "I'm going to do so much good there, too. They'll all be thrilled to have me back.''

"Look, Nat, I'm just not sure if that's entirely true.''

But Maggie could see that her employer had tuned

her out, a familiar trick with Natasha when the conversation wasn't proceeding to her liking.

"They were wonderful to me," Natasha said in a dreamy voice. "All those people in Crystal Creek. And when Jerry..."

Cue the tears, Maggie thought wearily.

Two bright trails of moisture slipped down Natasha's cheeks. "When the word came that Jerry was...that he was dead...those people gathered me to their hearts and never let me go. They saved my life."

Maggie, who had heard this all a great many times, sighed and rubbed her aching temples.

Natasha Dunne had made a movie in the Texas Hill Country when she was twenty-two years old. She'd actually stayed in the Crystal Creek Hotel during its filming. The movie, *Wild Land,* became one of the most famous westerns ever made, and the tragic story of its lead actress had certainly added to the gross income. The film still earned huge amounts of money in both domestic and foreign syndication.

At the time of filming, Natasha Dunne had been newly married to actor Jeremy Calder, the square-jawed, dark-eyed dream lover of women everywhere. Theirs had been practically a royal wedding, the fantasy of millions around the globe.

Soon after the wedding, Jerry was drafted and went to Vietnam. Women cried and held round-the-clock prayer vigils for his safety. Every magazine in the country carried the poignant photograph of lovely young Natasha standing on a windswept hilltop with one hand on her breast and another shading her eyes as she gazed at the sunrise, crying for her absent husband.

The nation was paralyzed with grief when news flew across the airwaves that Jeremy Calder had been killed in combat, shot out of the sky to die in a jungle swamp, with a picture of Natasha, it was said, in a waterproof case next to his heart.

The new bride was inconsolable. She finished her contracted work on *Wild Land,* though most of the final scenes were rewritten to omit the star, or done with the help of a body double. For two months afterward she went into retreat, staying in Crystal Creek and crying her eyes out in her hotel room.

Reporters and photographers camped out in the town, trying to catch glimpses and photos of the grieving young widow. Though the studio tried to guard her privacy, Natasha Dunne and Jeremy Calder had become a famous symbol of everything that was wrong with the Vietnam war...the flower of American youth being cut down in its prime.

Finally the studio whisked their star away from Crystal Creek and hid her in a secret place unknown to anybody. It was months before she reappeared, paler and lovelier than ever, and more poised somehow, as if her youth had vanished in the flames of sorrow and a new, stronger woman had emerged.

Despite her beauty and fame, Natasha never remarried. And though she hadn't been able to endure going back to Crystal Creek in the intervening years, the town had always haunted her, as she often told Maggie.

Now she wanted to buy the place, make it her own and become its patron saint, possibly its goddess.

Maggie sighed, almost too tired to think.

"I've decided I also want to live there," Natasha was saying. "A good part of the year, at least."

As exhausted as she was, this still got Maggie's attention. "You want to live there? In Crystal Creek? Oh, please, Nat, tell me you're kidding."

"I'll need a house," Natasha went on, ignoring her again. "Something that's a decent size, of course, with lots of room for guests, because I'm sure we'll be having…"

Natasha brightened and sat erect, clapping her hands, looking almost like her old self in spite of the scars.

"I know!" she said. "We can buy the hotel, and convert it to a private residence!"

Maggie stared at her employer with bleary dismay. "Natasha, that's just not—"

"It was such a beautiful old place." Natasha's voice sounded quiet and faraway. Her puffy lips stretched into a wistful smile. "All that beautiful woodwork, and views of the hills from every room on the second floor. I'm sure a good architect would be able to—"

"Nat, listen to me."

The actress stopped talking and blinked slowly. "What's the matter, dear?"

"You can't buy the Crystal Creek Hotel."

"Why not? It's perfect." Natasha's enthusiasm began to mount again. "We'd have tons of room and lots of bathrooms. Honey, does it still have that big extra lot next door? You know how I love to have privacy and trees all around me so I can hear the birds singing. I hope nobody's built on that lot, Maggie?''

"No, the vacant lot is still there, and it's full of big pecan and cedar trees. You can hear birds singing in there all the time."

"Oh, that's wonderful." Natasha reached out to squeeze Maggie's arm gratefully. "I'm so glad you came to me, darling. See, I'm better already. You always make me feel that way."

"Natasha…"

"How much do you think the hotel will cost us? Of course, I'd always intended to buy it along with the rest of the downtown businesses. But now that I have this idea, we'd better raise our offer so you can get it right away. I want to bring an architect in and—"

"The hotel's not for sale," Maggie said bluntly, stemming this flow of words.

"Not for sale?" Natasha said. "How is that possible? I just told you, Maggie, I'm willing to pay whatever I have to."

Maggie squeezed her employer's hand. "All these years," she murmured, only half teasing, "and the lady still hasn't learned there are some things money can't buy."

"Yes I have," Natasha said with a thoughtful, sad tone that Maggie found a little surprising. "I've learned it all too well. If you only knew."

Maggie watched her in silence.

"But when it comes to tangible things," Natasha said with a flash of shrewdness, "my experience is they're usually for sale if the price is right."

"Well, that may be true," Maggie admitted, "but not in this case, I'm afraid."

"Who owns the hotel? I know you told me once, but I forgot."

"Well, you won't forget him after you meet him," Maggie said dryly.

While Carla moved quietly around the room sorting out Natasha's clothes and makeup, Maggie told the story of Doug Evans. She described his arrival from Scotland and his passionate love for his adopted home, his disapproval over Maggie's concocted story of a movie company buying up local property.

"Well then, I'll just have to speak to him myself," Natasha said firmly when the story was finished. "Once my face is healed, I'll go to Crystal Creek. I can actually stay in the same old room where I lived during that…" Her voice trembled, then steadied. "During that awful time. This man will soon change his mind when I'm there in person."

Maggie thought about Doug Evans, his piercing green eyes and tender smile. "I don't think he'll change his mind," she said.

"I'm very famous in Scotland," Natasha said with a note of touching pride. "They even named a street after me in Glasgow. Did you know that, Carla?" she asked, rolling her head on the pillow. "It's called Dunne Street, a lovely walkway down near the water."

"Lots of streets are named after you in Mexico, honey," Carla said in her musical voice. She smiled fondly at her employer. "Now, should we let Maggie get some sleep?"

"Yes, of course. I'm so sorry," Natasha said with

childlike contrition. "It's just lovely to see her again."

Maggie got up and bent to kiss the bandaged head. "Good night, Nat," she murmured. "I'll sleep for twenty hours or so, and feel great in the morning."

"Can you sleep without pills?"

"At the moment, I could drink a gallon of coffee and still sleep." Maggie looked at the battered face with sudden suspicion. "Why do you ask?"

"Oh, don't worry," Natasha said with a hoarse chuckle. "I don't have any drugs to share with you. Carla's been feeding me sugar pills, did you know that? And the silly girl thinks I'd fall for that," she added placidly. "As if I'm a complete idiot."

Carla stood with hands on hips, staring down at the bed. "Now, how did you know that?"

"I'm not the silly goose you all think I am." The bruised face on the pillows contorted into a faint smile. "But I do love you for taking such good care of me. You're the only family I've got, you two girls and Terry. I love you all."

Again tears shone in Natasha's eyes.

"Now, for goodness' sake, don't start crying," Maggie said briskly, "or those incisions will sting, and then you'll be sorry."

"Because I have no painkillers for you," Carla said with a hearty burst of laughter. "Only sugar pills."

Natasha giggled, then winced at the pain.

"Well, you big fraud," Carla said comfortably, "now that you've stopped pretending to be at death's door, what do you want for dinner? Should I order up some nice scampi and asparagus for you from the kitchen? You always like that.''

''And a bottle of wine,'' Natasha said forcefully. ''Maybe a good French cabernet.''

''Whatever you want.''

While Carla and Natasha were discussing food, Maggie went into the other bedroom and dragged her clothes off, then fell into bed, sighing with bliss, lulled by the gentle rocking motion of the ship.

She was satisfied with what she'd accomplished by this grueling trip. Natasha was soon going to be her old lovable, infuriating self again.

Now, if only the actress would drop this whole nonsensical idea of buying a Texas town, life could start getting back to normal.

CHAPTER EIGHT

ABOUT A WEEK LATER on a raw, windy February afternoon, Douglas Evans sat behind the reception desk in his hotel and frowned at six people who were assembled in the lobby, all wearing expectant looks.

Ralph and Gloria Wall sat stiffly together on the love seat. The druggist looked hot and sweaty in dress pants and a stiff new cardigan with leather elbow patches, perhaps a recent Christmas gift.

Doug was grimly amused to note that Gloria had even bullied her husband into wearing a tie for this important occasion.

The chair of the school board looked as placid and queenly as usual in a red polka-dot dress with deep ruffles around the neck. She wore matching shoes and carried a huge plastic handbag, also bright red.

Stella Metz, who worked at the town hall, wore a mauve pantsuit and sat in one of the wing chairs. She was a thirtyish woman, thin and predatory, with puffy blond hair and fingernails like purple talons.

When Doug caught her eye she smiled with automatic flirtatiousness, but he didn't respond. Stella turned away deliberately, scowling and clicking her nails on the wooden chair arm.

Jilly Phipps was on the sofa. The voluptuous red-haired schoolteacher also tried to catch Doug's attention, but he ignored her, pretending to be busily occupied with the papers at his desk.

Stella and Jilly owned a small house together over on Elm Street, and it wasn't hard for Doug to guess what they were doing here.

Julia and Steve Brown made up the last of the small group, a wholesome couple in their fifties who owned the hardware store. Both of them looked miserable. Doug sympathized, knowing how hard it must be for them to be part of this group, incurring the wrath of many longtime neighbors.

But everybody in town knew the Browns had been having financial troubles for years, and the hardware store was about to go under if they couldn't somehow meet their bank loan.

"Are you sure she's coming back this afternoon?" Gloria asked with a challenging glance in Doug's direction. "We've been waiting almost an hour already."

Doug glanced up at the woman with a gaze so level and steady that she was forced to look away, her plump cheeks coloring with annoyance.

"I have no idea what schedule Maggie Embree keeps," he said at last. "Her brother told me she was coming back this afternoon, and I passed the information on to you."

As if summoned by the mention of his name, Terry opened the lobby door and stepped inside. Robin and Moira were with him, their faces glowing bright red from the chill of the breeze. Robin's mouth was smeared with chocolate ice cream, and she held tightly on to Terry's hand, laughing. Her older sister skipped along at his other side. Though usually a solemn child, Moira also looked happy at the moment.

"Mr. Embree!" Gloria said loudly, accosting Terry at once. "Is your sister coming back this afternoon, or isn't she?"

Terry looked a little taken aback at the woman's peremptory manner. He glanced at Doug, who shrugged again in noncommittal fashion and looked down at the papers on his desk.

"Who wants to know?" Terry asked the group.

"All of us do," Gloria said. In any assemblage of people, Gloria Wall was usually the self-appointed spokeswoman. "We've come to talk business with her."

"I don't know if she's going to feel like talking business," Terry said mildly. "Maggie's coming back from a long trip, and when she gets here I'm betting she'll be completely exhausted."

"We just need a few minutes of her time." Gloria waved off this objection with a lofty swipe of her red handbag. "Besides, it's not such a long trip out here from California."

"California?" Terry asked.

The little girls tugged at his hands, trying to draw him toward the back of the hotel.

"We happen to know your sister works for a big movie company," Gloria told him, "and that she's gone back to talk to her boss about buying up a lot of property in Crystal Creek to make a movie here." She indicated the rest of the group. "And we're fixing to get in on the ground floor."

Terry looked at the woman with some indecision,

then shook his head and followed the two girls who were talking excitedly about a treasure hunt.

But at last good manners triumphed over any other emotion he might be feeling, and he paused at the back door of the lobby.

"Maggie should be back any minute," he said to the group near the window. "Her plane was supposed to land in Austin just after lunch, and she planned to drive straight out from there."

Then he disappeared along with the children. Gloria settled back in her chair with an air of triumph, shooting a venomous look at her husband. "See? I told you," she muttered.

Ralph shifted uncomfortably and tugged at his tight shirt collar.

Under any other circumstances, Doug would have found the whole situation funny, but today he was not at all disposed to amusement.

Because when Maggie Embree walked in that door this afternoon, the unpleasant business of selling off Crystal Creek was going to begin. And he was damned if he'd sit quietly by and watch it happen without a fight.

He stared at an invoice from the Double C winery, but the figures swam in front of his eyes. All he could see was her face, the long-lashed eyes and high cheekbones, the sweet mouth and errant dimple and glowing skin, those eyebrows like dark wings...

Doug shook his head and rubbed a hand across his forehead.

Maybe, he thought hopefully, she wasn't as beautiful as he remembered. Maybe it had all been an illusion, just because of her sophistication and the elegant way she wore her clothes.

No doubt when he saw her again, knowing what to expect, her looks would leave him cold. He'd be able to concentrate on what she was doing, not the way she made him feel.

While he was forming this thought, the lobby door opened and Maggie trudged into the lobby carrying a couple of leather traveling bags.

She wore jeans and a loose red sweater, and her hair was pulled back into a casual French braid. She looked tired, almost dropping on her feet, and so lovely that his heart skipped a couple of beats, then began to pound erratically.

He wanted to take her into his arms, kiss the tiredness from her face and carry her off to his bedroom. He wanted to rub her feet, caress her temples and stroke her body until she relaxed. He wanted to make love to her with gentle tenderness and then let her fall asleep in his arms, safe and warm and cherished.

Daft, he thought in despair.

This woman was an enemy to Douglas Evans. She was on a mission to destroy everything he held dear. In fact, the group sitting here in his lobby would help her strike the first blow in her campaign.

Doug knew he had to remain cold and remote, and plan his defenses carefully. He couldn't let himself think about her eyes or her mouth, or the way her breasts moved so enticingly under that sweater as she approached the reception desk.

"Hi, Doug," she said with a wan smile, pausing next to him. "God, I'm so tired. Still working on your spreadsheet, I see?"

Her smile was almost timid, as if she hoped he might forget about their disagreement and just be friends. Again Doug felt himself painfully torn.

"So, has anything been going on?" she asked, shifting the heaviest bag to her other shoulder. "Any messages for me?"

With a curtness he didn't entirely mean, Doug inclined his head toward the group in the lobby.

"They're all waiting for you," he said without looking at her. "And they're getting a wee bit impatient, so you'd best deal with them right away."

MAGGIE RECOILED a bit, hurt by the coldness of his tone. For the first time she realized just how much she'd been wanting to see him again. In fact, during the long trip to Texas, as she stared out the windows of various airplanes, she'd somehow convinced herself that she and Doug could even make a new start.

Maggie would explain the conflicts of her loyalty to Natasha and her own deep reservations about this project, and then they'd talk things out and leave the hostility behind.

But now, back in his hotel, when she looked at his lowered head and the grim set of his jaw, those hopes plummeted.

Uncertainly, she turned to study the group in the lobby. She recognized Ralph Wall, the druggist, and her heart sank even further.

"Oh, no," she said, backing away. "Please, not now. I just got back from a very long..."

"We won't take much of your time." This firm statement was from the big woman in ruffles who sat next to Ralph Wall. "I'm Gloria Wall, and we want to be the first to speak to you about what you're planning here in Crystal Creek. As a group, we represent two prosperous downtown businesses,'' the woman added importantly, "and three very nice homes.''

Maggie exchanged an involuntary glance with Doug, and was chilled by the icy look in his eyes.

"I'm not really in any state to talk business," she said apologetically to the woman in the red polka-dot dress. "Honestly, if you all knew how tired I'm feeling right now..."

But her pleading was clearly lost on Ralph Wall's spouse. Gloria got to her feet and moved across the lobby in majestic fashion, gesturing for the others to follow her.

"We've been waiting all week for you to get back, and sitting in this lobby for over an hour,'' the woman said accusingly. "We have a right to some kind of assurance that our properties will be considered first. It won't take long.''

"All right," Maggie said in defeat. "Can you all just come upstairs?'' she said wearily, "and we'll—''

"No!'' Doug said from behind her, his voice like a whiplash.

Maggie turned to look at him.

"This is my hotel," he said calmly, though his face was hard, his eyes piercing. "If you're planning the appropriation of this town, my bonny lass, you won't do it on my property.''

In spite of her feelings for him, Maggie felt her stubbornness rise at his high-handed manner.

"I'm renting my room," she said. "And that gives

me the legal right to do whatever I want inside that room after I've closed the door, providing it's not against the law.''

"It may give you the legal right.'' He met her eyes with a look of cold challenge. ''But I'm telling you I won't allow it. If you take those people upstairs, or anybody else you intend to do business with, I'll throw you out on the street.''

The group stood around watching, their mouths agape, while Maggie stared at the handsome Scot.

Finally she nodded tightly and reached in her shoulder bag for a room key. ''Then I'll just take this luggage upstairs,'' she told the group, ''and splash some water on my face. Can I meet you all down at the Longhorn in fifteen minutes?''

Mrs. Wall gave Maggie a grudging nod. She and her followers trooped out of the lobby.

Maggie paused on the way up the stairs, and turned to look at the silent man behind the desk. ''Do you know where my brother is?'' she asked.

"Playing with my nieces in the kitchen,'' he said coldly. ''As usual.''

Maggie couldn't tell if he was just annoyed with her, or also angry about her brother and his contact with Rose's children. At the moment she was too tired to ask.

As she dragged herself up the stairs she thought wistfully about pulling the drapes and falling asleep, forgetting all about that group of property owners down at the restaurant.

But of course, that wasn't possible, because Maggie Embree was a person who took her responsibilities seriously. And as long as she was employed by

Natasha Dunne, her first responsibility was to her job.

Fifteen minutes later, when she went back downstairs carrying her leather briefcase and feeling only slightly refreshed, Doug had vanished from behind the reception desk.

Maggie looked at his empty chair and the blinking computer screen. Even Dundee was nowhere in sight. She felt suddenly so overwhelmed with sorrow that it was all she could do to hold back the tears.

Just exhaustion, she thought as she headed into the biting wind toward the restaurant. All she needed was a good night's sleep, and then Doug Evans and his furious disapproval wouldn't matter to her nearly so much.

AT LEAST her first business interview with a group of Crystal Creek townspeople seemed to go well enough.

Maggie was still prepared to be evasive about Natasha and her plans, but these citizens didn't seem to care who she worked for, or what use their property would be put to. All they wanted was an assurance that their homes and businesses would be purchased for cash and rented back to them, and that the whole transaction would be "legal and aboveboard," as Gloria Wall stressed, fixing Maggie with a suspicious gaze.

"We'll bring our own lawyer, and you may feel free to use any legal representation you like," Maggie said, taking a hungry bite of the Longhorn burger on a plate in front of her. "Or if you prefer, we can have the papers drawn up by a local real estate sales-person.''

"Doug Evans is the only one in town who sells real estate," Jilly Phipps said. "And I don't think he'd be too happy about being involved in any of this."

"No, I doubt if he would," Maggie said gloomily. Ridiculous how the mere mention of his name unsettled her, as if she were a high-school girl with a crush.

"We could always bring out a real estate man from Austin," Steve Brown suggested. "I have a friend who's really good, and won't charge an exorbitant commission."

"I don't know about you, Steve Brown, but I'm not paying for somebody just to draw up a set of legal papers!" Gloria said.

"You're tighter than a tomato skin, Gloria," the hardware proprietor retorted calmly. "You always have been."

Stella Metz entered the fray in Gloria's defense, and Maggie let them argue for a while. She looked from one face to another as they exchanged insults.

"Why are you all so anxious to sell your property?" she asked finally, making them pause and turn to stare at her. "I mean," she went on, "you've all lived here quite a long time, I assume. Doesn't it bother you that when this process is concluded, you'll just be tenants, not owners?"

The Browns both looked uneasy. "We really need to sell," Julia said at last, with a look of anxiety that wrung Maggie's heart. "We can't get another bank loan, not even from Cody Hendricks who's always been real good to us. And nobody wants to buy a hardware store in a little town like this.''

Her husband shot her a warning glance, and Julia's face colored with embarrassment.

"Nobody but you, I mean,'' she murmured.

Maggie touched her arm. "Well, we're very eager to buy your store, and we'll give you a fair price.'' She looked at the druggist and his wife, then at the two single women. "What about the rest of you? It doesn't bother any of you to sell?''

"Money's money,'' Stella said philosophically as the others nodded agreement. "We all want the cash, and we don't care who owns the house. Why should we?''

"Especially if we get a signed agreement from you that we can rent the property back and go on with our lives just like we always have,'' Ralph said hoarsely, tugging at his collar.

"That will be an integral part of the deal,'' Maggie told him. "We certainly don't want to turn the place into a ghost town. Our…my employer's goal is for Crystal Creek to remain vibrant and fully populated, just as it's always been.''

"Well, without some help, that's not going to happen,'' Steve Brown said bluntly. "The town's already emptying because taxes are so high. Next month we're even voting on whether to close the middle school.''

He cast an accusing glance at Gloria Wall, who glared back at him. "You all know we can't afford that school,'' she said. "We need to get rid of it.''

"I know how much you hate Lucia Whitley,'' the hardware owner said. "That's where a lot of this comes from, Gloria. Your war against the middle school's got nothing to do with lowering our taxes.''

Mottled color rose in Gloria's face. She was about to make a furious rejoinder, when Maggie spoke out, trying to forestall more hostility in the group.

"So if you all sell your properties and don't have high taxes to worry about, will you vote next month to keep the middle school?'' she asked.

"We will,'' the Browns said in unison.

"Me too,'' Jilly Phipps contributed. "Hell, I work there. If the middle school goes, I'm out of a job.''

"We don't need that school,'' Gloria said loudly. "Ralph and I both feel that very strongly. Don't we, Ralph?''

Her husband remained silent. Gloria poked him sharply with her elbow, and he grunted something inaudible.

"How about you, Stella?'' Maggie asked the blonde in the mauve outfit. "Would you vote to keep the middle school?''

The woman shrugged. "Who knows?'' she muttered. "That snooty Lucia Whitley keeps saying the school is so important, though I don't see what it would hurt to bus the kids a few miles, I really don't. But I'd hate to see Jilly lose her job,'' she added hastily.

"So you're neutral at the moment,'' Maggie said. "And you'd be more likely to vote in favor of the school if you didn't have to worry about high taxes?''

"Well, yes,'' Stella said with some reluctance. "I reckon I would.''

"That's good to hear.'' Thoughtfully, Maggie

made a mental note to use this point in any future discussion with Doug Evans on the topic.

If the man ever deigned to speak with her again.

Natasha Dunne's purchase of Crystal Creek, as dramatic and grandiose as the whole thing seemed, might turn out to save some of the town's long-cherished institutions.

She made appointments with the members of the group to view their properties, and promised that offers to purchase would be forthcoming after the appraisals had been completed.

Finally, washed under by a deep, heavy wave of tiredness, she got up and gathered her papers, excused herself and plodded back to the hotel, wondering if Terry would be there.

And maybe Doug would be behind the desk again, perhaps waiting for her, his dark head lowered over the bookwork that he hated so much...

Against all reason, her mouth curved into a wistful smile and she quickened her steps.

What she wanted, in all honesty, was to lean against his hard body, rest her head in the curve of his shoulder and feel his arms around her, holding her. She wanted the sweet burr of his husky voice in her ear, and the smiling warmth of those green eyes.

When she went into the hotel, the lobby was still empty. Her spirits plunged immediately. She trudged up the staircase to her suite, which was also vacant and cheerless.

Again she felt a tug of concern, then shook it off. It wasn't late, no matter how exhausted she felt. In fact, it was barely past six o'clock. Maybe Terry was down having a hamburger in the bar, or playing darts with some of the locals.

Terry didn't usually make friends so readily, but he seemed to fit in well with the residents of this little town.

She remembered Doug's cold announcement earlier in the day that Terry was with Rose's children. "As usual…" Wasn't that how he'd put it?

Maggie brooded as she soaked in a blissfully hot bath, wondering if Terry's relationship with Rose was anything she should concern herself with.

All her worries fled when she heard a discreet scratching at the door. Maggie opened it to find Dundee standing in the hallway, gazing up at her with a look of lofty disinterest.

"Well, hello," Maggie whispered in delight, kneeling to stroke the cat. "Hello, you big sweetie. Where on earth did you come from?"

Dundee rubbed briefly against Maggie's legs, then stalked past her into the room and made a beeline toward the corner of the suite where Terry, bless his heart, had apparently been putting out cat food and water, along with a litter pan.

"Dundee!" Maggie said. "You've moved in with us!"

Dundee took a few bites of the dry cat food, then followed Maggie into the bedroom.

Thoughts of Natasha and her real estate acquisition, of greedy townspeople and Doug's coldness and Terry's preoccupation with Rose Murdoch…all drifted out of Maggie's mind.

She found herself in the four-poster bed with the big tabby nestled cozily at her side, and then she was tumbling into a sleep full of troubled dreams, most of them about Doug Evans.

CHAPTER NINE

MAGGIE AND DOUG lay on a tartan blanket, their faces close together as they smiled at each other. They were on a hillside overlooking a still blue lake, above a village of slate-roofed cottages. Beyond them, misty hills lifted away to the sky. A soft rain was falling all around them, but it felt as warm as sunshine.

Nearby, Maggie could see a haystack and the big red barn from the farm where she'd grown up, along with a couple of the Holstein cows her father had been so proud of.

Briefly she was diverted by the sight of the cows and the barn, and the way her childhood and Doug's had somehow become entwined. But then her attention went back to him, because he'd stood up among the heather and was taking off his clothes.

He stripped away his jeans and shirt and loomed above her, splendidly naked, rigid with desire. The raindrops glistened on his skin and dark hair.

Maggie reached up toward him and then realized she, too, was naked. Alarmed, she tried to cover herself, but he knelt and pulled her hands away, kissing her with lingering passion.

"So beautiful," he said huskily. "Maggie, you're

so beautiful. But I want to see your hair loose on your shoulders..."

He unfastened the braid at her neck while she kissed his chest and shoulders, delighting in his warm nearness. The rainfall had become a drift of flower petals that skittered across the tussocks of grass and caressed her skin.

Her hair was loose and free, lifting in the wind, dancing like bright flower petals. Doug buried his face in it and murmured something she couldn't hear, then lay full length on the blanket and gathered her tenderly into his arms.

She could feel his big body with all of her own. From his large bare feet to the crown of his dark head, he was hard and strong, thrusting and urgent, warm and fine as silk.

"I love you," she whispered.

He laughed. "How can you love me, lass?" he teased. "You barely know me."

"But I do know you." She caressed him, emboldened by passion. "I've always known you."

"And I you," he told her, all the teasing gone from his voice. "And I you, my darling."

His body moved against hers, and Maggie cried out with pleasure. Soon she was lost in the fiery sweetness of his lovemaking and the thrilling, satisfying movement of his body against hers.

He was powerful and tireless, pounding, pounding, pounding...

DOUG CONTINUED to hammer at her door, but there was no answer. He glanced at his watch.

Nine-thirty.

Maggie had gone up to the room more than three hours ago and not come down again. He knew because he'd been watching for her through his office door.

Terry was still over at Rose's house, and Doug was very anxious not to miss this chance for a private conversation with Maggie.

But clearly she wasn't going to answer the door. Maybe, he thought with a quick touch of embarrassment, she'd been so exhausted that she'd fallen asleep already, and here he was pounding at her door like an inconsiderate boor.

It would probably be best if he just...

At that moment the door swung inward and she stood gazing up at him.

Doug forgot everything he'd been planning to say and stared back at her, feeling his throat tighten with emotion.

She wore a knee-length white terry-cloth robe, hastily belted over some kind of brief red silk nightwear. Her beautiful face was scrubbed and free of makeup, and her hair tumbled loose onto her shoulders.

Involuntarily, he reached out a hand to touch the shining mass, then moved closer to her. Her silky hair clung to his fingers, and he caught an enticing fragrance of shampoo and sleep.

"I'm sorry," he said, clearing his throat. "I've wakened you. I didn't mean to."

He couldn't stop himself from stroking her hair, and she made no move to prevent him. Her beautiful eyes still seemed dazed with sleep, wide and almost frightened, as if she was looking at a ghost. She had an odd, vaguely guilty look that intrigued him.

"Did I startle you?" he asked, letting the door swing shut behind him.

Now they were alone in the sitting room of the suite. He was urgently conscious of her nearness, and the rumpled four-poster bed just beyond her open door.

"I was...sleeping." She shook her head, finally ducking away from his hand. He let it fall, watching as she moved off and hugged her arms nervously. "I didn't realize you were knocking on the door. It was...for a while it was...part of my dream."

For some reason her face warmed with a delicious flush that crept upward from the collar of her robe and made her look once again like a little girl caught in some kind of mischief. Doug was so enchanted by her that he had to battle an almost overwhelming urge to take her in his arms and cover her face and throat with kisses.

But at that moment Dundee wandered out from the bedroom, stretching and yawning. Doug stared at his sleek tabby, then back at the sleepy woman with her disheveled hair.

"Margaret Embree," he said with mock sternness. "Have you stolen my cat?"

"She just...comes up here sometimes," Maggie said vaguely, blushing again.

"Ah, I see," Doug murmured, trying not to laugh. "Just wanders in for no reason, does she?"

"I don't know why..."

By now Maggie was obviously waking up, and had begun to look worried.

"Is something the matter?" she asked, frowning. "Is Terry…"

"Nothing's wrong," Doug assured her. "I just wanted to talk with you, that's all."

"In the middle of the night?"

"It's barely half past nine," he said mildly. "I didn't realize you'd be asleep already."

"Yesterday at this time, I was in Athens." Maggie yawned. "And it's really tiring to travel that far in one day."

"I'm sorry." He moved away, cursing himself for his lack of thought. "I'll go now, and talk with you sometime tomorrow."

"Oh, that's all right," she told him. "Now that I'm awake, I'll probably have a hard time going back to sleep anyhow. I've really been out like a light for the past few hours."

"What were you dreaming about?" He watched as she sat on the couch, took a pair of socks from an open suitcase and pulled them onto her slender feet.

"Nothing in particular." She looked away from him, her cheekbones touched with pink again.

Doug was intrigued by her obvious embarrassment, but decided not to pursue the question. Instead, he sank into the chair opposite her and watched her face closely.

"Did you have a good trip, apart from the rush to get home?" he asked.

"It was better coming back. I don't get as jet-lagged when I travel west," she said, clearly making an effort to compose herself.

"How's your employer?" he asked.

"She's getting better."

"Was she unwell?"

"She's recovering from surgery," Maggie said.

"On a cruise ship? That's an odd place to recuperate, isn't it?"

"The surgery was…cosmetic," Maggie told him. "She needs to be somewhere far from home where her privacy won't be compromised, at least until the worst of the damage heals."

"But all kinds of people get cosmetic surgery these days," Doug said mildly. "Your employer must be very sensitive indeed about her privacy."

Maggie pulled the hair back from her shoulders. He watched regretfully as she took a scarf from the suitcase and tied the dark mass out of sight at her nape.

"Yes," she murmured absently. "I guess you could say that."

"Say what?" he asked, still thinking about that cloud of hair, and the warm, silky feeling of it against his fingers.

"My employer is very protective of her privacy."

"Any particular reason?" He extended his legs comfortably and leaned back in the chair.

Her face was so expressive that he could see her hesitation, even sense the exact moment when she decided to tell the truth.

"My employer is Natasha Dunne," she said.

Doug stared at her, openmouthed, too shocked to respond.

Natasha Dunne, the movie actress, was one of the most famous women in the world. Even during Doug's boyhood in Scotland, her face had been almost as well recognized as the queen's.

"If the press knew about her surgery," Maggie went on, "they'd be hanging around in droves trying to catch a picture of her while she's still in bandages. We wanted to get her somewhere as far away as we could."

"But…what does Natasha Dunne want with Crystal Creek?" he said at last.

"She wants to own it."

"Own it! Surely you're joking."

Maggie gave him a wry, sad smile that tugged powerfully at his heart. In spite of the tumult in his mind, Doug had to fight another urge to take her in his arms and make love to her right there on the couch.

"Look, I'd hardly joke about something like this," she said.

"Why would a famous movie actress have any interest in this Texas hill town?"

"Natasha Dunne made a movie here, way back in the sixties."

Maggie put her stockinged feet on the coffee table. Her legs were long and slender, exquisitely shapely, with a warm tan despite the winter chill outside. Doug had a hard time looking away.

"And I suppose your Ms. Dunne makes a habit of buying up every town she makes a movie in," he suggested. "It's sort of a hobby, the way some women collect spoons?"

Maggie was obviously too tired to respond to his sarcasm. Instead, she shook her head against the back of the couch.

"She was a new bride when she made that film," Maggie said. "She'd just married Jeremy Calder, and while they were filming he was killed in Vietnam. Natasha was crushed with grief. She stayed here a couple of months after the filming was done, right in this very hotel, as a matter of fact. The townspeople were so good to her that she never forgot their kindness.''

"I remember something about that story now," he said, frowning. "Though I'd forgotten the town was Crystal Creek."

"And now," Maggie went on, "Natasha's in her fifties, starting to feel rootless and a little nostalgic, I guess. Whatever the reason, she wants to go back and recapture that part of her life."

"Even though it was a very sad part?"

Maggie looked at him frankly. "You know, I find it a little hard to understand that, too. But Natasha's always been an actress above all else. Maybe she feels that if she goes back to the scene of her pain, she can rewrite the script somehow."

"None of us can rewrite the script. We have to play it out and move on."

"That may be true for people like you and me. But when you have as much money and power as Natasha Dunne, you don't pay any attention to the word *can't*. Even the people closest to you are afraid to say it."

"But why would the woman want to own a whole town?" Doug said, frowning. "What possible benefit could it have for her?"

"Terry and I often speculate about that ourselves, but Natasha hasn't enlightened us. I think maybe she wants to feel this is her place, a bit of the world that really belongs to her."

"It's incredible that a woman could have so much money and fame but still feel the need to buy power."

"Not when you think about it," Maggie said. "The major problem with money and fame is the way it tends to hold you hostage. I believe what Natasha really wants is to buy a big enough piece of property so that she can feel herself surrounded by safety. It's a sort of buffer zone, I guess, between her and the public."

"But that buffer zone would make her a very lonely person," Doug suggested.

"Yes." Maggie gazed at him, her eyes wide and thoughtful.

"The lovely Natasha Dunne has nobody really close to her?"

"Just my brother and I, and a longtime personal maid, and a few other close staff members."

"So she wants to buy herself a hometown." Doug shook his head in disbelief. "Well, that's just absurd."

Maggie watched him but didn't respond. She was clearly wide awake now, and a great deal more composed. An alert, cautious look had returned to her eyes, and Doug knew he had to proceed carefully.

Dundee reappeared from behind an armchair, licking her whiskers in suspicious fashion. She jumped lightly into Maggie's lap and curled up, purring noisily. Maggie petted the cat with long caressing strokes, her face so gentle that Doug was moved in spite of himself.

"Speaking of my brother," Maggie said after an

awkward silence, "I haven't seen him since I got back. Do you have any idea where he is?"

"I think he's with Rose and the girls," Doug said reluctantly. "I believe they planned to rent some cartoon videos and make popcorn tonight."

"You look upset." Maggie watched him closely. "Does it bother you?"

"A little."

"Why?"

"My sister is a very sensitive woman," Doug said, "and she's been through a great deal of misery. I wouldn't want to see her...get hurt."

"Terry would never hurt anybody," Maggie said with conviction. "He's always been the kindest, sweetest person I've ever known. And he's very shy, too," she added with a frown. "If anybody's going to get hurt in a relationship, it's likely to be Terry."

"Well, then, perhaps they're two of a kind."

"It's more likely," Maggie said, "that he just likes being around the kids. Terry's always craved a real family, ever since our mother died. And he adores children."

Doug glanced at the flowered drapes, drawn closely against the winter chill. He could hear the howl of the wind sweeping up the empty streets and around the eaves of the old building. The cold outside made the room feel intensely intimate, a little island of warmth that he shared with the woman who sat on the couch, watching him in silence while she stroked the cat.

"So," he said at last, "did you buy all their properties tonight? Is Natasha Dunne now the owner of the Crystal Creek hardware and drugstore?"

"Of course I didn't buy them," Maggie said. "First we need to have the properties appraised so we can arrive at a fair price. And when we do make a deal with any of the townspeople, our offers to purchase would still be conditional on Natasha acquiring a certain percentage of all the taxable properties."

"So what you're saying is, if Natasha can't have the lot, she doesn't want any?" he said with renewed annoyance.

"That's right. It doesn't do her much good to own a house or a business here and there. She wants the whole thing."

"My God," he muttered.

Maggie drew the robe closer around her legs and adjusted the collar to conceal a bit of red silk that peeped out at her bosom.

In spite of his anger, Doug felt deep regret when the sexy lace vanished.

"Look," she said at last, "since you're here, there's something business-related that I need to talk to you about."

"And what's that?" he asked, still struggling with the concept of this arrogant movie actress actually buying herself a town.

The whole thing was simply too outlandish, too incredible to grasp...

"Natasha wants very much to buy this hotel from you," Maggie said. "She's hoping to convert it to a private residence for herself."

HE WAS QUIET for so long that Maggie began to wonder if Doug Evans had heard what she said.

"Maybe you didn't understand me," she ventured at last. "I was saying…"

"I heard you," he told her curtly. "And I understand well enough, believe me."

Dear God, how he must disapprove of her.

Still, there was a strange, enigmatic expression in his eyes, something Maggie couldn't grasp and was afraid to think about.

For an unsettling moment, she recalled the dream he'd wakened her from with his noisy pounding at her door. It had been so intensely vivid, she could still feel the hard strength of his body, the warmth and sweetness of his lovemaking.

All this was so unfair, she thought miserably. Doug Evans was angry with her solely because of Natasha's silly plan. None of it really had anything to do with Maggie, who was only doing her job, and yet he seemed to consider her a bad person.

Well, she thought with rising stubbornness, if Doug Evans disapproved of her, that was just too bad. She wasn't about to turn her back on Natasha's friendship, a wonderful job and years of generosity, just because this handsome Scotsman disapproved of her employer.

"I take it," she said, matching his coldness, "that you're not interested in selling your hotel?"

"Damn right I'm not. Your movie star will have to find herself another property that suits her selfish purposes. And you are quite free to pass my words on to her."

"What if the rest of the townspeople decide to sell?" Maggie asked. "Do you plan to be the only holdout?"

"I will never sell my property to Natasha Dunne," he said in a quiet, chilling tone. "Not if she offers me ten million dollars, and not even if this hotel should turn out to be the only property in her town that doesn't belong to her."

"You're a very obstinate man, aren't you," Maggie said thoughtfully.

"I'm a decent man. I ask nothing of anybody except that they leave me alone. And I don't use other people for my own purposes. I consider that a despicable way to behave."

"Do you think that's what I'm doing?" Maggie asked, stung by his words. "You think I'm just a hard-hearted manipulative person who's trying to take advantage of your neighbors?"

"I don't know what to think of you, Maggie." He regarded her steadily.

In the shaded glow of the lamp, his eyes were very dark green, and hard to look at directly. Soft light flickered on his cheekbones and his mouth, touching them with a lingering fire.

Maggie shivered, forcing herself to look away.

"I don't particularly care what you think about me," she murmured after a long, tense silence.

"Don't you?"

"Why should I?" she asked.

"Maggie, tell me, what do you honestly think about what you're doing here?" Again he watched her with that probing gaze. "Do you not feel any guilt at all?"

"Guilt?" she echoed. "Why on earth should I feel that way? I'm doing nothing wrong."

"Did you have a hometown back in Ohio? What

would you have thought if somebody came in and bought that town out from under your neighbors?''

Startled, Maggie recalled the sleepy farming community that had been home to her for all of her childhood.

Not for the first time, she thought about what it might be like for the people of Crystal Creek to see their town being divided up and sold to the highest bidder. As always, the image made her shiver a little.

But she couldn't let this man see her wavering. He was far too clever, such a dangerous opponent.

She continued to caress the sleepy cat, thinking about her answer.

"Why should you care so much?" she asked. "This isn't your town, after all. You didn't come here until you were a grown man."

"Do you think a person can only form these attachments in his youth? It's not possible for a grown man to fall passionately in love?"

When he spoke about falling in love, her dream returned with shattering clarity. Maggie bit her lip and looked down, nervously pleating the belt on her robe. "Who's talking about love?" she asked.

"I love this town. I feel at home here. It's the place that holds my heart, more than anywhere I've ever lived. Can you not understand that?"

She shook her head. "Nothing holds my heart," she said quietly. "I've never felt like that."

"You've never truly loved a place?" he asked.

Maggie couldn't understand why she was talking to him this way. Maybe it was because of the wind sobbing around the corners of the building, or the feeling of weariness that still dragged her down, or the passion of her dream followed so abruptly by the man's actual presence across from her.

Whatever the reason, she found her anger fading, replaced by a desire to talk to him, to pour out her heart and ask for his understanding.

"I think it has something to do with being adopted," she said, her voice not quite steady. "Although I always felt loved, I've never really felt like I belonged anywhere. In fact, it makes me sympathetic to Natasha, because I believe she feels the same way."

"Your parents told you early on, didn't they? You knew that you weren't their natural child?"

"As soon as I could understand, they made me realize I was a chosen baby, and that they loved me more than anything."

"But you still didn't feel as if you belonged to them?"

"I couldn't help wondering about that poor little schoolgirl who was my mother." Maggie swallowed painfully. "When I was in my twenties and finished university, and both my parents were dead, it started to obsess me so much that I went looking for my birth mother. I tried to gain access to my birth records in Cincinnati. I was so sure it would help me to feel...more grounded, I guess."

"But it didn't?"

"No, it was awful. The records had been expunged. All the names and addresses were removed, anything that might lead back to my birth family."

"Did anybody tell you why?"

Maggie twisted her hands in her lap, thinking about that miserable time.

"I remember my father saying my birth mother came from a wealthy family in Cincinnati, and they'd hidden all traces of her pregnancy. I guess they wanted to protect her. After all, she was only sixteen. But when I found those records and saw how thoroughly they'd blocked out any possibility of ever finding her...it made me feel rejected all over again."

"So you've never found her?"

"It's impossible," Maggie said. "The trail's thirty years old by now. And obviously she never wanted me to find her in the first place. Still, there are times when I can hardly bear thinking..."

"What?"

"That somewhere my mother's reading or sleeping or watching television at this very moment," Maggie whispered, swallowing painfully. "She's in her mid-forties, very likely married and living in Ohio. She's raised a family who are my brothers and sisters. And I'm still out in the cold."

"Is that why you're so sympathetic to what Natasha wants to do in Crystal Creek?"

She looked away from him, staring at the lamp. "I don't know," she confessed at last. "There's such a feeling of roots and history in this little place. It's really appealing. Maybe that's what Natasha—"

"You can't buy a heritage, Maggie," he said gently. "You have to build it."

"I can't build anything."

"Why not?"

To Maggie's horror, her eyes began to sting with tears. "Because I have no foundation. There's no way to find out who I really am, and both the people

who were my adoptive parents are dead. I have nobody but Natasha and Terry.''

"That's more of a foundation than a lot of people
have. You also have the memory of a lifetime of
security and people who cared about you. I'd say
that's enough to start building a life."

"You don't understand." She tried to hold back
the tears, but they were beginning to gather in her
eyes and trickle down her cheeks. "How can you
possibly understand the emptiness, and the feeling
that I'll never…''

Her voice broke.

"Oh, Maggie.'' He got up and moved close to her,
lifting the cat gently to the floor. Then he pulled
Maggie to her feet and drew her into his arms.

Maggie was too upset to resist. She let herself be
gathered into his embrace, and burrowed against his
solid chest. It was so much like her dream that she
was both confused and aroused. He even smelled the
way she'd imagined, warm and clean, with a healthy
scent of maleness and shaving cream.

"Poor Maggie,'' he whispered against her ear.
"You're tired out and stressed. And it doesn't help
that I'm up here badgering you, does it?''

"Don't feel sorry for me.'' She nestled closer to
him. "You're right, it's just that long trip. I'll be fine
in the morning.''

Doug's mouth sought hers, and he kissed her. His
lips were hard and sure, moving hungrily against her
own.

Maggie felt herself drowning in sensation. Everything fled from her mind.

Worried thoughts of Terry, of Natasha, of her job

in Crystal Creek and Doug's opposition to it, blew away like the flower petals in her dream. All she wanted was to hold him, and stay here in his arms forever. She wanted him to lift her and carry her to bed, and make love to her all night long.

If he tried, she would make no move to stop him. In fact, she'd be shameless about stripping off her clothes and offering herself to him. But even as she pressed ever closer to him, excited by a growing recklessness, his mouth stilled on hers, and he drew away.

Maggie glanced up at him in time to see that hard, shuttered look returning to his face. He controlled himself with a visible effort and turned away from her toward the door.

"I'm sorry," he said over his shoulder, with a formal tone that chilled her to the core. "That was unforgivable of me. It won't happen again."

"Doug," she whispered.

But he was gone, vanished into the night like the images in her dream, and there was nothing left but the harsh sobbing of the wind.

Even Dundee was gone, apparently the cat had chosen to leave with her rightful owner.

Maggie was truly alone.

CHAPTER TEN

THE NEXT WEEK PASSED in a rapid and confusing whirl of activity.

On the following Sunday night, fully recovered from her whirlwind trip to the Mediterranean, Maggie was working at the computer in the little sitting room. Methodically she entered details on the properties that had been appraised so far, doing a running total of the financial outlay and her best projections for rental income.

She leaned back and stretched her arms, frowning at the spreadsheet she'd composed and thinking about what was happening in Crystal Creek.

Every day, more residents came forward, usually looking furtive and guilty, to inquire about the sale of property. Since Doug still wouldn't allow Maggie to hold interviews in her suite, the corner booth at the Longhorn was now her makeshift office, and she'd developed an active craving for Longhorn burgers and home fries with gravy.

It was near the end of February, with the plebiscite regarding the middle school only two weeks away. Almost half of the town's businesses and a third of the residential properties were on Maggie's list of potential acquisitions.

By now her budget allocations were climbing past

ten million dollars, and still people kept coming to see her.

The mood in the town was a strange mixture of anger and euphoria. At conversations in the beauty parlor, the barbershop and the pub, people spoke of little else besides Natasha Dunne, whose name and purpose were well known by now.

Opinions remained sharply divided. Some were delighted at the unexpected windfall of cash along with a promise that their lives would continue unchanged.

Others, like Doug Evans, grew more furious with every day that passed, and more insistent that the townspeople should stand firm against this reckless takeover bid by an outsider.

Old-timers, like the McKinney family, were trying hard to mobilize community sentiment against acquisition. Regular meetings were held at the Double C ranch, as well as Carolyn Trent's place and Bubba Gibson's, to plot strategies for blocking Natasha's scheme. But all the passionate rhetoric, it seemed, couldn't outweigh the lure of instant cash.

The battle even eclipsed the argument that had been raging for months over the Crystal Creek middle school. As Maggie had foreseen, the school issue was shoved almost completely into the background. Most people seemed to feel that if they could escape the burden of property ownership and their current high taxes, they wouldn't mind keeping the school.

"Let Natasha Dunne buy the school, too," many of them said. "She can pay the taxes to keep it open. Then nobody will have any problems."

This was a powerful argument on Maggie's behalf,

and it had even brought a few more of the stubborn holdouts to sit reluctantly with her at the booth in the Longhorn and talk business.

But not Doug Evans...

She sighed and leaned back, running a weary hand through her hair.

Terry was with her for once, lounging in the flowered armchair with a paperback novel and Dundee asleep in his lap. He looked up from the pages.

"Hey, what's the matter?" he asked. "You sound so tired."

"I'm okay." She frowned and punched in some more numbers. "Maybe I'm eating too many burgers down at the Longhorn. I'd better start ordering the spinach salad instead."

He laughed. "You'd have to be crazy to pass up a Longhorn burger for salad. Nora Slattery's burgers are food for the gods."

"Oh, that's so true. I never tasted anything that delicious." Maggie smiled at her brother, then looked back at the computer screen.

Suddenly she heard a faint, haunting sound from somewhere beyond the hotel. Frowning, she got up and crossed the room to pull the drapes aside, then drew her breath in sharply.

Doug Evans stood down in the vacant lot by the live oak trees, practicing on the bagpipes. His tall figure was silhouetted against the sunset sky and a withered drift of leaves. His profile looked austere, drawn in concentration, even a little sad, but the music he made was intensely sweet and stirring.

Maggie shivered and rubbed her arms. She let the curtain drop and went back to the computer.

"So, has Doug warmed up to this idea at all?" Terry asked. "Is he coming over to your side?"

"Not so you'd notice," Maggie said dryly, though her heart leaped and fluttered as it always did at the mention of the man's name.

"Is he still mad at you?"

"I don't know. If he is, there's certainly no evidence of it."

"Well, that's a sign you're making progress, right?" Terry asked.

"Not really." Maggie frowned, staring at the computer screen. "Doug's far too clever and pragmatic to go around being mad. In fact, he's been very charming to me for the past week."

Except that he took care never to touch her, Maggie thought gloomily.

Their passionate kiss the day she returned from her trip now seemed as long ago and impossible as that sweet, sexy dream his visit had interrupted...

"Charming?" Terry asked with a grin. "Our host is charming to you?"

"Oh, yes." Maggie chewed the end of her pen. "He takes me out for walks and shows me the beauty of Crystal Creek. On Tuesday we even drove up to Rimrock Park to study the fossils and natural vegetation. He keeps threatening to take me horseback riding, too, out at the Double C ranch. It makes me wonder what he's up to."

"Maybe he's forgotten you're a farm girl, and thinks you'll be at a disadvantage on a horse," Terry suggested. "Or," he added with a brotherly grin, "it could be he's planning to shove you off a cliff somewhere and put an end to his problems."

"That could very well be," Maggie agreed. "I'm pretty sure Doug Evans wouldn't mind watching me fall over a cliff."

"If he hates you so much," Terry asked, "why does he still let you give him computer lessons?"

"Partly because the price is right," Maggie said grimly. "And you know what? I suspect he thinks he can still win this one if he stays close to me."

"How?"

"Doug probably believes that if he can figure out what makes me tick, and gain my confidence, then maybe he can convince me to talk Natasha out of this crazy plan to buy the town. I'm sure that's why he spends so much time with me."

Terry grinned again and raised a mocking eyebrow, but Maggie ignored him.

The whole conversation was beginning to make her uncomfortable.

She didn't like to think about all the time she and Doug spent together working on the hotel computer system, or walking and talking while they looked at the local countryside and explored the charms of Crystal Creek.

Every hour she passed in his company made Maggie more painfully conscious of the man, and brought back with greater vividness the feeling of being in his arms with his mouth on hers.

Maggie had had the same dream several times now, where Doug made love to her with breathtaking passion on that windy Scottish hillside while her father's Holstein cows grazed placidly nearby.

And to complicate the issue even more, she was growing increasingly attracted to the town of Crystal

Creek. It was truly a beautiful place, filled with vigorous and eccentric people who shared its history and contributed to its unique character.

Maybe Doug's subtle campaign was working. When Maggie saw the town through his eyes, she had to battle her own growing discomfort over Natasha's plans for Crystal Creek.

But in their telephone conversations, Natasha seemed more happy and excited than Maggie had ever known her. And the actress remained adamantly opposed to Maggie's frequent suggestion that she donate money to the town instead of buying up the property.

Worst of all, several of the townspeople themselves appeared surprisingly resigned to the whole plan.

"So, how does our little surgery patient feel nowadays?" Terry asked. "Have you talked to her lately?"

Maggie dragged herself back to reality. "Oh, much better. The bandages are all off, and apparently she's healing nicely. Natasha feels great about the way her surgery turned out. In fact, she sounds more chipper than she has in ages."

"No wonder," Terry said with gentle sarcasm. "It's not every woman who gets a new face and a whole town of her own to play with, all at the same time."

"I talked to her this morning. She's getting tired of staying in Greece. The villa has spiders, she says, and there's no decent cheese within miles."

"Spiders," Terry echoed, opening his book again.

"And no cheese. Poor Natasha, nobody should have to put up with horrors like that."

Maggie set her pen down and stared at her brother. "Terry, why do you always make fun of her this way? You know how lonely she is, and how good she's been to us."

For once his teasing grin vanished and he met her eyes steadily. "I don't like what Natasha's doing to this place, Mags. In fact, I happen to believe it's immoral."

Maggie's eyes widened. "You're kidding. Buying all this property is immoral? You never said anything like that before."

"You've never asked," he said with a detached note in his voice that troubled her.

"But Terry...most of the people who live in the town don't feel that way. They really need the cash we'd be pumping into their economy. Our purchase of all these properties will actually save their middle school for them."

"You're wrong," he said with that same cold expression. "It'll save the school for Natasha. Because by the time you're done with all this, it won't be their school anymore, will it? Nothing will belong to these people. They'll be guests in their own town, and Natasha will own everything."

"Not quite everything," Maggie said with a bleak smile, looking around at the cozy confines of their sitting room.

"Well, that's true. Thank God for Doug Evans, and the McKinneys and Gibsons, and a few others who can't be bought."

Maggie was a little surprised by how much his criticism hurt.

"Terry...I can't believe you're doing this."

"Doing what?"

"Taking sides like this. You've turned away from me and Natasha to side with a..." Words failed her.

"With a man of principle like Doug Evans?" Terry said curtly. "Well, you'd better believe it, Mags. I think it's wrong to sweep in here with millions of dollars and buy this town. I think it's selfish and divisive, and I want no part of it."

"But you are part of it," Maggie said. "You can talk about your lofty ideals, Terry, but the fact is, you're living here in the hotel with me. And when Natasha comes down next week, you'll still be here."

"No," he said quietly. "I won't be here, Maggie. I'm leaving before the end of the week."

She gripped the pen, immediately forgetting all about their conflict in her concern for him.

"But...where will you go?" she asked blankly. "Your apartment won't be ready for at least two more weeks. And you still need to finish your book. Didn't you tell me you have two hundred pages to go?"

"Yes, that's about right. The book's going really well. I can probably finish it in a couple of months if I have a peaceful place to work."

"So where will you go?" she asked again. "I'm sure Natasha will rent you an apartment somewhere if you need to—"

"I don't want anything from Natasha, for God's

sake!'' he snapped, then looked apologetic when Maggie stared at him in hurt surprise.

"But, Terry, you know she wouldn't mind at all. Natasha loves to help.''

"I know she likes being generous,'' he said. "But I haven't accepted any of her generosity since I was a teenager, Maggie.'' He picked up the book again. "Besides, I have my own plans.''

"But where will you live?''

Terry studied his sister's face for a long, thoughtful moment. "I'm going to marry Rose Murdoch, and live with her and the little girls in their house by the river.''

Maggie's jaw dropped, and she struggled vainly for some kind of reply. Terry grinned amiably at her thunderstruck expression, looking almost like his old cheerful self.

"You're going to marry her!'' Maggie said at last. "Terry, I had no idea you and Rose...you felt that way about each other. I just thought you were having fun with the kids.''

"We don't feel that way,'' he said, a flush mounting on his sunny open countenance. "At least, Rose doesn't.''

"And yet the two of you are actually planning to get married?''

"Well, I haven't exactly asked her yet.'' Terry stared gloomily at the book in his lap. "I intend to pop the question tomorrow.''

"But, Terry, if she doesn't love you, don't you think...'' Maggie floundered, still struggling with this incredible revelation.

"Rose needs a husband. She needs to marry an

American citizen so she and the girls won't be sent back to Scotland right away, and she can have a better chance of getting a green card.''

"Yes, I can see what Rose gets out of this," Maggie said. "But what's in it for you?"

"I get to live in the nicest little house in the world, and spend my time with people I care about. And I also have the satisfaction of knowing I've done a very good thing for a wonderful woman and her kids.''

"So this will be...it's a platonic relationship?" Maggie asked. "You're doing it just to help with Rose's immigration problem?"

"Of course," he said, looking uncomfortable. "Rose has never given the slightest indication that she feels anything for me except sisterly friendship.''

"But you feel something for her?" Maggie asked, watching him closely.

"I'm in love with her," Terry confessed. "I've never felt this way about anybody, Maggie. I guess I'm hoping that if we have enough time together, and I treat her really well, maybe she'll eventually come to feel the same way.''

"But there are no guarantees," Maggie told him gently. "You've got to realize that, honey. If the feelings aren't there...''

"I know," he said. "You don't have to warn me about anything, Maggie. I've given a lot of thought to what I'm doing, and this is what I want more than anything in the world.''

She stared numbly at the computer screen, completely at a loss for a reply.

"Are you upset about this because of Doug's op-

position to your project?'' Terry asked. ''Does it
worry you that a family connection might complicate
things?''

''The situation can hardly get more complicated
than it already is.'' Maggie shook her head. ''I guess
I just don't know what to say, Terry. I'm speechless.''

''Well, that's a welcome change,'' he said with a
teasing smile, though Maggie could still see the concern in his eyes.

''I just want you to be happy,'' she said softly.
''You know that.''

''Oh, yes, I'm happy.'' He leaned back in his
chair, staring thoughtfully at the ceiling. ''Scared as
hell, but happy.''

''Well, that's good.'' Again Maggie looked at the
screen and tried to sort out the numbers that swam
in front of her eyes.

''Maggie,'' he said.

''Yes?''

''Don't say anything about this to Doug, all right?
I want to talk to Rose first.''

''I'm sure he's going to find out about it soon,''
Maggie said.

''I know he will, but I haven't even asked her yet.
Promise me you won't tell him.''

''Okay, I promise.''

Terry nodded and returned to his book.

The silence in the room grew oppressive, and
Maggie was too unsettled to work. Finally she got
up, switched off the computer and grabbed a sweater.

''I'm going downstairs for a while,'' she said with

forced casualness. "I might even go out for a walk, so don't wait up."

"See you tomorrow," he said without looking at her.

Maggie watched him from the doorway for a moment, but he was totally absorbed in the book. Still worried, she shook her head and wandered down to the lobby, where Doug was just coming in from outside. The bagpipes were nowhere in sight.

He settled behind the counter and glared at a stack of file folders.

As always, Maggie was powerfully moved by the sight of him. More and more, the man filled her heart and mind. She spent hours thinking about the smallest aspects of his appearance, like the shape of his hands and the way his hair grew on the nape of his neck, and the sudden, unexpected radiance of his smile.

Still, the reality of his physical presence was always a shock, and it took a moment for Maggie to recover her equilibrium before she could speak to him.

"Hi," she said, opening the little gate and walking behind the reception desk. "What's all that you're working on?"

"More tax stuff from the accountant. I need to start sorting all this out. It's getting too late to put it off any longer."

"Do you want some help running this accounting program?" she asked, settling in the other chair.

"Why? Are you in a mood to help me, Maggie?" He looked her over thoughtfully, close enough that she had to restrain herself from reaching to touch his arm or stroke his cheek.

Or brush that lock of dark hair away from his forehead…

She looked away hastily, then switched on the computer.

"Sure, why not?" she said casually. "After all, there's nothing much to do around Crystal Creek on a Sunday night."

He opened one of the files, and again she was reduced to helpless longing just by the sight of his hands.

Doug had such beautiful hands, with square palms and strong, blunt fingers…

"You were telling me the other day about deferred capital cost allowance," he said, apparently unaware of her discomfort. "But I still have a hard time wrapping my mind around the concept."

"Here, let me show you."

Deliberately she hitched her chair close enough to his that their arms were touching, then blushed at the warm electric thrill of his nearness.

"You see this?" She pointed at a column on the screen. "All new equipment, like things you'd use in the kitchen or the pub, can be depreciated by a larger percentage in the first year, and then written off gradually against income in any of the following three years. But when you make a substantial profit, it's probably a better idea to take the rest of the depreciation allowance in the next fiscal year."

He nodded thoughtfully, then turned to look at her, resting his arm on the back of her chair so she felt almost enclosed in his embrace.

"So, Maggie, how are you doing with your theft of my town?" he asked, though his smile belied the sharpness of his words.

"Things are going very well," Maggie said calmly. "A lot of the property owners are pretty well committed by now."

"And you're ready to proceed?"

"Fairly close. Natasha will arrive sometime this coming week. Then we'll look over the appraisals and make our final decision."

He nodded, still circling her lightly with his arm. "You must be very excited."

"Don't make fun of me, Doug. This is no pleasure for me. I'm only doing my job, and you know it."

"I know." He gazed at the deserted lobby. "Maggie, what are you planning for tomorrow?"

"Why?"

"It's going to be a beautiful day. Do you want to go for a drive?"

"I think I have a meeting with some property owners late in the afternoon," she said. "But I'll be free until then."

"Okay," he said placidly.

"Doug," she ventured, sitting close to him and trying to ignore the fact that their arms were still touching.

"Yes?"

"I don't suppose you've changed your mind about selling the hotel?"

He looked at her fully, but she kept her gaze lowered, pretending to study the files littering the desk in front of them.

"You know I'll never change my mind, Maggie. How can you even ask?"

"I just thought I'd check one more time," she said with forced casualness. "If you won't sell, I need to find some other place that would be suitable as a residence for Natasha."

"And I suppose you want my help?"

"Look, all of this is going to happen, Doug," she told him. "You can't stop people from selling their property, and I can't seem to change Natasha's mind. So you might as well go along with it and help me if you can. The whole town's going to benefit."

Doug frowned, his handsome face thoughtful. "I was thinking the Carlson place might be a suitable home for your movie star," he said at last. "It's really a beautiful house."

"Carlson?" she frowned. "I don't recall seeing that name."

"Jeb Carlson keeps pretty much to himself. When he retired, he built a big house on the cliffs above the river, just south of town."

"Really?" Maggie felt a stirring of excitement. "And you think he might be interested in selling?"

"A few months ago he was telling me it's a big place to look after all on his own. He asked me to keep my eye open for a buyer."

"This man's a bachelor, then?"

Doug gave her a teasing grin. "Yes, indeed, and a very handsome one, too. Maybe a bit old for you, but some women like that fatherly image."

Maggie smiled back, despite some niggling suspicion about Doug's sudden helpfulness. "So would you be willing to take me out there tomorrow?"

He shrugged. "Why not? You're going to get there somehow, so I might as well be the one to introduce you to Jeb."

"Thank you," she said. "I'll be ready to go anytime you want."

"Let's leave at about ten," he suggested. "I need to pick up some crates of whiskey in Fredericksburg. We can have lunch down there, and stop in at Jeb's on the way back."

"That sounds good." Maggie tried to keep her voice noncommittal.

In fact, it sounded absolutely wonderful. Because the truth was, despite the unsettling effect he had on her, spending time with Doug Evans had become the most enjoyable part of her life.

But Maggie couldn't help wondering how Doug was going to react when he heard about Terry's plan. She battled a disloyal urge to confide in the man at her side, even though she'd promised Terry to keep the news to herself.

Doug had been looking after his sister and his nieces for more than a year. Surely he had a right to know what Terry was doing.

But maybe the whole marriage idea was a fantasy of her brother's, and Rose would simply laugh at the suggestion. Probably it was best to wait until tomorrow night and ask Terry what had happened with his strange proposal.

She sighed, and Doug gave her a friendly hug. "Are you tired?" he asked. "Would you rather wait until another time to do this?"

Maggie pulled away from him hastily, almost

overcome by the longing to nestle into his embrace and kiss that hard, smiling mouth.

"I'm fine," she said. "Just a touch of spring fever, I guess."

"Really?" He grinned, eyes dancing. "That sounds interesting. What are the symptoms?"

She ignored his teasing and looked at the file again. "Let me explain what I mean about deferred capital cost allowance," she said. "And this time, pay attention."

"I'll hang on every word," he assured her.

Maggie sighed, trying not to think about the dangerous hours they'd be spending together in the morning, all alone under the warm Texas sun.

CHAPTER ELEVEN

THE FOLLOWING DAY Rose Murdoch stood behind the reception desk in the hotel lobby, making careful entries in the register.

Her brother was on a ladder in the middle of the big room, changing a lightbulb in the antique hanging fixture. He wore jeans and a denim shirt, and looked lean and handsome.

"You're becoming a real Texas cowboy," Rose told him. "Nobody could tell you weren't born right here in Crystal Creek."

"At least until I open my mouth." He smiled down at her. "That Scottish accent of ours is still a dead giveaway, Rosie."

"Even your brogue is fading. Except for the bagpipes, soon you'll be a Texan through and through."

"Well, that's good to hear." Doug frowned, removing the old light bulb fixture. "Because you know I'm planning to make this place home for the rest of my life."

"Even after Maggie's boss has become the owner of the town?"

His face hardened. "That's just not going to happen, Rose."

"How can you stop it?" Rose leaned on the counter, resting her chin in her cupped hands.

"I don't know," Doug said, climbing down from the ladder. "But there's got to be a way."

"Natasha Dunne is coming next week, you know. Maggie's already booked the rest of the second floor for her and the maid."

"How exciting," Doug said bitterly. "We can all line up to get autographed maps of Crystal Creek from the famous lady herself."

"You're very angry about this," Rose said, watching him thoughtfully.

"Of course I'm angry." He folded up the stepladder and carried it toward the door. "It's a horrible, unconscionable thing the woman is doing. How can anybody think that just because she has so much money and power it somehow gives her the right to disrupt people's lives this way?"

"Do you resent Maggie for having a part in it?" Rose asked curiously.

Her brother paused by the door. "I'm really disappointed in Maggie," he said at last. "You know, I can't help thinking if she was as nice as she pretends to be, Maggie would see how awful this is and tell Natasha Dunne to—"

He stopped abruptly, looking up the staircase. Rose followed his gaze and saw Maggie partway down the steps, dressed in khaki trousers, a white cotton shirt and red cardigan, her dark hair pulled back in a braid and tied with a tartan scarf. Dundee was at her heels, looking more than usually smug and well fed.

The cat paused when Maggie did, and the room was suddenly electric with tension.

"So, do you think I'm only pretending to be nice,

Doug?'' Maggie asked, clinging to the polished oak banister. "You still believe I'm actually some kind of selfish monster?''

"I don't know what you are, Maggie," he told her with a level glance. "I've said before, I just can't figure you out.''

Maggie descended the stairs slowly. "And I keep telling you I'm just doing my job. There's no big mystery," she said. "Nothing at all for you to figure out.''

"I see." Doug opened the front door. "Are you ready to go? I'll be leaving as soon as I put this ladder back in the shed.''

"You still want me to go with you?" Maggie asked. "Even though I'm such a terrible person?''

"Don't be daft," he told her curtly.

The two of them were so focused on each other that they'd apparently forgotten all about Rose behind the counter. She watched her brother, torn with sympathy at the look on his face.

There was no doubt in Rose's mind that Doug cared a great deal for Maggie Embree, more than he would ever admit.

Possibly more than he even knew himself.

"Daft?" Maggie paused at the foot of the stairs, still pale with tension. "What seems really daft to me is the idea of spending a whole day with somebody you obviously despise.''

"Oh, for God's sake," Doug said impatiently. "Let's not make a huge deal out of this, Maggie. Come on, help me carry the ladder outside and then we'll head down to Fredericksburg.''

"I hope you realize I'm only going with you,"

she said coldly, "because I want to see this house you were telling me about."

"Oh, yes, Maggie. I know well enough why you're going with me."

"Just so you understand that. Oh, Rose, I didn't know you were there." Maggie tried to smile, catching sight of Rose behind the counter when she turned to lift the other end of the ladder.

"Hello, Maggie," Rose said uncomfortably. "I hope you have a nice day."

"With this brother of yours?" Maggie gave a short, humorless laugh. "Terry thinks Doug is probably planning to shove me over a cliff, or maybe he'd prefer to throw me in front of a wild bull."

"Not a chance," Doug said, obviously beginning to recover his equilibrium. "A stubborn, hardheaded woman like you might hurt that poor bull."

Rose watched as they went outside. The door closed behind them but she could see them through the window, still arguing as they put the ladder away and headed for her brother's truck.

She finished making the entries in the register and glanced into the bar at Casey Leach, their part-time bartender, who was washing glasses. Rose smiled at the woman, then went back to work in the kitchen next to the bar, where Terry was chopping vegetables.

Rose took a place at the counter and began methodically to prepare individual salads, cover them in plastic wrap and stack them in the roomy interior of the big stainless-steel fridge.

Terry worked at her side, dicing green peppers and tomatoes for her, slicing mushrooms and piling them onto a plate at her elbow. From time to time he opened the door to check on the girls, who were playing with an old doll carriage in the backyard.

"When does Moira need to start her school-work?" he asked, coming back to Rose's side.

"I thought I'd let her play for an hour or two yet," Rose said. "The sun is so nice and warm today. And she's worked ahead on everything except her social studies report. She can do that this afternoon when Robin's having her nap."

"Okay. You're right, it's probably a good idea to give her a little break."

"How about you?" Rose asked. "Shouldn't you be working, too?"

"No doubt," he said cheerfully. "But this is a lot more fun."

He grinned down at Rose and she looked away quickly, her hands trembling.

Rose Murdoch adored Terry Embree with a passion that had turned her whole world upside down.

After the long nightmare of her marriage, and the anxiety of bringing her children to this big strange country, Rose had thought love would never happen to her. She was too timid, too plain and ordinary, not at all the type of woman to arouse any sort of passion in another person.

Besides, she'd given up believing in the existence of a man like the one who now stood at her elbow, calmly slicing peppers.

Terry was such a nice person, with his sunny blond good looks and his casual manner. And he was genuinely interested in Rose's little girls. He complimented Rose on her cooking, admired her housekeeping and seemed to enjoy talking to her about his thoughts and ideas.

A week earlier, Terry had given Rose the opening chapters of his first novel to read. She'd been worried the book might not be good, and she'd either have to be dishonest or risk hurting his feelings.

But Terry's novel was wonderful, a luminous story of childhood and self-discovery, so beautifully written and absorbing that Rose could hardly wait to read the rest of the book.

When she'd told him this, his boyish face had shone with happiness. Remembering, she had to battle an impulsive urge to give him a hug.

"It looks like Doug and Maggie are fighting again," she said abruptly, pushing the treacherous thoughts out of her mind.

"What set them off this time?" Terry lifted another pepper and examined it, then cut a dark spot away from the bottom.

"Doug and I were in the lobby, and he was telling me how upset he is over this business of selling the town. Maggie came downstairs and heard him." Rose frowned, remembering Maggie's hurt expression. "I think she was really upset by what he said."

"She can look after herself," Terry said. "Besides, she already knows how Doug feels, but it doesn't seem to stop them from spending a lot of time together."

"Do you think they...like each other, underneath all the squabbling?"

"I don't know. Maggie's never been the type to have a lot of boyfriends. And she's really buttoned up about her feelings."

"Doug's the same way," Rose said. "But he seems different with Maggie, somehow."

"I think it's more likely they're just using each other," Terry said. "Maggie would love to get Doug to help her with this project, and he wants to talk her out of the whole thing."

"Well, that makes sense." Rose carried more salads to the fridge. "Although it sounds a bit manipulative."

"Rose, how do you feel about two people using each other, if they're both benefiting from it?"

Something in his tone seemed strange to Rose, who'd grown so accustomed to the man that she understood his every inflection by now.

Terry was still chopping peppers with a show of casualness, but she could see the sudden tension in his hands as he gripped the paring knife.

"I suppose it's all right." She glanced at him curiously. "Anyhow, it's not our business, is it?"

"Then let's talk about our business, Rose," he said, still not looking at her.

"Our business?"

"What if we decided to use each other?" He looked up at her, smiling cheerfully though she could see the nervousness in his eyes.

"I don't know what you mean," Rose said. She felt suddenly awkward, almost frightened.

"I'm suggesting that you and I make…a little arrangement," he said. "For our mutual benefit."

"What kind of arrangement?"

"I was thinking…" Terry lifted a tomato and set it carefully on the cutting board. "I think we should get married."

Rose stared at him, her jaw dropping. "Married? You and I?"

He nodded, concentrating on the tomato.

Rose looked down at her hands, feeling a hot wave of bewilderment and shame. "Terry," she whispered, "are you making fun of me?"

"Of course I'm not. Think about it, Rose," he said earnestly. "If you had an American husband, you'd have less risk of immediate deportation. It would allow a little breathing space for you and the girls."

"But...what about you?" Rose asked, her mind whirling. "You'd do such a thing just to help me?"

"Well, partly," he admitted. "But I'd benefit from it, too."

"How?"

"I'd get to live in your house for a while, and I love the place. I could take that empty bedroom for myself and set up my computer in there. I know I could write in that room, Rose," he told her. "From the first time I saw your house, I've wanted to work there."

"But, Terry..." She wrung her hands helplessly.

"Besides, I need to get away from this hotel now that Natasha's coming," he said. "I hate what she's doing here, Rose. I don't want to be part of it. And there's always such a circus around the woman, wherever she's living. I can't stand the uproar. It interferes with my work."

"People don't get married just so they can have a peaceful room to work in," Rose said. "I'll rent the place to you if you like it so much."

"But that's not fair to you. Look, just think about this for a minute." He dropped all pretense of working on the vegetables, set his knife down and turned to face her. "It's a good bargain. You get a fighting chance for a green card, and I get a place where I can finish my book in peace. You'll look after the cooking and cleaning and all that for me. I'll have the girls around to play with whenever I need a break. And then later on, after you and the girls are settled…"

He paused, looking out the window.

"Yes?" she prompted. "After we're settled, what happens?"

"We can get a divorce," he said. "I already checked into it. We can even get an annulment, because the marriage won't ever…be consummated."

Rose felt her cheeks warm. In spite of herself she pictured the two of them consummating the marriage he proposed. She saw Terry's handsome face on the pillow next to her, felt his arms around her and his husky voice in her ear, telling her he loved her.

She turned away and clenched her hands into fists to stop their shaking.

"I don't think this is a good idea," she said at last.

"Come on, Rose," he pleaded. "Just think about it. Once you get over the shock, you'll see that it's a good deal for all of us. I get a comfortable place to work and everything looked after for me. In return, I can buy some time for you and the girls."

Rose looked out the window to where her daughters were playing.

A day or two earlier, Robin and Moira had found a box of old baby clothes in the attic of their house.

And sometime within the past few minutes they'd captured Dundee and dressed her up.

The big cat crouched inside their doll carriage, looking extremely annoyed, her yellow eyes mere slits under the frill of a bonnet tied beneath her chin. "Oh, dear. Poor Dundee. Our cat would never stand for that kind of treatment."

Terry followed Rose's gaze and laughed, breaking the tension in the room.

"Come on, Rose," he urged. "The kids are so happy here. Say you'll do this for their sake, if not your own."

"A marriage of convenience," she said numbly, her hands working with automatic skill as she forced herself to slice lettuce and arrange it into bowls. "Just for purposes of citizenship."

"And a divorce as soon as you say the word," he promised. "It's really nothing more than a practical way to make sure the girls are safe here."

Rose thought about her ex-husband who waited in Scotland, angrier than ever since she'd taken the girls so far away.

"Come on," Terry said, watching her. "This is the only way for the girls to be safe."

"When…when would we do it?"

"Whenever you want. Tomorrow, if you like. I'll apply for the license right away, and then we'll just go over to the town hall."

"So soon?" she asked, her mind beginning to whirl crazily.

"I want to get out of this place," he told her. "Rose, you don't know how much I'm dreading the thought of Natasha arriving in a few days. Besides, if we're going to do this, we need to get our marriage registered right away, before somebody comes out here and says you have to go back.''

"I can't think straight," she whispered, putting down the knife and covering her face with her hands.

"You don't need to think. Look, I'm the writer here," he said in the boyish, teasing voice she could never resist. "I'll do the thinking, and you do everything else. What could be fairer than that? Please say yes, Rose."

She was amazed to feel herself nodding helplessly.

"Really?" he asked, his face lighting with happiness. "You'll really do it?"

She nodded again, unable to speak.

Terry gave her a hug, then went outside to look at the cat in the doll carriage.

His embrace had been casual and brotherly, but even after he was gone Rose tingled all the way to the core of her being. She gazed through the window at him, overcome with fear at this incredible, unbelievable thing they appeared to be doing.

CHAPTER TWELVE

MAGGIE WANDERED along the streets of Fredericksburg, enchanted by the little Texas hill town. Most of the shops and restaurants had a Bavarian theme, and on this mellow spring day she could almost believe she was walking through one of the small European villages that Natasha loved to visit.

Doug was busy at the moment, negotiating with the distributor who supplied his whiskey, so he'd left Maggie to her own devices until lunch. She was relieved to be away from him after their stilted, awkward trip south from Crystal Creek.

Hours later, Maggie still couldn't forget the shock of coming down those hotel stairs and hearing him in conversation with Rose.

Eavesdroppers never hear good of themselves, her father used to say.

Moodily, she stared at a window display of dried-flower arrangements and wreaths, thinking about Doug's comment that if she were "as nice as she pretends to be," Maggie would be trying to talk Natasha out of going ahead with her project.

His cold appraisal was unexpectedly painful. Maggie could hardly bear to think of the man weighing her conduct in his mind and deciding that her behavior was a disappointment to him.

In fact, she was surprised at herself for being so sensitive to his opinion.

Normally Maggie lived her life in a calm, detached kind of fashion, comfortable with herself and her own moral standards.

But Douglas Evans, with his hard handsome face, his probing gaze and quiet measuring silence, shattered her peace...

Maggie shivered briefly though the morning sun was warm on her back. Abruptly she pushed the thoughts aside and went into the little gift shop, to look for a gift for Rose's children.

Soon she was so absorbed in the search that all thoughts of Doug Evans and his disapproving attitude were submerged for a while. But to Maggie's dismay, they came flooding back when it was time to meet him at the restaurant down the street.

He stood waiting for her in the lobby, studying a framed map of Germany that hung on a brick wall near the reception desk.

At first he was unaware of her arrival. Maggie took advantage of the moment to study him covertly. What a wonderfully attractive man, she thought. If only the two of them could have met under different circumstances.

When he turned and saw Maggie in the doorway, his eyes kindled with a hungry enigmatic look that thrilled and disturbed her. But as always, he masked his expression at once and moved forward with automatic courtesy to take her elbow.

"They've got a table for us." He nodded at the shopping bags in her hand. "You've been making good use of your time, I see."

She smiled. "This place is really a shopper's dream. you should see all the fabulous little gift shops out there."

He ushered her into the dining room and seated her near the fireplace, where a soft blaze flickered on the hearth in spite of the springtime warmth outside.

A cheerful waitress arrived to take their order, dressed in an embroidered pinafore and apron, with blond hair coiled in tight braids over her ears.

Against her better judgment, Maggie ordered potato salad and bratwurst, and was pleased when Doug followed suit.

"That sounds like a nice Scottish meal," she teased, hoping the man was ready to relax and be a little more friendly.

"I believe in cultural diversity." He stretched his long legs comfortably under the table.

"Well, this town is definitely the place for you, then. What a marvelous little bit of Europe, right in the middle of Texas. Natasha would just adore it."

"Why not bring her down here?" he suggested. "Maybe she'll fall in love with Fredericksburg, and leave Crystal Creek alone."

Maggie's spirits plummeted. "Please, Doug," she said, looking at him directly. "Can't we call a truce, just for lunch? I'm tired of fighting."

He considered her for a moment in thoughtful silence. "All right," he said at last. "No fighting. So what did you buy?"

Maggie dug into one of the shopping bags and took out a tiny embroidered outfit that was similar to their waitress's costume, but with frilly white pantaloons.

"It's for Robin's teddy bear," she said in response to his questioning glance.

Doug leaned forward to examine the bright little costume. "Robin will love it," he said, his voice softening into a brogue, as it always did when he was moved. "Did you get something for Moira as well?"

Maggie brought out a chunky velvet case and opened it to reveal a silver brooch shaped like a small mesh handbag. Inside the bag were a handful of miniature silver charms. She showed him a lipstick, comb and mirror, each of them no larger than a scrap of fingernail.

Doug gazed at the little objects, then looked up at Maggie with frank admiration. "You obviously understand little girls," he said.

She shifted awkwardly under his direct gaze. "I was a little girl myself once," she said with an attempt at lightness. "It's not so hard to remember the kind of things I liked."

"What did you like?"

She gazed at the fire, considering. "Well, I wasn't much for dolls and things," she said. "I mostly preferred jumping off the haystack, and playing with my chemistry set."

"So you were a tomboy, then?" he asked with a teasing smile.

"Most of the time. But when I got a bit older I collected miniatures, like these things in Moira's handbag. My father built me a dollhouse and I spent hours and hours of my free time making furniture and decorations for it, and putting up bits of wallpaper in every room."

"Do you still have it?"

"Of course." Maggie smiled. "It's back in the apartment in New York. Natasha had a big glass display case made for it."

"My nieces would love to see that dollhouse."

"Yes, I'll bet they would. Most little girls like dollhouses." Maggie glanced up at him, and their eyes met and held for a moment.

She was relieved when the waitress arrived with their salads and a pitcher of ice water. Maggie murmured her thanks to the young woman, then picked up her fork to begin the salad.

"Do you like it?" he asked.

She nodded. "This is the German style. They use oil and vinegar instead of mayonnaise on their potato salad. I love it."

He was still watching her, his face hard and intense.

"Maggie," he said.

"Yes?" She took another bite of the salad, but it was difficult to concentrate on eating when he looked at her with such concentrated emotion.

"How can you be so..."

"So what?" she asked when he fell silent.

"I keep telling you, I can't understand what you really are. Sometimes you seem like a country girl, all wholesome and excited about simple things. Other times you're a jet-setting Hollywood deal-maker. Which of those is the real Maggie?"

"Both of them are," Maggie said. "Nobody's one-dimensional, Doug. Every person is a bundle of contradictions. In fact, you're every bit as hard to figure out as I am."

"That's not true." He began to eat his salad. "I'm a very ordinary and boring man. What you see is what you get."

"Oh, right," Maggie scoffed gently. "You're really boring, Doug. A perfectly ordinary man who looks after his sister and nieces, and buys a small-town hotel thousands of miles from home, runs three businesses, is the town mayor and plays the bagpipes at local functions while dressed in a kilt..."

His face broke into the charming grin that always unnerved her. "How did you hear about the kilt and bagpipes?"

"People talk," she said primly. "In fact, I know all kinds of things about you."

"Do you now? Like what?"

"I try not to listen when they discuss you," Maggie lied. "After all, I'm not in Crystal Creek to talk about their eccentric mayor."

"We all know why you're in Crystal Creek," he said, his smile fading as quickly as it had appeared.

Maggie put down her fork and gave him a level glance. "Look, Doug, what would you have me do?"

He met her eyes steadily but didn't answer.

"I really mean it," Maggie said. "Natasha is my boss, and she's set on doing this. Would you prefer that I quit my job just to please you?"

"I'd prefer that you didn't help the woman disrupt life in Crystal Creek."

"But how?" Maggie asked. "I'm not arguing with you," she added earnestly. "I really want to know. Should I tell Natasha to forget this plan because if she goes ahead with it, she's going to have to do it without me? Is that what you think I ought to do?''

"You must have some influence over her," Doug said after a moment's thought. "I saw that message she sent you from the cruise ship. Obviously she's very dependent on you."

"And you think I should be taking advantage of my employer's dependence to make her give up something she wants so badly?''

"It's wrong, this thing she wants," he said passionately. "Surely you've got to agree with that, Maggie."

"I know you believe it's wrong," Maggie told him. "But a lot of the people in your town are thrilled about selling their properties and getting out from under that tax burden. Isn't there even a tiny possibility some of those people could be right, and you could be wrong?''

"Not a chance in the world," he said curtly. "Our tax problems will be solved when the economy improves. Nothing's going to be helped by selling the town to the highest bidder.''

Maggie stared at a row of ceramic beer steins ranged along the mantelpiece. "My relationship with Natasha is more than just an employer-assistant one. I owe her a lot," she said at last. "And you're right, Natasha does depend on me. She's actually a lot more vulnerable than you'd expect, and I want to see her happy.''

"No matter what the cost?" he asked, taking a sip of water.

"You're the one who's decided this is a costly endeavor," Maggie told him. "Really, Doug, I wish

you could just try to see the other side and understand maybe it's not as terrible as you think. It's
possible Natasha honestly does have the best inter-
ests of the town at heart, and what she's doing could
be a real benefit to Crystal Creek.''

He shook his head.

Maggie's heart sank when she saw his face take
on the familiar shuttered look. ''I guess nobody can
convince you of anything,'' she said. ''You're so impossibly stubborn.''

''I see. And you're not?'' He raised his eyebrows
in sardonic fashion.

Wistfully, Maggie remembered his look of warmth
when she'd shown him the gifts for the two little
girls. But the closeness between them was gone, and
they finished their meal in a silence broken only by
occasional polite comments.

A COUPLE OF HOURS LATER, Maggie glanced at his
austere profile, then looked out again toward the
greening hills.

They were on their way back to Crystal Creek,
driving north through rural countryside alive with
color and sunshine. ''How far away is this place
we're going to?''

''Just another mile or so. Jeb Carlson built on the
cliffs above Crystal Creek so he could face south
across the river valley and see the lights of town at
night.''

As he spoke, Doug turned the vehicle and headed
down a narrow road of white crushed rock, leading
over a hill to a commanding view of the Claro River.

Maggie drew her breath in sharply when she saw

a sprawling flat-roofed bungalow of pale sandstone, built into the cliff so that it blended with the surrounding countryside.

"Oh my," she breathed. "What a lovely setting."

"Jeb had the house designed and decorated by an architectural firm in San Antonio."

"How much does he want for it?" she asked as Doug parked and got out of the truck.

He joined her on the flagged sidewalk. "I haven't discussed price with him. Probably it would go for about a million and half on this market."

She frowned, examining the house and property. "And what's the square footage?"

Doug glanced at her with a wry smile. "Could you stop being a businesswoman for just a few minutes, Maggie?" he said. "Remember, we're only here for a visit at this point."

"All right," she agreed. "But you know, if this place is as beautiful inside as it looks from here, and if it's really for sale, I'm going to want to talk business pretty soon."

"Well, I suppose that's better than having you hanging around trying to buy my hotel out from under me," he said, then stepped up to ring the doorbell before Maggie had a chance to reply.

The door was opened by a tall, handsome man with a balding head and a clipped gray mustache. Jeb Carlson was probably about sixty, Maggie thought, but he looked lean and fit.

"Hello, Doug," the man said with pleasure. "How nice to see you. Please come in. I'm tending to some plants in my greenhouse."

"This is Maggie Embree," Doug said. "Maggie, meet Jeb Carlson, one of my favorite people."

Maggie shook the man's hand and was instantly charmed by the warm sweetness of his smile.

"Hello, Mr. Carlson," she said. "It's very generous of you to let me come and see your house on such short notice."

"Doug twisted my arm a bit," the man said. "And please," he added, "call me Jeb."

Maggie and Doug followed him through a series of cool, beautiful rooms decorated in earth tones, with rough-plastered walls and Mexican-tile floors. Maggie saw fine pieces of art and sculpture, jewel-like Navajo rugs and masses of plants.

"It's lovely, Jeb," she said. "You have a beautiful home."

Their host led them to a glass-roofed atrium at the center of the house. Mounds of soil lay on the tiles, and tall ferns nodded in the soft breeze generated by banks of overhead fans.

"I like gardening," the man told Maggie, who continued to gaze around in admiration. "Here, have a seat and I'll bring out some iced tea."

Jeb indicated an arrangement of wicker furniture, couches and chairs fitted with deep soft cushions. Then he vanished through an archway leading to another part of the house.

Maggie stared at the cool forest of greenery, and the tall windows with their sweeping view of the town, the distant hills and the sparkling river far below.

"How can he bear to leave this place?" she asked Doug, who was watching her in thoughtful silence.

"He says it's lonely."

"But where will he go if he sells?"

"You mean you really care?" Doug asked.

"Of course I do. Why would you ask that?"

"Because," he said, "it seems to me you're not all that concerned about the people in town whose properties you're buying up right and left."

Maggie flushed and was about to respond sharply, when their host reappeared carrying a tray with glasses, a pitcher of iced tea and a plateful of cookies.

"It's Emily's day off," he said with a shy smile of apology. "I found what I could in the fridge and cupboards, but I'm afraid I don't know my way around the kitchen very well."

"This is perfect," Maggie assured him. He looked vaguely familiar, though at the moment she couldn't think where she might have seen him before.

"I really love your home, Jeb" she said, sipping her tea. "Doug was right, it's just beautiful."

"And Doug tells me your employer might be interested in purchasing this place?" The man seated himself in a chair opposite his guests and gave Maggie a thoughtful, penetrating glance.

"Did he also tell you who my employer is?" Maggie asked.

Jeb grinned, his eyes crinkling pleasantly. "He didn't have to. Emily and her children have been talking of little else this week."

"They're right." Maggie returned his smile. "My employer is Natasha Dunne."

"And my cook tells me that Miss Dunne wants to buy Crystal Creek."

Maggie looked up at the man quickly, wondering if she'd caught a teasing note in his voice. But Jeb Carlson's expression remained calm and impassive, politely interested.

"Yes," Maggie said. "Natasha has very fond memories of the months she spent here, although it was quite a long time ago."

"I remember those days," Jeb said unexpectedly. "I was living here in the county at that time, you know."

"Really?" Maggie asked. "Did you ever have a chance to meet Natasha?"

"I probably did," he said, his voice noncommittal. "I was quite a young man at the time, working on the Double C ranch as a trainer. We supplied almost all of the horses they used in the movie, so I met a lot of the movie people."

"That's so interesting." Maggie looked at the older man, fascinated, then glanced around at the luxurious house.

Jeb caught the unspoken implication and laughed aloud. "Hardly the kind of place you'd be likely to afford on a horse wrangler's wages," he said. "Is that what you're thinking, Maggie?"

She shifted awkwardly and exchanged a glance with Doug, who was sipping his tea and listening in silence to their conversation.

"I didn't mean to suggest…" Maggie began.

"That's quite all right," their host said. "In fact, I left Crystal Creek a very long time ago. I finally quit messing with horses, made use of my college education and got a job as a civil engineer. I also made a lot of money in oil stocks back when this state was booming. All in all, I've been a very lucky man.''

"How long have you been back?" Maggie asked.

"Just a couple of years. But people are right, you know," Jeb said, his smile fading. "You can't ever go home again."

"So if you sell your house, you won't stay in Crystal Creek?"

He shook his head, gazing at the majestic sweep of land beyond the windows. "No, I don't think so."

"Where will you go?" Maggie asked.

"I'll probably move west, out to some of those wide-open spaces."

"I honestly don't know how you could bear to leave this place," Maggie said, finding herself liking the man more and more as their conversation progressed.

Jeb winked at Doug. "This is not exactly the approach your client should be taking," he said cheerfully, "if she wants to make a good real estate deal."

"The poor wee lassie doesn't know much about business," Doug agreed, laughing. "I'll need to have a private chat with her, won't I?"

Maggie made a face at him, then got up and moved toward the windows, staring in fascination at the green valley and the expanse of rolling hills.

The men continued to talk together quietly as she looked around the comfortable room, furnished with soft leather couches and armchairs. Like the rest of the house, this room was largely decorated with plants, from banks of exotic cacti to tall ferns that brushed against the beams of the vaulted ceiling.

"It must take a whole day just to water the plants," she said over her shoulder.

"Oh yes, it does," Jeb agreed. "And I have to warn you, they go with the house. I couldn't even begin to move all of them."

Again Maggie wondered why anybody would want to sell such a beautiful home. She turned, about to ask Jeb Carlson about the number of bedrooms, when her eye fell on a small table near the window. Transfixed, she stared at a flash of gold and glass, tucked partly out of sight behind a heavy ceramic lamp.

The half-hidden object was a framed studio photograph of Natasha Dunne.

CHAPTER THIRTEEN

SHE CAST a furtive glance over her shoulder at the two men who were still deep in conversation, then leaned closer to study Natasha's young and lovely face.

Maggie spent much of her time handling the various souvenirs and relics of Natasha Dunne's career, which were presently being organized for donation to a select group of museums. Throughout the years, Natasha's publicists had used about half a dozen photographs for distribution to fans and the media. Millions of those pictures were now scattered across the country and around the world.

But Maggie was quite certain she'd never seen this particular portrait.

Natasha looked very young, probably in her early twenties.

About the same age she'd been when she filmed *Wild Land* and lost her adored young husband...

Maggie cast another quick glance at the two men, then lifted the photograph and carried it into a shaded alcove near the fireplace to study Natasha's face in the light from the windows.

It was a studio portrait, but more casual than the ones the publicists always favored. Maggie was shocked to note that the face hadn't been retouched at all. A small blemish actually showed near one of Natasha's famous cheekbones.

Even more peculiar was the fact that Maggie could find no inscription of any kind on the photo. Since the beginning of the star's career, full-face glossies had always been stamped with Natasha's sprawling signature, accompanied by the phrase "Lots of love and kisses from Natasha."

In the photograph, Natasha looked happy, sparkling with beauty and vigor. Obviously the portrait had been taken before Jeremy was killed. In the years following that tragedy, the actress had never quite recaptured this air of childlike delight. Her later photos showed a thinner, even more exquisite woman, but one whose eyes looked hurt and wary....

"She was very beautiful," a voice said quietly at Maggie's elbow.

Maggie looked up with a guilty start to find Jeb Carlson standing near her, looking remote and strangely awkward.

"I'm sorry." She flushed with embarrassment as she hurried to replace the photograph. "I didn't mean to pry. This just...caught my eye."

"I must have forgotten to put that photo away along with the others," Jeb said.

"The others?" she asked, confused.

He didn't reply, just moved the picture out of sight behind the big table lamp.

"I thought you said you...didn't actually meet her back then," Maggie ventured, a little surprised by the sadness in the man's face, and a sudden air of tension in his manner.

"Our paths may have crossed once or twice," Jeb

said, gazing out the big window. "As I told you, the McKinney ranch supplied most of the horses for the film."

So that was the explanation, Maggie thought in relief. Probably all the horse wranglers on the set had been given this particular photo. No doubt many of them would have kept it, just as Jeb Carlson had, to prove they'd been in contact with a very famous woman during a tragic and emotional part of her life.

Still, it was surprising that she could find no signature on the portrait.

"Doug's gone outside to check the foundations," Jeb said. "He asked me to escort you out to the truck whenever you're ready, because he needs to be back at the hotel soon."

Maggie smiled her gratitude. "You've been very kind. And if you're really interested in selling your home, I'd like to bring Natasha out someday next week to have a closer look at the place."

"That would be fine," he said courteously, walking with her toward the door.

"You'll have a chance to meet Natasha again." Maggie paused in the foyer. "That should be interesting for both of you, after so many years."

Jeb Carlson's pleasant face was suddenly distant and hard. "If Natasha Dunne is coming to my house," he said formally, "then I can assure you I'll be absent on that day."

"Why?" Maggie asked.

He smiled and touched her arm. "The lady's not going to be interested in an old horse wrangler. She'll just want to look at the house, so it's best if I stay out of the way."

"That's not necessary at all," Maggie protested. "I'm sure Natasha would be..."

But he'd already guided her out onto the sun-washed terrace where Doug waited by the truck.

They said their goodbyes and headed off toward town. Maggie looked back through the window and saw Jeb Carlson watching them in the growing distance, all alone at the entrance to his magnificent house.

"What a nice man," she said to Doug. "I really liked him."

"You know, Jeb reminds me of somebody," Doug said, frowning at the narrow road. "I never realized it until today."

"Me too." Maggie glanced over at him in surprise. "Who is it, do you know?"

"I can't put my finger on it."

"Maybe he resembles one of those really big Hollywood stars from the fifties," Maggie suggested. "Somebody like Cary Grant or Jimmy Stewart. He has that same look of distinction, wouldn't you say?"

Doug nodded thoughtfully, then pulled the truck off the road, bumping across the open pasture and behind a sheltering grove of trees to a high point of land that looked over the river valley.

"Come on," he said, parking and getting out. "You've got to see this."

While Maggie clambered from the truck and looked around, shading her eyes with her hand, Doug rummaged behind the truck seat and pulled out a clean tartan blanket, spreading it out on the tufted grass at the edge of the cliff.

Maggie stared at the blanket.

"Hey, what's all this?" she asked, trying to keep her voice light. "I thought you were in a hurry to get back to the hotel."

"Not that big a hurry." He sprawled on the blanket and leaned back comfortably on his elbows. "This view is too good to miss. We can spare a few minutes to enjoy it. Come and sit down, Maggie."

Still hesitant, she moved closer and sat beside him, then forgot all about his nearness for a moment as she gazed down into the valley.

The river moved slowly below, a bright ribbon of silver in the midday light. Fields ran down to the water's edge in neat squares and rectangles, dotted with livestock and machinery that looked minute in the distance. An eagle soared and drifted gracefully on the currents of air rising from the valley floor, flying high above the land, his wings outstretched.

"This is pure heaven," Maggie said, awed by the beauty all around her. "No wonder you love it here, Doug."

He smiled and reached over to touch her shoulder, his hands warm and caressing. "You really are a country girl at heart," he said huskily. "Aren't you, Maggie?"

She hugged her knees and rested her chin on them, watching as the eagle vanished into the drift of blue hills to the east.

"I don't know what I am," she confessed. "I've lived in so many places with Natasha that sometimes I don't seem to have an identity at all anymore."

"Then maybe it's time you found one," he suggested, his hand moving up across her shoulder to fumble with her hair.

"What are you doing?" Maggie asked nervously.

But she felt so warm and content, still seduced by the gleaming sunshine and the magnificent vista beyond them.

"I'm undoing your braid. I want to see that hair loose in the sunshine."

"No, please don't…"

Still she couldn't summon the will to protest, not when the sun was so warm on her face, and he was near enough that she could have nestled into his arms if she wanted to.

"You've been very quiet since you came out of Jeb's house," he said, his fingers still moving gently at the nape of her neck. "Did something happen to upset you back there?"

"Not really," she said. "I just feel sorry for the poor man, planning to leave that house and all his beautiful plants. It makes me sad."

Her hair was free by now. Doug combed it with his fingers, lifted the silky mass and let it fall around her face. He stared at her with a concentrated intensity that made her shiver, and continued to stroke her loosened hair.

"Beautiful," he whispered. "Maggie, you're so beautiful."

She tried to edge away from him on the small blanket. "Doug, we really should be…"

But he gathered her into his arms and buried his face in her hair. "You smell like sunshine," he murmured. "And sagebrush, and roses."

"Well, you smell like sunshine, and leather and shaving cream."

"And do you like that, Maggie?"

She pressed her face against his throat, surprised by the silkiness of the skin just below the rough stubble along his jawline.

"Yes," she whispered, terrified by her flood of emotion. "Actually, I like it a lot."

His hands moved over her body, stroked her back and hips, touched her hair again. Then his mouth found hers and he unbuttoned her shirt, reaching inside to cup one of her breasts.

Maggie shuddered in his embrace and moaned softly. Doug unfastened her bra, opened her shirt and bent to kiss her breasts, his hair tickling a little against her bare skin.

"We really shouldn't be doing this," she said with the last of her vanishing self-control.

"Why not?" He glanced up at her, his face so near that she could see the tiny laugh lines radiating from his eyes. "Don't you want me, Maggie?"

"Of course I do. I'm human, after all," she said. "And you're a very attractive man. But don't you think…"

"Have you ever made love under a bright afternoon sun, Maggie?" he whispered. "With cows and eagles watching you?"

Suddenly she recalled the dream that haunted her regularly. This was uncannily similar, from the tartan blanket to the misty hills in the distance, even the barns and cattle.

But that was ridiculous, Maggie told herself. Just

because she had some kind of bizarre recurring fantasy, it didn't mean she was supposed to...

At that moment a handful of flower petals came skittering across the grass and drifted softly all around them, touching her lips, lodging in Doug's hair and eyelashes.

With the gentle kiss of those flowers, Maggie was fully lost in her dream, gripped by a hot, passionate wave of sexual need so overwhelming that she had no defense against it.

Their clothes seemed to melt away with the same magical ease that Maggie always experienced in her dream. Without really knowing how it happened, she found herself lying naked on the blanket, aware of the soft prickly wool beneath her back, the warm glow of sunshine on her legs and breasts and the big hard-muscled presence of the man in her arms.

Doug's body seemed both strange and oddly familiar. His chest was matted with dark hair, more than she'd expected, and he was even bigger and more powerful than the image from her nightly dreams.

Still, there was a sweet familiarity about their embrace that soothed her constant hunger, at least for the moment. She sighed, breathless with passion, and strained him close to her, running both hands up and down his naked back.

"Did you know I keep dreaming about this?" she whispered in his ear. "Almost every night. I'm going to need therapy if it doesn't stop."

"You dream about sex?" he asked, his voice rough against her ear.

"No, I dream about this," she said. "You and me,

making love outdoors on a blanket, just like we're doing now. What do you think that means?"

He pulled away to smile at her, their faces almost touching. "I'm guessing it means you like me just a little bit, lassie," he whispered. "And for that, I'm a very thankful man."

"But don't you think it's a weird coincidence that we—"

"For God's sake, woman, stop talking," he murmured. "How is a man supposed to kiss you when you're always talking?"

She laughed and hugged him, then felt her body begin to move against his with urgent purpose.

Their tender, playful lovemaking, under the golden Texas sky, with the eagles soaring overhead, was the most richly satisfying sexual experience Maggie had ever known. No other man had ever brought her this kind of happiness, this utter completion and joy.

"So, tell me, Maggie girl, was it as good as your dream?" he asked when they lay in each other's arms, sated and still.

"Much better," she whispered, hugging him fiercely when he made a slight move to draw away. "Don't leave me yet, Doug. I love the feeling of you."

"My back will be getting sunburned," he teased.

"Oh dear," she whispered, releasing him. "You're right, it will. I guess that's the danger of outdoor lovemaking. But you know, I never seem to think about it in my dream."

He rolled gently away from Maggie and gathered her into his arms, covering both of them with the free edge of the blanket, to keep the sun and the breeze from their naked skin.

"Why would you be having sexy dreams about me, Maggie Embree?" he asked, kissing her face, her eyelids and throat and the tip of her nose.

"I don't know." She watched a lacy drift of clouds that covered the sun for a moment, casting dappled shadows on the hills.

"You know what I think?"

"No." She turned to smile at him lazily. "But I'll bet you're going to tell me."

"I think it's a sign we're supposed to be lovers, not fighters, you and I."

"Really?"

He nodded solemnly, then reached under the blanket to stroke her body with long gentle caresses that rose from her hip into the curve of her waist, all the way up to her breasts, over and over again.

Maggie stretched and luxuriated under his touch, nestling closer to kiss his chin. "If I were Dundee, I'd be purring. Wouldn't you love to be a cat, Doug, and sleep all day in the sun?"

"Quit trying to change the subject. Don't you think we should call a truce?"

"What would happen after the truce?"

"You'd leave my town alone," he said earnestly. "You could talk your movie star into buying something else to play with. And then you and I would be able to do this all the time. We could…"

Maggie leaned up on one elbow, the blanket dropping away from her breasts as she stared down at him thoughtfully.

"Hey, is that what this was all about, Doug?" she asked, trying to keep her voice light.

He stroked her hair idly. "What do you mean?"

"You made to love to me so you could talk me into doing what you want with the town?" Maggie rolled away and began to gather her clothes. "Could it be you only see me as a means to an end?"

"Don't be daft," he said. "You never gave me a chance to finish what I was saying."

She pulled on her panties and jeans and buttoned her shirt, then found she'd forgotten her bra. Maggie stared at the scrap of lace for a moment, and stuffed it into the pocket of her jeans while Doug watched in silence.

"Don't you want to hear what I was going to say?" He began to put on his own clothes.

"Not really. I'm afraid I might not like it."

Doug ignored her, calmly buttoning his shirt. "I was going to say, after you get that woman out of my town, you could come back and stay with me. We could run the hotel together, and make it a nice thriving business, and maybe have…"

He paused, watching her abrupt gestures as she pulled on her socks and shoes.

"Have what?" Maggie asked.

"We could have a couple of wee bairns with hair like this," he whispered, touching the loosened mass around her shoulders.

She pulled away from his hand. "I don't think this is the time to be talking about…babies." Her voice broke, then steadied. "Not when you feel the need to keep reminding me about these problems between us even while we're making love."

Doug touched her shoulder and cupped her chin in his hand. "Maggie," he said softly. "Maggie girl, please look at me."

But she got up and walked to the truck, climbed inside and sat waiting for him, staring straight ahead through the window at the rolling hills that vanished into the misty horizon.

He joined her, switched the truck into gear and backed up from the hillside, circling out onto the road that led away from Jeb Carlson's house.

ON THE WAY HOME they made perfunctory, stilted conversation for a little while, then lapsed into an uncomfortable silence. Maggie was afraid to look at him; her resistance was even lower because her body felt so richly satisfied, so warmed and fulfilled by his lovemaking.

If only everything was different between them, she could happily have curled up and gone to sleep in his arms…

When Doug stopped at the hotel, she got out and hurried off without a backward glance, hoping she wouldn't encounter anybody before she got to her room.

Fortunately Terry was out. Welcoming the solitude, Maggie washed her hair, ran a hot bath and soaked for a long time, trying to wash away all traces of Doug's lovemaking.

But Maggie knew she was going to dream about him again tonight. She told herself how much she dreaded the prospect, though another treacherous part of her could hardly wait to fall asleep and welcome him back into her arms.

After all, there wasn't much chance she'd hold Doug Evans again in real life.

At last she climbed from the bath, dried herself and wrapped her wet hair in a towel, then pulled on her terry-cloth robe and belted it around her waist.

When she wandered out into the sitting room in search of her hair dryer, she found Terry sitting by the window with his laptop on his knees, pecking idly at the keys.

"Are you working?" Maggie asked.

"No, just playing solitaire. I haven't been able to get much work done lately." He leaned back, stretching his arms. "There's just been too much going on."

Maggie stood by the window to look down on the tree-lined street. "It's this place," she said gloomily. "I can't wait to get away from here."

"But if Natasha buys all this property, you'll never escape. She plans to spend a good part of the year in her very own town, doesn't she?"

"Oh, God," Maggie said wearily. "I wish I could talk her out of it, Terry. But you know she's like a bulldog once she gets an idea."

"So how was your trip to Fredericksburg?" he asked. "Did you and Doug have a nice time?"

Unbidden, Maggie thought of smiling green eyes and a lean naked body of sex and sunshine and broken whispers of endearment. To her shame, she was flooded with a hot, urgent hunger.

I want him again, she thought in despair. God help me, I want him right now, this minute...

"It was all right," she said aloud, leaning her forehead against the cool glass of the window. "Fredericksburg is a magical place. And we saw a really terrific house out on the edge of town, and met the nice man who owns it.''

"So is Natasha going to buy his house?"

"I don't know. Probably she will," Maggie said moodily, still gazing at the deserted street. "After all, that's what Natasha does, right? She buys everything she ever wants."

"Are you all right, Mags?" he asked.

"Sure," Maggie turned and forced herself to smile at her brother. "What about you?" she asked. "How was your day?"

"I talked to Rose," he said. "This morning, right after you left."

Maggie looked at him blankly for a moment, then remembered the incredible plan he'd confided the night before.

"Terry!" She hurried across the room to grasp his arm. "I've been so wrapped up in my own problems, I forgot all about what you told me. So you've actually talked to Rose about getting married?"

He nodded solemnly.

"And what did she say?"

"You'll never guess." Terry smiled at her, his gentle blue eyes dazed with happiness. "Maggie, she said yes."

CHAPTER FOURTEEN

TWO DAYS LATER, just before noon, Doug Evans stood frowning at himself in the mirror as he knotted his tartan tie. He was in his suite of rooms on the main floor of the Crystal Creek Hotel, preparing to serve as best man at his sister's wedding.

The whole thing was still unbelievable to Doug. He couldn't even wrap his mind around the fact that Rose was getting married, let alone try to feel any happiness for her.

The knot in his tie was crooked again. Impatiently he yanked it loose and prepared to start over.

Robin appeared in the doorway, wearing a long plaid dress with a white lace collar. Her socks were dazzling in their whiteness, and she had a brand-new pair of black patent shoes that seemed to fascinate her.

Moira stood behind her sister, similarly dressed and looking unusually happy.

"See, Unca Dougie?"

Robin held up her teddy bear, splendidly outfitted in the Bavarian costume that Maggie had bought in Fredericksburg. Doug felt a harsh stab of pain when he looked at the bear's solemn furry face, remembering that sweet, magical afternoon under the Texas sky.

"And I've got mine on, too," Moira announced, touching her thin chest where she'd pinned the tiny silver mesh handbag.

"What about all those wee things that belong inside?" Doug asked, trying to smile at his nieces. "Do you still have them?"

"Of course I do," Moira said loftily. "Robin isn't allowed to touch any of them, so they'll never, ever get lost."

Rose appeared suddenly behind her girls, wearing a simple blue dress and a corsage of white orchids. She looked nervous and a little flustered, but astonishingly pretty.

"Here, let me do that," she said, coming into the room and taking the tie from her brother's hands.

Doug submitted while Rose put the length of tartan around his neck, knotted it expertly and then smoothed the fabric so it lay flat.

"I do wish you'd change your mind and put on the kilt," she said. "I don't see why you can't, Dougie. After all, it's my wedding day."

"I only wear the kilt for happy occasions," Doug muttered. "And this is no wedding. It's nothing but a sham, Rose."

She stood on tiptoe to smooth his hair. "You're just cranky because Natasha Dunne is coming to town this afternoon. Come on, Doug, get into the spirit of the occasion."

Doug looked down at his sister's glowing face.

Surely she didn't place some kind of emotional significance on this bizarre arrangement she'd made with Terry Embree?

After all, the man was only using her to get a home and a place to write his damn book.

Doug scowled and tugged on his tweed jacket while Rose and the little girls watched.

Maggie Embree and her brother, and the soon-to-arrive Natasha Dunne...they were users, all of them, Doug thought. And he and his family had somehow become their victims. Now even Rose and her children were caught up in all this.

"It's going to be all right," Rose whispered, standing on tiptoe to kiss his cheek. "Truly it will, Dougie. This is for the best, you know. It's going to help keep the girls safe."

Strains of piano music drifted in from the hotel lobby, and Robin came over solemnly to grasp her uncle's hand.

"We have to go now," she told him. "Moira and I are supposed to walk with you."

Flanked by his nieces, Doug walked slowly into the hotel lobby where a few people sat on chairs facing the fireplace. Howard Blake waited near the hearth, his silver hair gleaming in the sunshine that glimmered through freshly cleaned windows.

Terry stood in front of the minister, looking boyish and unexpectedly happy for a man who was sacrificing his freedom to help some strangers in their fight for legal citizenship.

Doug took his place next to the young blond man and reached in his pocket to make sure the ring was there. At that moment Mamie Gibson, the town's favorite pianist, began to play the wedding march.

Doug looked up and caught his breath as Maggie came slowly down the staircase. She wore a simple flowing dress of taupe jersey, and carried a small arrangement of local wildflowers. Her only concession to adornment had been to leave her hair loose to her shoulders, swept back on one side and held with a jeweled clip.

Doug's heart began to pound. He wondered for a crazy moment if she'd done that for his benefit, knowing how much he loved to look at her hair.

Briefly he closed his eyes and allowed himself to forget the chasm that separated them. Instead, he imagined that he, not Terry, was the groom, and this lovely woman was his bride, coming down the stairs to join herself to him forever.

It soothed his pain to pretend she loved him after all, that she wasn't angry with him and none of those hurtful things had ever happened.

Soon Maggie would slip her hand into his and repeat the lovely ageless vows at his side. Tonight she would be in his arms, laughing with him in the darkness as her slender body eased this fiery hunger that the sight of her always aroused.

And from then on, for the rest of their lives, they would stand together as they watched the seasons come and go in Crystal Creek, living the small-town life that was dear to him...

Doug was so deep in his reverie that he was startled when Howard Blake began to speak.

Robin stood at his side, quietly removing the lacy pantaloons from her teddy bear. She studied them for a moment, biting her lip in concentration, then turned them around and began to tug them back over the bear's bottom.

Moira gave her little sister a fierce nudge with her

elbow. Robin let out a small squeal of protest and glanced up at her uncle, who smiled reassuringly and stroked her hair with a gentle hand.

The little girl burrowed against his leg, cast a bitter frown at Moira and finished dressing her bear, then jammed a thumb in her mouth and continued to lean against Doug as the service proceeded.

"If any among you know of any reason why these two should not be joined together, let him speak now or forever hold his peace," the minister told the hushed assemblage in the hotel lobby.

Involuntarily, Doug caught Maggie's eye as she stood next to Rose, holding her simple bouquet.

Doug suspected Maggie had deliberately chosen such quiet garb so that the maid of honor would not eclipse the bride on this special day.

A few minutes ago he'd been thinking of Maggie as a user. Now he was acknowledging that she was thoughtful and considerate of others.

The woman had him tied in knots.

He studied the sweet line of her cheek and mouth, the steady honesty of her eyes, the drift of freckles across the bridge of her nose.

Her slim body had been so delicious in his arms, opening to him with playful, womanly passion.

Dear God, how he lusted after the woman, and how hopeless it all was!

Maggie still spent her days lining up properties for purchase, with much of the downtown block committed by now. And since their sweet interlude above the Claro River, she'd barely spoken a word to him.

Worst of all, her damn employer was arriving this

afternoon from Greece. The woman would be settled right here in Doug's hotel by nightfall.

And after that, the painful process of breaking up the town would begin in earnest...

Doug came back to himself with a start. Terry was nudging his arm gently, looking a little anxious.

"May we have the ring, Doug?" the minister said, also with a concerned expression that indicated it wasn't the first time he'd asked.

Hastily, Doug rummaged in his pocket, brought out the velvet case and opened it, handing the antique gold wedding band to Terry.

It was really a beautiful ring. Doug wondered where his new brother-in-law had managed to find that gorgeous piece of jewelry on such short notice.

Terry slipped the ring onto Rose's slim, work-hardened hand, and the two of them repeated their final vows.

"I now pronounce you man and wife. You may kiss the bride," Howard Blake intoned, his eyes sparkling with pleasure. There was no doubt the man loved performing weddings.

Doug wondered how many of his Crystal Creek neighbors had been joined in marriage over the years by this kind man.

He tried to catch Maggie's eye again but she was watching her brother and his new bride.

Doug followed her gaze and saw Rose as she lifted her face shyly to be kissed.

Something in his sister's expression caught Doug's eye. He stood transfixed, his mind whirling.

Rose was actually in love with the man!

Doug had been close to his sister all his life, and

was able to read emotions that Rose hid from everybody else. Now he saw the tenderness in her eyes, and the wistful curve of her mouth as Terry bent to drop a hasty, cautious kiss on her cheek.

Doug looked around once more for Maggie, but she had moved off across the room and was chatting with Lucia and Jim Whitley. The teacher and principal stood next to the window with their arms entwined, probably thinking about their own recent marriage.

Doug kissed his blushing sister and shook hands with his new brother-in-law. He turned away to exchange conversation with a few of his neighbors, feeling intense gratitude to the people of Crystal Creek for setting their conflicts aside long enough on this day to attend his sister's wedding.

Finally he made his way into the pub to check on lunch preparations.

As he went, he brooded about Rose's timid smile as she'd raised her face for that kiss from her husband.

This was a new complication, and one he hadn't figured on. If Rose had actually fallen in love with the man, then she was in danger of being badly hurt, and Doug didn't know what he could do to protect her.

"Damn them all," he muttered aloud, standing by the hearth and gazing down at the fireplace that brightened the dim recesses of the pub.

"Damn who?" a voice asked at his elbow.

Maggie stood there, wearing jeans and a sweater, her hair pulled back into its customary ponytail.

Doug glanced at her with rising unhappiness.

"That was quick," he muttered. "Will you not even stay for the wedding lunch, then?"

"Natasha's plane gets in just after two o'clock. I have to leave right away or I'll be late."

"You mustn't be late for Natasha," he said coldly, turning to head back to the lobby.

"Please, Doug." She reached for his arm.

He paused.

"You and I are actually kind of related now," Maggie said awkwardly. "I'm sort of…your sister-in-law, I guess. So let's try not to have hard feelings between us, all right?"

He met her eyes, aching with sorrow and sexual need. "Don't worry, Maggie. There's nothing between us," he said quietly. "Nothing at all."

Before she could answer he strode away, back to the lobby where his sister and her new husband were surrounded by a group of laughing well-wishers.

A COUPLE OF HOURS LATER, Maggie sat in the arrivals hall of Austin's gleaming new airline terminal, waiting for Natasha's flight. She leafed idly through a magazine, wondering what sort of mood her employer was going to be in after this trip.

Like many of her colleagues, Natasha Dunne owned a third share in a luxurious private jet based out of Chicago, which she and her staff used whenever they needed to travel. But the plane had been unavailable on such short notice, so Natasha had been forced to take commercial flights from Greece to Texas.

This was an experience the reclusive actress dreaded, even though her travel agent always tried to purchase at least half a dozen seats in the first-class section to guarantee a buffer zone around Natasha.

The big plane drifted onto the runway and taxied up to its port, and passengers began to disembark. With a sinking heart, Maggie noticed the familiar buzz within the terminal and realized that Natasha's presence had already been noticed.

"Great," she muttered, tossing the magazine away.

Now there'd be hell to pay. Hopefully Carla had at least managed to dress her employer in something unobtrusive.

But to Maggie's astonishment, Natasha herself came swirling along the covered walkway, wearing a white woolen cape and looking radiant. From this distance, at least, there was no evidence of the recent surgery. Natasha's famous crown of red-gold hair had been freshly tinted, and her tall slender figure and perfect oval face were as lovely as ever. She was flanked by a couple of airline attendants for protection, but paused graciously along the rope line to sign autographs and chat with fans.

When she saw Maggie, her face broke into a smile of genuine delight.

"Darling!" she exclaimed, hugging Maggie and clinging to her.

"You're looking just great, Natasha."

"It's so lovely to see you," the older woman whispered. "Maggie, you simply can't imagine how happy I am to be back in Texas after all these years."

"Welcome home. Where's Carla?" Maggie asked, disengaging herself gently.

"She's gone down to arrange for the luggage. Is your car nearby?"

"Right outside." Maggie smiled her thanks to the flight attendants. Then, with the ease of long practice, she took Natasha's arm and hustled her to the curb where Maggie's car was waiting.

Before most of the people in the terminal even knew what was happening, Natasha had been safely tucked inside the Mercedes, and Carla was approaching with the luggage cart.

Still, Maggie didn't fully relax until they were clear of the city, driving westward toward Crystal Creek. "I always worry about you in public places," she said to Natasha, who gazed out the window with a bemused expression. "I'd rather have about six armed guards traveling with you at all times."

"When I live in Crystal Creek, I won't need any guards at all," Natasha said dreamily. "The whole town will be mine, and I'll just have a safe, normal existence like everybody else."

In the rearview mirror, Maggie exchanged an eloquent glance with Carla, who sat quietly among stacks of shopping bags from the duty-free shop at Heathrow.

"I brought lots of presents for the two little girls," Natasha said happily. "I can hardly wait to meet them. Since they're Terry's stepchildren, they'll be almost like my own grandbabies. Won't they, Maggie?"

"Sort of," Maggie said noncommittally, thinking about Terry's peculiar marriage. "Moira and Robin are really nice girls."

"And Terry's happy?" Natasha said anxiously. "This Rose… She's a nice person?"

"Yes, very nice." Maggie took a deep breath. "But it's not a real marriage, Nat. You mustn't get all starry-eyed and romantic over this, the way you tend to do," she warned. "Terry just married this woman so she and the girls could apply for American citizenship and hopefully put off being deported."

"But does he care about her at all?"

Maggie remembered Terry's confession, and her own promise not to give away his secret. "I think he's quite fond of Rose," she said carefully. "But they're not…in love with each other."

"Nonsense." Natasha made a lofty, dismissive gesture, her graceful hand flashing with rings in the sunlight. "What woman in her right mind wouldn't fall in love with Terry?"

"Just don't get involved, Natasha, all right?" Maggie pleaded. "You know how upset Terry gets when he thinks we're meddling in his business. He wants a life of his own."

"Did the ring arrive on time?" Carla asked from the back seat. "Natasha was frantic about that ring. We had to make at least a dozen phone calls to get our hands on it."

"Yes, the ring arrived in Crystal Creek with about two hours to spare." Maggie smiled, her face softening. "It was our mother's wedding ring, but Terry would never have had it in time for the ceremony if Natasha hadn't pulled all those strings to get it out of the safety-deposit box in Malibu. I'm sure he's very grateful to you, Nat."

"Nonsense." Again the actress waved a casual

hand. "It was a pleasure for me to help." Natasha gazed out the window of the Mercedes again, watching the hillsides with their covering of mesquite and stunted cedar.

"I'd forgotten how lovely it all is," she murmured, enchanted. "You know, darlings, I haven't been back to the Hill Country since Jeremy...since he..."

Carla leaned forward from the back seat to drop a hand on her employer's shoulder. Natasha patted the hand gratefully, dabbed at her eyes and turned to Maggie with a dazzling smile.

"So you told me things are going well. I want to know details," she commanded.

"I'll fill you in later," Maggie said, still concentrating on the road in front of her. "I think you'll be pleased with the progress we've made. Except for the hotel, of course," she added, her throat tightening with pain as she recalled the cold expression on Doug's face, standing there by the fireplace in his pub.

"Well, that's wonderful!" Natasha said, oblivious to the sudden change in Maggie's tone. "You're such a clever, efficient girl, Maggie. I just knew I could count on you."

Maggie bit her lip, battling a sudden urge to burst into tears. "Why are you all alone?" she asked. "Where's that security detail I paid so much for?"

Natasha waved airily. "Still in New York. I gave them a week off."

Maggie stared. "Why?"

"I wanted to come back to my old town all alone," Natasha said. "We slipped away yesterday.

Just Carla and I. Even the press didn't know about it. I wanted this to be a private time for us. So do you really like the new me?'' she added, touching her face with a timid gesture that made Maggie even more emotional.

"You look fabulous,'' she said honestly. "Except for that little bit of pinkness, nobody would even know you'd had the surgery.''

"And I truly look younger?'' Natasha took a gold compact from her handbag, flipped it open and studied her reflection anxiously.

"You look about the same age as me,'' Maggie said. "But a lot less tired,'' she added ruefully.

"My poor darling.'' Natasha caressed Maggie's shoulder. "This has been so hard for you. As soon as the loose ends are tied up and I really own the whole town, we'll send you on a nice long holiday. Where would you like to go?''

"Scotland,'' Maggie said without thinking.

"Really, dear? Well, in that case, we should call the—''

"Never mind,'' Maggie said hastily. "I was just kidding. I don't even know why I said that.''

"Maggie?'' the other woman said, looking at her closely. "Darling, are you really all right? What's been going on in this town?''

"I'm fine,'' Maggie said. "You're right, I probably just need a holiday.''

"Carla, what should I do with these children?'' Natasha said gaily, shifting to address the quiet woman in the rear seat. "I turn my back on them for just a few minutes, and I come back to find my little

Maggie worn out and completely frazzled, and Terry off getting married to a stranger…"

"Nat, we're not children," Maggie said.

"I suppose you aren't." Natasha settled back against the seat, looking out contentedly at the Texas countryside, then glanced at Maggie again.

"You're sure he won't sell the hotel? I'd so love to own that building."

"I'm sure," Maggie said curtly. "But," she added to soften her reply, "I did find another house I think you'll like."

While Natasha listened, Maggie described the lovely home on the river cliffs above Crystal Creek, going into detail about the privacy, the marvelous view, the well-planned and luxurious interior with its cool masses of greenery.

"Why would anybody want to sell such a beautiful place?" Carla said from the back seat.

"The owner says it's too lonely. I think he plans on moving to west Texas."

"What's his name?" Natasha asked absently, frowning at a chip in the glossy nail polish on her thumb.

"Jeb Carlson," Maggie said, then jumped a little in surprise when Natasha gripped her arm.

"What?" the actress said. "What did you say this man's name is?"

Maggie stared at the woman beside her in concern. Natasha's face had turned so pale that in the afternoon light all the minute scars from her surgery were clearly visible. She seemed utterly terrified.

"Natasha," Maggie said. "What's the matter?"

"This man's name," Natasha whispered hoarsely. "Did you say it was…Jeb Carlson?"

"Yes, that's the name. Why, do you know him?" Maggie looked away from the road to gaze at her employer.

Carla, too, watched anxiously from the back seat. "Natasha," she said, "what's wrong, dear?"

"Nothing." Natasha huddled in the passenger seat, wrapping the cape tightly around her as if for comfort. "Nothing's wrong."

"But do you know this man that Maggie's talking about?"

Numbly, Natasha shook her head.

"Are you sure?" Maggie exchanged a worried glance with Carla in the mirror.

"Will I have to…to talk to the man if we buy his house?" Natasha asked in a frightened whisper.

"Of course not," Maggie said, increasingly puzzled. "Doug Evans is the local real estate salesman and the listing agent, so he's the one who'll handle the transaction. Besides, Jeb Carlson already told me he didn't want to be around when you came to see the house."

Natasha licked her lips. "He…said that?"

"Yes, he seemed very considerate. He's a lovely man, Nat. I really liked him. I can't imagine why he wants to go away."

Natasha turned without speaking and gazed out the window again

Maggie glanced over at her from time to time, still feeling uneasy.

It must be the effects of jet lag, she told herself, because she was almost certain that Natasha's ebullient mood had faded, and she was now crying softly.

CHAPTER FIFTEEN

DESPITE ALL THE YEARS of her involvement with Natasha Dunne, Maggie was still continually amazed by the actress's ability to seize the spotlight and dominate every situation.

This always appeared to happen without effort on Natasha's part.

But never was it more evident than during Natasha Dunne's arrival in Crystal Creek. The lovely actress seemed to recover quickly from her unexpected bout of sadness in Maggie's car. By the time they emerged from the Mercedes in front of the Crystal Creek Hotel, Natasha was as gracious and glamorous as ever.

Maggie whisked her employer past small knots of curious townspeople, then hurried her through the lobby and up the stairs.

Doug stood on the upper landing, repairing a faulty window lock. He turned as they approached, his face impassive.

"Natasha Dunne," Maggie said, feeling suddenly uneasy. "This is Douglas Evans, the hotel proprietor."

"Mr. Evans! How wonderful to meet you at last!" Natasha extended her jeweled fingers and turned on her most brilliant smile.

Doug shook her hand courteously, but seemed

completely unmoved by the presence in his hotel of one of the most glamorous women in the world. "Hello, Miss Dunne," he said. "I'll go down and get your luggage." He turned without another word and descended the stairs to the lobby.

Maggie watched him stride through the door before she took Natasha's arm again, then led her down the hall to the suite.

"We've changed things around a bit up here, Natasha," she said after Doug had delivered the luggage and gone silently back downstairs. "The whole floor is reserved for us. Now that Terry's gone, I'm giving this connected suite to you and Carla. I've moved my own things into the next room, and we'll use the one across the hall as a temporary office, if I can talk Doug into getting a few more phone jacks for us."

"What a gorgeous man he is," Natasha said reflectively. "I don't think I've ever seen anybody quite so handsome. But," she added, frowning, "he seems quite distant, doesn't he?"

"Don't worry," Carla told her employer wryly as she rolled one of Natasha's garment bags into the larger bedroom with the four-poster bed. "He's a man, isn't he? So you'll soon have Mr. Evans completely won over and eating out of your hand, dear."

But Natasha wasn't listening. She left the suite and wandered along the hall to a room near the other end of the building, where the windows looked over the town and the hills beyond.

Dundee was there. A furry, inert ball, the cat drowsed on a quilt near the old-fashioned radiators.

She didn't even stir when the group of women entered the room.

"This is where I slept!" Natasha told Maggie and Carla, who'd followed her. "Back when we were here filming *Wild Land.*"

"Really?" Maggie stopped behind her and peered in. "This very room?"

Natasha nodded dreamily, running a hand over the cotton bedspread. "And this is the bed where…" She flushed and straightened, covering her face with her hands. "Where I was lying when they told me Jeremy was dead," she whispered, her voice muffled.

"Come along," Carla said. "Twelve hours of sleep for you, my dear, and you'll feel like a new woman. And a good thing, too, because I think tomorrow will be a busy day."

CARLA'S PREDICTIONS turned out to be correct, except for the one about Natasha having the hotel proprietor eating out of her hand. In fact, Doug seemed to go out of his way to avoid his famous guest.

After a comfortable night's sleep, Natasha went to the Longhorn with Maggie for lunch the next day and met the residents of "her" town, thrilled both with the ambience of the restaurant and the freedom of small-town Texas.

"I won't even need to hire bodyguards here," she said excitedly across the gingham-checked tablecloth. "Oh, Maggie, this place is exactly the way I hoped it would be."

"What do you mean, Nat?"

Natasha waved a jeweled hand at the other patrons. "These people know I'm here, but none of them are making a big fuss. They just say hello as if we're already neighbors, and then go on about their business. And when they look at me,'' she added, her eyes misting with emotion, ''you can tell how much they love me.''

''That's because they're counting on you to take their worries away by giving them a ton of money,'' Maggie said dryly over the vinyl-covered menu, then regretted her words when she saw Natasha's hurt look.

They ordered coffee and fried-chicken fingers with sweet-pepper sauce, one of the Longhorn's richest delicacies, and ate in silence while Natasha watched her assistant gravely.

''Why are you upset about this, Maggie?'' she said at last.

''Who says I'm upset?''

''You don't have to say anything. I can tell by the set of your mouth.''

''It just seems…a little presumptuous to buy a whole town,'' Maggie said awkwardly. ''A lot of people are upset about it.''

''On the contrary, most of these people seem utterly thrilled about it.'' Natasha gave Maggie a surprisingly shrewd glance. ''But not your delicious Scotsman, I take it.''

''He's not my Scotsman!''

Natasha took a sip of coffee. ''That isn't what Terry tells me,'' she said.

''Oh, for God's sake!'' Maggie stared at her employer. ''You've already talked to Terry about this?''

''They gave Carla and me a lovely cup of tea early this morning in their cute little house, and then Terry and the girls walked us back to the hotel. Terry thinks you're passionately in love with this Scotsman.''

''Well, that's just ridiculous!'' Maggie shifted angrily in the chair, remembering sunshine and silky naked warmth, and flowers and sweetness…

''Ridiculous?'' Natasha raised an eyebrow. ''Why?''

''In case you haven't noticed, the man despises me and everything I'm doing here.'' Maggie said stiffly. ''So let's not talk nonsense, all right? Doug Evans is the furthest thing from my—''

''Speak of the devil,'' Natasha murmured, waving gaily to somebody at the door.

Maggie turned to see Doug standing in the entry with his nieces. Her heart began to pound noisily, as it always did at the sight of him.

Moira and Robin, who by now were fully enraptured with their glamorous visitor, ran toward the booth. Natasha pulled the two little girls in beside her, draped an arm around each and let them share the last of her chicken fingers while Maggie watched with a rueful smile.

Over their heads she exchanged a glance with Doug who waited by the door, his face carefully inscrutable.

''Moira, is your uncle ready to take us out to Mr. Carlson's house?'' she asked.

Moira nodded, swallowing the last bit of chicken. ''He says me and Robin can go too.''

''Robin and I,'' Maggie corrected automatically.

''We get to see the big house that Natasha's going to buy,'' Robin added, clutching her teddy bear.

"Oh, what fun," Natasha said, clapping her hands. "So, girls, let's all go see this wonderful house, shall we?"

Her voice was bright, her famous smile dazzling. But Maggie caught an undercurrent of fear and uneasiness in her employer's words, and wondered again what was going on in Natasha's mind. With such an accomplished actress, it was never easy to tell.

They rode out to the Carlson place in Maggie's big car. Doug lounged silently next to Maggie in the front seat, while Natasha insisted on sharing the back with the two little girls, who examined her rings while Natasha told how she'd acquired each one.

"I love this shiny blue one," Moira said. "Where did it come from, Natasha?"

"That sapphire was a gift to me from the king of Jordan, where I made a movie and got to be friends with his wife. She's American, you know."

"What about this gold one?" Robin asked. "It looks like leaves all wound together."

"In a minute, dear." Natasha dropped a kiss on the little girl's bright hair and leaned forward. "Doug, could you tell me something?"

"Yes?" he asked courteously, glancing back at her.

"Maggie says the owner of the house…this Mr. Carlson…he won't be home this afternoon when we look at the place?"

Doug shook his head. "Jeb left a key with me and drove up to Abilene for the day. He prefers for me to represent him completely in the business deal, and he says if it's finalized he'll move his things out as soon as possible so as not to inconvenience you."

"I see. That's very kind of him." Natasha sounded relieved as she settled back and turned her attention to the two little girls again.

But Maggie was watching her in the rearview mirror and she was once again puzzled by the look on Natasha's lovely, expressive face.

If she hadn't known better, she could have sworn that Natasha was disappointed that she wasn't going to be meeting Jeb Carlson on this bright March afternoon.

THAT NIGHT Maggie sat upright in bed, propped on a mound of pillows, reading through property lists and adding sums of figures by the glow of the bedside lamp. A knock sounded at her door.

"Come in, Natasha," she called, expecting one of her employer's cozy late-night chats. "The door's still unlocked."

But it was Doug who came into the room, then locked the door carefully behind him.

Maggie set the papers aside and sat erect, pulling the blankets up cautiously around her waist, grateful that she'd chosen to wear flannel pajamas tonight instead of a flimsier nightgown.

When they were together, the situation was always volatile enough without added fuel...

"I like your pajamas," he said, crossing the room to sit in the chair by the window.

"Why are you here, Doug?"

"I wanted to see if you're comfortable. It's too

bad you had to give up that nice bedroom down the hall.''

"This arrangement works better for everybody," Maggie said, wishing the man didn't have such a shattering effect on her.

Whenever Doug was in the room, Maggie wasn't aware of anyone else. And she wanted him so much, with a wild, ever-increasing hunger that brought her almost to the brink of despair.

"Then it's a good thing Terry left, so your boss and her maid could have the suite."

"Yes, it is." Maggie stared at the flowered drapes, wishing he'd go away.

She felt so tired and drained. The last thing she needed was more of his disapproval over what she and Natasha were doing.

But when he spoke, his words surprised her.

"Maggie," he said, "what do you really think about this marriage?"

"You mean Terry and Rose?"

He gave her a shrewd glance. "Who else would I mean?"

Maggie flushed and hugged her knees, hiding her face briefly.

"I'm so tired," she muttered. "Whenever I'm away from Natasha for a while, I tend to forget how much she wears me out."

Doug watched her in grave silence.

"The marriage?" he prompted after a few seconds.

"It's not a marriage," she said. "It's a business arrangement."

"Why did your brother do it?"

"Who knows? He wanted a nice quiet place to work. He likes her house and her kids." Maggie frowned at the list of numbers. "Maybe he just wanted to do something generous for Rose."

"I don't want her to get hurt," Doug said, fingering the edge of a chintz cloth draping the lamp table. "And I already told you, Terry would never hurt anybody."

"Pardon me if I'm not exactly in a position to be impressed with your family's consideration for others."

"Oh, come on, Doug," she said with a flare of annoyance. "That's just not—"

But he waved his hand in a weary, dismissive gesture. "Look, let's not get into this, Maggie. I'm as tired as you are."

Her anger faded. She looked over at him in concern, noticing how exhausted and drawn he looked. They sat for a moment in a silence broken only by the spring breeze whistling at the corners of the old building.

"Do you think she's going to buy the Carlson house?" he said at last.

"Oh yes, she loved it. I knew she was going to. It's exactly Natasha's style."

"You'll need to add some heavy security if she's actually going to live out there."

"We're used to that," Maggie said. "For people as famous as Natasha, security is just a constant part of life."

She was silent a moment, toying with the edge of the paper.

"Doug…"

"Yes?"

"Have you ever noticed a portrait of Natasha that Jeb Carlson keeps on that low table in the living room?"

"Once or twice," he said. "I guess Natasha was every young man's fantasy back when Jeb was a horse wrangler in Crystal Creek. It's a funny coincidence that she'd turn up one day and buy his house, isn't it?"

"I saw the picture when you first took me to the house, but today it was gone from the table. He deliberately took it away before Natasha came. I just wondered…"

Doug looked at her directly. "Does it make you nervous?"

"A little," she confessed.

"Actually, it's not so strange." Doug leaned back in the chair. "Jeb's a really nice man, Maggie. He may have had a bit of a crush on your boss, but he's probably a little embarrassed—which is why he removed the picture."

"Natasha seems…" Maggie hesitated.

"What?"

"I don't know. She's acting funny about the whole thing. I can't figure her out."

"I suppose it's got to be an unsettling experience for her to come back to a place where she endured such terrible pain."

"You're probably right," Maggie said. "After all, she was so crazy about Jeremy Calder, and they'd only been married a few months when he was killed."

"So do you think she's changing her mind at all about buying the town?"

Maggie shook her head. "If anything, she's more determined than ever. She loves the place, Doug. Natasha says she feels safe here."

"My God," he muttered.

"Please," Maggie ventured, "can't you just try to look on this from our point of view? Maybe it's not as bad as you think."

He shook his head. "I come from a small country, Maggie, with a long history of oppression and conquest. We Scots understand in our bones that being taken over is never a good thing."

"But Natasha is hardly a conquering army," Maggie said dryly.

"Yes she is. She just uses money as her weapon, instead of bullets or broadswords."

"Life here will hardly change at all," Maggie argued. "Except that the names on the land titles will be different, everything's going to go on just as it always has."

"Oh, come on, Maggie!" he said impatiently. "You're too bright a girl to believe that. You must realize that everything in Crystal Creek will be completely different from now on."

"How?"

"The individualism will be gone. All the character of the town will vanish," he said passionately. "We'll lose our eccentrics, who'll move to Lampasas or Llano or somewhere else so they can live free. The only people left here will be the toadies who enjoy having a famous woman call the tune while they dance."

"That's far too harsh," Maggie told him. "And you know it. I wish I could get you to just look at my point of view for a change."

"All right." He settled back in the chair. "Tell me your side."

"Well, for one thing, there's this plebiscite about the middle school," Maggie said. "It's happening in two days. And you know what?"

"What?"

"Before I came here and started talking about property acquisition, the middle school didn't have a hope of winning that vote. Not a chance in the world. But do you know how it stands now?"

"Oh, I'm sure you'll tell me," he said with a brief smile that faded quickly as Maggie pulled out another sheet of paper.

"At Terry's wedding," she said, "Lucia Whitley told me the opinion in the town was now running almost fifty-fifty. Doug, they actually have a good chance of saving their school," she told him earnestly. "And that's all because of Natasha's plan."

"There are other ways to save the school," he said stubbornly. "The town council's been working on plans to lower the mill rate and come up with a fairer property tax. But there's nothing we can do if it's all taken out of our hands."

Maggie leaned back against the pillows, watching him. Despite the familiar difference of opinion, they weren't arguing as passionately as they had in the past. It felt almost comfortable to be having this late-night discussion with him.

Maggie was surprised how much she enjoyed having him just sitting there and chatting, without a lot of painful emotional intensity between them.

The thought crossed her mind that she and Doug were like a husband and wife talking things over at the end of the day. Regretfully, she pushed the image away.

Because that was one fantasy that was never going to come true. Not with Doug Evans...

"Well, at least it's kind of nice to talk to you without yelling," he said with a tired smile, echoing her thoughts. "We should try it more often."

"I don't know," she said a little shakily. "We don't seem to be very good at it."

"Maybe we could learn." Doug looked her over with a penetrating glance that made her body feel warm with yearning.

"Doug..."

"So, are those flannel pajamas nice and cuddly?" he asked.

"They're warm," she said with forced casualness. "A very good choice," she added pointedly, "for people who prefer to sleep alone."

"Do you prefer to sleep alone, Maggie?"

"It seems a whole lot less complicated," she said neutrally.

"And would you rather be free of complications than have somebody to cuddle you?"

"Why are you doing this?" she asked in despair.

"Doing what?"

"There's no point in flirting with me, Doug. We're on opposite sides of a major issue, and you can't win me over just by climbing into bed with me again.

I'm not sure what opinion you may have formed, but the truth is, I'm not that easily influenced.''

"Maybe not." He got up and came over to touch her hair. "But you're a woman who can recognize the truth when she sees it, if she only allows herself to have an open mind."

"And you would be the sole judge of what constitutes truth?"

"I'm a fair-minded man," he said. "If you ever spent enough time with me, you'd come to realize the truth of that, Maggie."

He was moving his hands through her hair with a slow, mesmerizing touch, lifting the long mass and letting it fall, smoothing it with gentle fingers.

The soft caresses made her want to reach out and pull him into bed with her, turn the light out and lose herself in his powerful, sweet maleness.

"Don't," she said in a choked voice. "Please, don't do this."

He stopped at once, drew back from the bed and moved toward the door.

"Good night," he said with a tone of formality that made her heart ache.

"Doug," she said when he opened the door to leave.

"Yes?" He glanced back at her.

"What makes you think Terry might hurt Rose?"

He watched her gravely for a moment. "Because I'm very much afraid my sister's in love with the man," he said at last.

"But..." Maggie stared at him in astonishment. "Doug, he loves her, too! Terry told me even before he proposed, and made me swear I wouldn't give his secret away."

Doug's face broke into one of those rare, shining smiles. "Really?"

"Really." Maggie felt a brief pang of guilt. "I shouldn't have said anything, but since you told me about Rose..."

He chuckled with genuine amusement. "How long do you think it'll take that daft pair to figure out they're in love with each other?"

"Do you think one of us should interfere?"

"We can't even manage our own love lives, Maggie," he said, his smile fading. "We'd best leave others alone, don't you think?"

She nodded, battling an urgent desire to call him back.

"You're right." She forced herself to pick up the papers again. "I guess we'll just have to let Terry and Rose work out their own problems. Good night, Doug."

"And after that," he said, pausing in the doorway, "maybe somebody will be kind enough to work out our problems for us."

"I doubt it," Maggie told him.

He seemed on the verge of a reply, then shook his head and closed the door quietly behind him, leaving Maggie alone in the warm pool of lamplight.

At least he hadn't noticed Dundee, who once again slept on the quilt near the radiators. Maggie suspected that if Doug knew his cat was here in the room with her, he'd come back and take Dundee away.

And right now Maggie desperately needed company, even if a sleek fat tabby—who was much more interested in food and a warm bed than any kind of companionship—was the best she could do.

CHAPTER SIXTEEN

THREE DAYS LATER, at his desk under the dormer window in Rose's upstairs spare room, Terry Embree sat and gazed outside. Afternoon sunlight sparkled on the slow-moving river like a scatter of diamonds. A pelican swooped low over the water, then rose and circled in graceful flight. Inside the room, Hippo, the cat, drowsed contentedly on a braided rug in a warm square of sunlight.

Terry sighed and looked back at the computer screen, where the final chapters of his novel continued to flow from his fingers with astonishing ease.

Too much ease, Terry thought gloomily. At this rate he'd be done in just a month or two. A new novel was already forming in his mind, so enticing that he could hardly wait to get started on it.

But once the current book was completed and polished and sent off to the agent, he'd have no excuse to stay here with Rose any longer. The deal was that he would only stay as long as it took for him to finish.

Unfortunately, Terry had been all too correct about this little house, and life with Rose and the girls. It was like a constant inspiration, effortlessly igniting his creative force.

Every day as he worked, words came tumbling

onto the computer screen, and the hours flew by before he was aware of them.

He and Rose already had a household routine comfortably established.

After breakfast each morning, his wife and the girls walked up to work at the hotel while Terry was writing. In the late afternoon, they came home, and Rose prepared a simple, delicious meal that they ate in the kitchen, sharing conversation and laughing with the children.

After dinner, Terry and the girls cleared up and then went for a walk to give Rose the chance for a long bath and some time to herself. Then they put the children to bed, watched television or read for a couple of hours.

Sometimes he and Rose put the books aside and talked about everyday things, or about Terry's work, or their childhood memories. Then they went upstairs to their separate beds.

It was an ideal life. Only two things made him lie awake at night... The fact that Rose was sleeping alone just down the hall from him, and the sure knowledge that he would soon have to leave.

Once his book was done and her citizenship application was under way, there would be no excuse for them to stay together.

Terry tried to imagine what his life would be like after he left this house. How could he survive without seeing Rose and the girls every day?

Or worse, how could he bear having to watch them move in with another man someday, maybe a handsome Texas rancher or oilman, somebody bold enough to win Rose's heart.

He grimaced with pain and forced his thoughts back to the words on the computer screen, but they danced and blurred before his eyes.

"Hello," the gentle voice he'd recognize anywhere said from the doorway. "Am I interrupting?"

He turned to see Rose standing there, looking adorable in a soft pink sweater and flowered dress.

As always, Terry's heart lifted at the sight of her. He had to turn away so she wouldn't see the blaze of happiness and love on his face.

Instead he looked at his watch, then frowned in surprise. "It's only two o'clock, Rose. Is something the matter?"

"I told you this morning," she said patiently. "In a few minutes we're supposed to be at the school to hear the results of the school plebiscite. Do you even remember that the vote was held yesterday?" she asked, her voice gently teasing. "Or do all of you writers just live in a constant fog?"

"I distinctly remember walking up there with you." He smiled back at her. "You wore a pair of khakis and your blue denim shirt that's exactly the same color as your eyes."

Rose watched as he switched off the computer and removed his backup disk. "What does my blue shirt have to do with the vote on the middle school?"

"Nothing." He took his jacket from the closet and joined her in the hallway. "I just have a novelist's eye for detail, that's all. Where are the kids?"

"They're walking over to the school with Doug. Robin was anxious to stop and play on the carousel for a few minutes."

Terry smiled fondly as he followed her down the

narrow staircase. "They both just love that old carousel, don't they?"

"I love it, too," she said. "It's like a symbol of all that's good about this town."

Rose took her handbag from the newel post and they left the house, walking together up the street toward the middle school.

"It seems too good to be true," Rose said, looking around contentedly, "that my girls might really grow up in this place. What a wonderful childhood they'd be able to have."

Terry gazed at the masses of willows along the river, the flowers beginning to bloom in gardens and hedgerows, the bright storefronts and the distant white spire of a church steeple.

"This is a nice place, all right," he agreed.

"It makes me feel so ashamed," she murmured at his side.

Terry looked down at her in surprise, but she kept her head turned away, so all he could see was the gentle curve of her cheek.

"Ashamed?" he said. "What would you possibly have to be ashamed of, Rosie?"

"I feel like I haven't ever thanked you enough for...what you did," she whispered. "It was really wonderful of you, Terry, giving up your freedom just to help us. I'll be so glad after the citizenship papers start going ahead and we can..." She hesitated, looking painfully embarrassed, then went on. "I'll be glad when you're able to leave again and get on with your life."

I don't want to leave, he longed to shout. *I want to stay with you forever, Rose. I love you.*

But he couldn't say those words aloud. If he ever did, their already bizarre situation would become unbearably complicated.

So he kept his silence, walking at her side with his hands jammed into his pockets.

"Do you think the school will win the vote?" she asked, clearly trying to change the subject.

"I don't know. It looked like sentiment was still pretty evenly divided yesterday. And that terrible woman who runs the school board...what's her name?"

"Gloria Wall," Rose said.

"Well, Gloria seems to have a lot of power around here."

"Not as much as she did before Natasha Dunne came to town."

Terry nodded gloomily. "Isn't it strange how something good can actually come out of something bad?"

"I guess something good can come out of almost anything," Rose said shyly.

Terry smiled at her, battling the familiar urge to take her hand or put his arm around her.

"Well, Mrs. Embree," he said, forcing his voice to remain light and teasing, "we'd better hope for our kids' sake that the school wins the plebiscite. Otherwise they'll have a long trip on a school bus every day."

Rose looked up at him, wide-eyed, then blushed the endearing shade of pink that he especially loved. Again it was all Terry could do not to stop right there on the sidewalk and gather her into his arms.

DOUG MANAGED to coax his nieces away from the old carousel with just a few minutes to spare, and hurried them up the street toward the Crystal Creek middle school where the whole town was gathering to hear the results of the plebiscite.

He could feel the tension, and see the anxiety on the faces of his neighbors.

Everybody was there, from J.T. and Cynthia McKinney whose daughter Jennifer would soon be old enough to attend middle school, all the way up to older people like Mamie Gibson, who had never married but still maintained a passionate love for her town and its school system.

Also present in the school auditorium were many hard-core supporters of Gloria Wall. These were the people who believed the middle school had to go, and the students should be bussed to a neighboring town to save costs.

Gloria, it was whispered, had a deeply personal dislike for the middle-school principal, Lucia Whitley, and would do anything to hurt her, even if it meant depriving Crystal Creek of a school it had maintained for almost a century.

Doug settled in a chair near the front of the hall with his nieces on one side of him. Moira was already quietly preoccupied in a video game that Natasha had brought for her. Robin was busy undressing her teddy bear who, as usual, wore the embroidered Bavarian costume purchased in Fredericksburg.

Doug glanced down at the furry toy and its bright dress. Again he remembered that sunny afternoon on the tartan blanket with Maggie in his arms. He almost groaned aloud as he recalled her silken nakedness, her slender body and shimmering hair, and the unexpected playfulness and passion of her response.

God, what a woman she was!

He shifted awkwardly in his chair, sharply uncomfortable at the sudden tightness in his groin, and tried to distract himself by looking around at the assembled townspeople.

Almost at once he caught sight of Maggie herself. She was sitting a few rows back, with Natasha Dunne at her side.

The famous actress was attracting surprisingly little attention. People already seemed to take her for granted in Crystal Creek.

The two women hadn't seen him yet, and Doug turned away quickly.

One thing he had to give Maggie credit for, she'd been right about the school plebiscite. Until the arrival of Natasha Dunne and her unexpected plans to buy up most of the local property, nobody would have given a plugged nickel for the school's chances.

Gloria Wall and her gang had done their work well. The whisper campaign had worked, and everybody had been convinced the school was too inefficient, too expensive and redundant to survive. They'd been anxious to get lower taxes, and many were prepared to sacrifice the school to get them.

Now the atmosphere seemed less tense and hostile, though it was still impossible to tell how the vote might go.

A hushed silence fell as Lucia Whitley walked out onto the stage, followed by the entire staff of the school. The teachers seated themselves in banks of chairs at the rear of the platform while Lucia waited quietly at the podium with a sheet of paper in her hand.

Doug looked anxiously at his friend on the stage. Lucia Whitley was a beautiful woman, though not at all like Maggie. The principal was blond, cool and fashionable, despite the growing bulge of her pregnancy.

But impending motherhood seemed to have softened Lucia a little, given her a kind of gentleness and a feminine glow that had been lacking in the past.

Love could probably do that, Doug thought, smiling at Lucia's new husband, Jim Whitley, who lounged behind her on the platform.

The lanky cowboy was one of the most popular teachers in the middle school. Many of Crystal Creek's residents had been surprised by his marriage to the elegant principal, and even more startled that Jim—who'd been a bit of a rolling stone—now seemed willing to settle down to the pleasures of domestic life.

But there was no doubt Jim Whitley was enjoying his marriage. He gave every appearance of a man who was completely satisfied with his life.

Apparently that was another thing love could do for you, Doug thought with a pang of yearning.

More than anything Doug wanted a partner to share his life and his dreams. But that partner, he realized in despair, had to be Maggie Embree.

No other woman would ever be enough for him, not after he'd held this one.

Again he felt that hard stiffening of desire. Doug

forced himself to concentrate on Lucia who had begun to speak.

"My friends and neighbors," she said in her clear,
cultivated voice, "we have all been through some
very trying times together in the past year. And as
you know, we've had a very difficult decision to
make."

The audience sat listening to her in tense stillness.

"All of us here at the school are very much
aware," Lucia went on, "that this place is expensive
to operate, and that many of you already suffer under
a heavy tax burden. We've tried hard to run our
school as economically as possible in order to lessen
the financial burden, but this continues to be very
difficult and requires a great deal of sacrifice."

Again the principal looked down at the audience
and caught Doug's eye. She nodded briefly in rec-
ognition, but didn't smile.

"Now, you've made your decision about the
school, and I am required to announce the results."

She put on a pair of reading glasses and consulted
the paper in her hand.

"Discounting spoiled ballots, the vote was sixty-
one percent to thirty-nine in favor of..."

For the first time, a smile softened the principal's
austere features. A stir of excitement began to ripple
through the assemblage.

"You have decided to retain the middle school,"
Lucia said simply. "And for that, my friends and
neighbors, I am so very grateful to all of you."

Tears glistened in her eyes. She brushed at them,
smiling, while Jim got up and came forward to hug
her. A roar of approval swept through the auditorium

as the citizens witnessed their elegant principal being cuddled tenderly in her husband's arms.

Gloria Wall got up and swept out of the room glowering. A few of her supporters followed, but most people were applauding furiously, yelling and stamping and whistling.

Lucia left her husband's embrace and moved back to the microphone.

"I'd like to call on our mayor, Douglas Evans, to say a few words," she announced, then returned to sit among her staff.

Startled, Doug got up and made his way to the stage amid more waves of thunderous applause. He raised his hand and the crowd grew quiet.

"If I'd known this was going to be a celebration," he said, "I'd have brought along my bagpipes."

This elicited a roar of laughter. Doug scanned the crowd until he found Maggie, who sat gazing up at him with a thoughtful smile on her face. He could see that she was genuinely happy about the vote to save the school.

"I want to thank all of you for what you did here," Doug told his neighbors. "I know you've made the right decision." He waited through another round of applause. "And now," he said, "I'd like to ask you to consider another decision."

The crowd grew silent and expectant.

"There's been a lot of talk lately about some big real estate deals in our town," Doug said. "Now, normally that would suit me just fine, because I'm the guy who sells real estate in Crystal Creek, and the market doesn't keep me all that busy."

He raised his hand to still the laughter at this little joke.

Maggie was watching him closely from the audience. Even from this distance he could see the sudden tension in her face, and the quick, anxious look she exchanged with Natasha Dunne.

"But this time," Doug told the crowd, "I'm not happy about the sudden boom in real estate. In fact, my friends, I hate it."

All laughter stilled. Nobody coughed, nobody shuffled their boots or whispered to their neighbors. The silence in the room was so intense that it seemed alive.

"I don't want you to sell your town," Doug said passionately, leaning forward over the podium to make eye contact with one person after another. "Steve and Julia Brown, you've run the hardware store for years. Surely you can weather some bad times and hang on to your family business."

The Browns glanced nervously at each other, looking miserable.

"Stella Metz," Doug said, looking down at the clerk from the town office. "And Jilly Phipps, right up here on the platform." He turned to the young red-haired teacher, sitting with her colleagues. "You ladies own a beautiful home in Crystal Creek, and its value increases with every year that goes by. Why would you want to sell it?"

People turned surreptitiously to glance at Maggie and her famous employer, obviously curious about their reaction to this public attack from the mayor.

Maggie was very pale as she listened to him, but

Natasha Dunne's beautiful face seemed quiet, almost contemplative as Doug spoke.

"I can fully understand why somebody would want to own a major interest in this town," Doug said, addressing himself directly to Natasha. "Especially when that person has fond and very special personal memories of the place."

Natasha nodded up at him almost imperceptibly, her face calm and unrevealing.

"But all of you have precious roots in Crystal Creek as well," Doug said to the rest of the crowd, "and some of them go back for decades, even into the last century. I want you to think very carefully before you give up your rights to this place where your ancestors settled, where you raised your babies, where you hope to live out a peaceful old age."

A restless stir ran through the crowd. He could see by the expressions on many faces that he was making several people uncomfortable.

They didn't want to hear what he was saying. Too many of them had already been seduced by Maggie's offer of instant cash, with an end to high taxes and all the burdens of ownership.

"I don't want you to sell your town and rent it back from a wealthy owner," Doug pleaded. "I don't want you to become tenants in this place you've worked all your lives to build. Please, my friends, think hard before you do this."

"We can't afford the taxes!" somebody shouted from the rear of the hall.

"Then give us a chance to work on that," Doug called back. "You've already decided you can afford your middle school after all. Now, let's all put our heads together and see if we can come up with some way to generate more income for the town and reduce the tax burden. Just don't sell Crystal Creek to the highest bidder. I beg you, my friends and neighbors, stop and think hard about what you're doing!''

He stepped away from the microphone, but this time there was no ovation. The crowd got up to leave, murmuring quietly among themselves. Doug had no way to tell if his impassioned plea had swayed them at all.

But he could see how upset Maggie was. She sat rigidly beside her employer, waiting for the crowd to thin before she and Natasha got up to leave.

Doug lingered on the stage among the teachers, who were all still jubilant over the school victory. Many of them congratulated him on his speech.

He looked down into the auditorium and saw that Robin and Moira had left their seats and gone back to join Maggie and Natasha. Terry and Rose were with them now, too.

Moira leaned against the famous woman's chair, entirely at ease, showing Natasha the intricacies of her video game. Robin nestled in Maggie's lap, watching contentedly as Maggie helped her to fasten the pinafore on the teddy bear.

Doug felt a constriction in his throat, and another sharp pang of sexual hunger. He excused himself from the noisy group of teachers, got up and walked down the steps, then out among the rows of empty chairs to join the little group.

Natasha gazed at him over Moira's smooth golden cap of hair. "Hello, Doug," she said quietly. "That was a very moving speech you just gave."

He was surprised by the movie star's lack of emotion. He'd virtually instructed the crowd to turn their backs on this woman and reject her offer, and he suspected Natasha Dunne was not a person accustomed to having her wishes denied.

Oddly enough, she didn't seem angry, just thoughtful and bemused.

But he could tell that Maggie was furious.

Doug looked with sinking heart at her pale face, the dusting of freckles on the bridge of her dainty nose, the tension in her face.

"I'm sorry," he told her over Robin's bright head. "But I needed to speak my mind, Maggie."

"If I'd had some fair warning," she said, "I could have offered a rebuttal. It was hardly fair of you to use this occasion to your advantage the way you did, Doug."

"Look, this isn't some kind of political campaign," he told her, oblivious to the silent, tense group who surrounded them. "It's a battle for the hearts and minds of this town, Maggie. It's a fight to preserve their heritage. I don't think the usurpers are necessarily entitled to equal time on the podium."

"They are if they're offering what the people want," Maggie said.

Natasha murmured something to her assistant, then looked up at Doug, still holding Moira in a casual embrace.

"Do you really feel so passionate about this, Doug?" she asked. "It's your belief that my plans will destroy the life of this town?"

"Yes," Doug said quietly. "That's my firm belief, Natasha."

She nodded and murmured something to Maggie again. Doug watched, feeling a sudden wild flare of hope.

Maybe the woman would cast aside this insane plan of hers, and go back to Hollywood where she belonged. If that happened, the threat to the town would end. And then, magically, the conflict between him and Maggie would be removed.

Doug would be able to court the woman he loved, and try his best to win her heart like any other suitor.

His hopes soared even higher when Maggie spoke.

"Natasha and I have been talking," she told Doug quietly. "And we've just reached an important decision."

"Yes?" he asked, his tension rising along with the optimism. "What's your decision, Maggie?"

But all his wild hopes were dashed with her next words.

"We've decided to go ahead with our plans, including the purchase of the Carlson house," Maggie told him. "I'd like to go out there with you tomorrow for another look at the place, and then tender a formal offer."

CHAPTER SEVENTEEN

THE NEXT MORNING—a warm March day with blue-bonnets beginning to appear in green fields—Maggie stared out of the truck window as she and Doug drove to Jeb's house. Spectacular drifts of Indian paintbrush, daisies and wild phlox sailed by. All the colors seemed too intense to be real. Deep green and vivid purple, warm red and yellow dotted the tall grass, while masses of cottony clouds sailed in a sky of delphinium blue.

This was such a magical place, Maggie thought. A wistful part of her actually wanted Natasha to buy the house and get rid of all her other homes, so they could live here all the time.

But Natasha Dunne was too restless to settle anywhere permanently. Before long she would begin craving the sunny warmth of a beach somewhere, or the sophisticated pleasures of Manhattan or Europe.

And then that lovely house above the river would have to be closed up and stand empty until it caught Natasha's fancy again.

But maybe Natasha would be different if she really owned this place, Maggie told herself.

The actress had been claiming for years that she wanted to put down roots, stay in one place and find a home where she could watch the seasons come and go. And there could certainly be no lovelier home than this majestic place in the Hill Country of Texas.

Privately, Maggie suspected what Natasha wanted more than anything was a man to share her life. There was no doubt that eternal commitment to a long-lost love could grow increasingly lonely as the years went by.

But the movie star never seemed to find a suitable partner, and often said that after Jeremy Calder, she couldn't possibly love anybody else.

Maggie shifted on the truck seat and glanced over at Doug, who drove silently along the crushed-rock trail toward Jeb's house. When they passed the turn-off to the spot above the river where they'd made love just a few days earlier, he caught her eye for a moment.

Maggie felt her cheeks flushing, but Doug's face stayed remote and expressionless.

He obviously didn't care, she told herself. Since he hadn't been successful at getting her to alter her plans, he'd probably just as soon forget all about her.

Briefly she wondered how awkward it was going to be when Natasha purchased the Carlson house, and Maggie was forced to spend at least part of the time here in Texas with her employer.

How could she bear to see Doug Evans all the time?

It simply wasn't possible.

"Great news that the middle school is going to stay in Crystal Creek," he said, breaking his long silence.

"Yes, but it wouldn't have happened without Natasha's involvement," Maggie said. "She's the one who really saved the school."

"Save your school, ruin your town," Doug said coldly. "Sorry, but that doesn't exactly sound like a good trade-off to me."

"I don't think…"

At that moment they reached their destination, and Maggie didn't have an opportunity to finish her thought.

She climbed down from the truck and waited silently next to Doug as he rang the doorbell.

Jeb Carlson appeared, wearing jeans, moccasins and a crisp white cotton shirt, looking as handsome and pleasant as Maggie remembered.

"So you've come back," he said with a smile at Maggie. "I take it your employer was at least a bit taken with the house?"

"She liked it very much," Maggie said. "In fact, Natasha's crazy about this place."

An odd, wistful look crossed Jeb Carlson's face. He seemed on the verge of saying something, then apparently thought better of it.

"Well," he said briskly, "where shall we start? I assume you'll want to have another serious look at the place before we start talking business?"

"Doug's already given me most of the measurements and statistics," Maggie said, "and he's worked out what he feels is a fair price based on current market conditions. Mainly, I wanted to check…"

She took a sheet of paper from her pocket and consulted it while the two men waited.

"We'd like to have a look at the chimneys, the

furnace and the foundations," she said. "Also, if we could go to the basement and check out the size of the water heaters, that sort of thing?"

"You're a good businesswoman, Maggie." Jeb smiled at her with such warmth that she was briefly startled. Again, she had the vague, elusive feeling of having met this man before.

He really was attractive, she thought, watching as he strode through the house, leading them toward the basement stairs. Still spare and erect, with that look of humorous intelligence in his eyes.

Jeb Carlson's eyes were an odd color, a very light brown that seemed darker because he had surprisingly dense eyelashes.

She followed the two men down the stairs to check out the utilities, then examined the rest of the basement. Jeb's house was built into the hillside, so both levels had full-length windows overlooking a breathtaking expanse of river.

Jeb had built several more bedrooms down here, along with a couple of bathrooms and a huge games room complete with twin billiard tables.

"You must have been planning to billet an army in this house," Maggie told Jeb when he came over with Doug to stand beside her.

They all looked down at the river far below, where pelicans swooped and soared.

Jeb shrugged. "Actually, I designed and built the place for resale," he said. "There's far more room than I'll ever need."

But Maggie thought she noticed a look of regret on his handsome, tanned face as he stared out the big windows. Again she felt some qualms over what

she and Natasha were doing, accompanied by the bizarre urge to talk to this man, to pour out her heart
and explain her part in the town's conflict.

"Well," Doug said beside her, "if everything's in
order, maybe we should go back upstairs and start
talking about price."

"You two go ahead," Maggie told them when
they reached the main floor. "Spend a few minutes
in Jeb's study and agree on an asking price between
yourselves. I'll wait for you out here in the living
room and look at the...gorgeous view."

Her voice faltered briefly as the reality of what
they were doing registered fully in her mind. Doug
gave her an intent glance, and she turned away.

"Maggie?" he said. "Are you all right?"

"I'm fine." She took a deep, steadying breath.
"Please, go ahead and decide on a price. I'd really
like to get this done so I can start closing deals on
the rest of the properties back in town."

Doug's face hardened. He and Jeb moved off toward a book-lined study on the other side of the
house.

Maggie wandered into the luxurious living room
and then paused. The framed photograph of Natasha
Dunne was back in its place on the low oak table by
the window.

She moved closer, studying Natasha's face with
narrowed eyes.

This was really such an unusual picture. She
picked the frame up to examine the photograph
closely; she noticed again that it hadn't been retouched or even signed.

Before she even knew what she was doing, Mag-

gie had turned the frame over to examine its backing.
The photograph was held in place by a square of
heavy cardboard with a stand attached to hold the
frame upright.

Holding her breath, Maggie tugged on the backing.
It slid easily out of the frame.

She glanced over her shoulder, then lifted away a
square of cardboard that covered the photograph. A
flimsy bit of notepaper fluttered to the floor while
Maggie studied the back of the picture, looking for
clues to its origin.

She found no studio stamp, no date or inscription,
nothing to give a hint about how Jeb Carlson had
come into possession of the mysterious portrait.

Utterly baffled, Maggie bent to pick up the scrap
of brittle, yellowed notepaper. Her heart began to
pound when she realized it contained a few lines
scrawled in Natasha's unmistakable handwriting.

Dearest Jeb, our baby was born today, a beautiful healthy child who is part of you and me,
and who has eyes exactly like yours. By the
time you get this note, it will all be over. But I
do love you, my darling, and I always will. My
heart is breaking. Please, please don't hate me
too much. Goodbye from your own Natasha.

Small faded blotches on the paper obscured some
of the words. Maggie realized that the smudges were
teardrops.

With shaking hands, Maggie folded the note and
put it in her pocket, then reassembled the frame and
stood it carefully back in place. Her knees were sud-

denly weak. She sank into one of the leather armchairs to study the note again.

For the first time, she noticed a date at the top of the page. She stared at it, her mind whirling.

But that wasn't possible, she thought, dazed. It couldn't possibly be. Because when Natasha Dunne had written this note, she was...

The two men came back into the room. Doug saw Maggie's face and moved toward her in obvious concern.

"Maggie," he said, "you're pale as a ghost. Is something wrong?"

She got up, still unsteady and confused. "I just...felt a little dizzy for a minute," she said. "Maybe it's a touch of flu. But I'll be fine," she added. "Did you...can we talk price now?"

"Not yet." Doug put a hand on her shoulder. "And that's probably just as well, considering how shaky you look."

Maggie glanced over at Jeb Carlson with new eyes, thinking how handsome he must have been thirty years ago, back when Natasha Dunne penned the incredible note that was now hidden in her pocket.

"We need to assess the land values again before we can arrive at a solid price," Jeb told Maggie.

She turned to Doug. "Can you do that right away?"

"This afternoon," he said. "I'll take you back into town and stop by the hotel to talk to Rose, then go to Austin and check with the main real estate office."

"All right. So I guess we'll talk to you later, Jeb."

Maggie left the house and went over to Doug's

truck like a woman stumbling through a dream, hardly conscious of his worried glances as they drove away from the Carlson property.

Again she stared out the window at the colorful array of wildflowers, but this time she barely noticed the landscape. She couldn't stop thinking about the note in her pocket.

Natasha had written that message to Jeb Carlson, telling him about the birth of a baby that belonged to both of them. The note had been dated five months after the death of her husband, the man whom all the world assumed was the only love of her life.

But Jeb Carlson's baby—Natasha and Jeb Carlson's—had been conceived while Natasha's beloved husband was still alive.

HALF AN HOUR LATER, Rose was in the hotel kitchen, marinating steaks for the early crowd expected at the pub. She put the steaks into a shallow baking dish, covered them with beer and added a bit of tabasco and seasoning, then set the bowl back in the fridge.

Doug came in and stood watching.

"Hi," Rose said, kneeling to haul some potatoes out from a lower cabinet. "Did Maggie buy the house for Natasha?"

"Not yet." He leaned against the counter. "We still need to agree on an accurate value for the land. I'm driving into Austin this afternoon to get some updated quotes."

"But do you think the deal will still go through?" Rose asked, troubled by the unhappy look on her brother's face.

"Probably tomorrow. And then," he said grimly, "the plunder will begin."

Rose began to wash potatoes at the sink. "Maybe Natasha will love the house so much, she'll be content to own it and leave the rest of the town alone."

"A lovely thought, but I don't believe it's too likely. Where are the girls, Rose?"

"They took Natasha down to see the carousel. And Carla went along to help look after everybody."

"No kidding," Doug muttered, idly hefting a salt-shaker fashioned to resemble a cob of fresh corn. "Is Natasha going to buy the carousel, too?"

"I think the carousel is part of the town," Rose said. "By the time she owns everything else, the carousel will automatically belong to her."

"God help us," Doug said bitterly. "What a daft plan it is, the whole thing."

Rose wiped her hands on a gingham towel and came across the room to give him a brief, comforting hug, then went back to her job at the sink.

"So what's Terry doing this afternoon?" Doug asked.

"He's at home, working," she said, trying to sound casual, though she couldn't hide a wistful smile. "He's been getting so much done these days. Terry says domestic life agrees with him."

"Does it agree with you?" Doug asked, watching her keenly.

"What do you mean?"

"Are you enjoying this arrangement you've made with Terry Embree? Is it working out all right?"

"It's lovely," Rose said simply. "In fact, the only bad thing…"

"What's the bad thing?" Doug asked, still fingering the ceramic corncob.

"Nothing," Rose said. "There's nothing bad. I didn't mean anything."

"Yes you did." He put down the saltshaker and leaned forward. "Come on, tell me what you were going to say, Rosie."

She looked up at him timidly. "I was about to say that I'll be sorry when it's over," she told her brother. "But I'll kill you if you ever pass that on, Douglas Evans."

"You'll be sorry when Terry goes away?" Doug said, still watching her.

"Yes, I will." Tears burned in Rose's eyes. She brushed at them with her forearm and went on scrubbing potatoes.

"Why would he go away?"

Rose stared at her brother in surprise. "Because it's only temporary," she said. "He's doing this as a favor to me, until he gets his book done. And at the rate he's working…"

"But you really love the man, don't you?" Doug asked gently.

Rose gripped the edge of the counter and took a deep breath. At last she nodded, unable to speak.

"Rose, listen to me."

Her anxiety was too great to bear. "Please, Doug," she said earnestly, "you must never, never tell anybody about this. I'd just die if Terry knew what a great fool I've been, falling in love with him when we agreed it was only supposed to be…"

"In your heart, you loved him before you ever went through with this marriage," Doug said. "Because you never could have done it otherwise, Rosie. Isn't that right?''

She nodded again, feeling numb with unhappiness. ''But I don't want him to—''

''Rose,'' her brother interrupted, ''stop talking and listen to me.''

She rummaged in the pocket of her apron for a tissue, wiped her eyes and then went back to work on the potatoes. ''I'm listening,'' she said.

''Terry's in love with you, Rose. Just as much as you are with him.''

''What?'' She threw her head up, staring at him.

''You heard me,'' Doug said calmly.

Rose felt a surge of anger. ''I don't see how you could joke about such a thing, Doug. If you had any idea of the way I feel…''

''Terry told Maggie that he was in love with you before he ever proposed to you,'' Doug said.

Rose studied her brother's face and realized he was telling the truth. Wonder dawned slowly in her mind, then a shining, incredulous joy.

''He did?'' she whispered. ''Terry actually said that to Maggie?''

''What a pair,'' Doug said with a fond grin, holding up the salt and pepper shakers. ''You've no more brains between you than these two corncobs. Living together all this time, and neither of you can figure out the other one's madly in love.''

But Rose was no longer listening. She took off her apron and set it aside, touched her hair nervously, looked at her reflection in the mirror next to the door.

''I have to…the girls won't be back for a while,''

she said vaguely. "I have to go home for a few minutes. If anybody comes in..."

Her voice trailed off and she was gone, leaving the hotel at a run and heading through the springtime streets toward her little home by the river.

THE HOUSE WAS QUIET when Rose entered, and her courage almost failed her as she paused in the lower foyer to look up the stairs.

Terry would still be working at his computer near the dormer window. But he was probably too absorbed to notice her coming up the walk.

Rose pressed her hands to her flaming cheeks and took a deep breath, trying to still the crazy pounding of her heart.

What if Doug was wrong, and she was about to make a huge fool of herself? It would be so painfully embarrassing for both of them...

But Rose found that she didn't care anymore. Even outright humiliation was better than this constant storm of longing that filled her days and nights.

Before she could lose her nerve, she climbed the stairs and paused in the doorway to Terry's room, looking at his broad shoulders, the glint of gold in his curly hair, the endearing way his shirt collar lay partly crumpled under the neck of his sweater.

"Hi," she said, making him jump a little. "Am I bothering you?"

He turned to smile at her, his eyes very blue in the afternoon light. "A diversion like you is always welcome," he said.

She crossed the room to stand next to him, reaching out automatically to straighten his shirt collar, patting it so it lay smooth against his sweater. His nearness, and the sweet reality of touching him, was enough to make her dizzy.

"I thought I'd just make you a pot of tea," she murmured. "I'll bet you'd never give yourself a break otherwise."

"That's so nice of you, Rose." He leaned back, stretching his arms. "Nine pages so far. One of my best days yet," he told her.

"I'm glad."

Rose stared blindly out the window and wondered what to say.

But her courage failed her. She moved toward the door, feeling awkward. "I'll call you when the tea is ready," she said.

He nodded and went back to his computer. Rose watched him for a moment from the doorway, her heart aching with excitement and dread, then left and went downstairs to put the kettle on.

She moved around the kitchen, setting out a platter of cookies, arranging teacups on the table along with sugar and cream. When the kettle began to sing, she poured water into the pot along with a couple of tea bags, then went back to the base of the stairs.

"Terry," she called. "Tea's ready."

He clattered down with a boyish smile and paused by the newel post to stroke the carved wooden dragon, then came into the kitchen, looking around with pleasure.

"What a nice surprise," he said. "Not many guys are lucky enough to live with somebody who comes home and makes tea for them in the middle of the afternoon. I'm spoiled, Rose."

"I'm spoiled too." She moved away to feel the sides of the teapot. "You always help me with the girls, and say such nice things to me all the time, and never raise your voice or get angry."

"Well, I should hope not." He came closer and looked down at her. "Are you all right, Rose? You seem a little tense. There's nothing wrong, is there?"

Tears burned in her eyes again. She brushed at them ineffectually.

"Rose!" He took her shoulders and gripped them, trying to see her face. "What is it? Tell me what's making you cry."

"I love you, Terry," she whispered.

"What?" He stared at her. "What did you say?"

"I said I love you." Rose took a deep breath and looked up at him. "I always have, from the first moment I saw you in the hotel lobby that day. When you suggested this marriage idea, I thought it would be a wonderful way to spend more time with you. But now…"

She was in his arms, nestled against his chest, and nothing had ever felt more wonderful.

"What?" he whispered against her ear. "You were going to tell me something else, Rose."

"I can't bear it if you leave," she sobbed. "I can't imagine not having you with me, Terry. I'll be so lonely…"

And then, miraculously, he was kissing her, and all her world was ablaze with joy.

"I'll never leave you, darling," he whispered. "My sweetest little Rose, why would I leave you when you're the only woman I've ever loved?"

Rose drew away to look up at him, wide-eyed and

incredulous. She wanted to tell him everything, let him know the way she felt and how wonderful he was in every way.

Then he was kissing her again, and she couldn't find the words to say.

But it didn't matter, she realized, lost in happiness, loving the warm sweetness of his embrace.

It didn't matter at all.

CHAPTER EIGHTEEN

WHILE ROSE AND TERRY held each other, laughing and crying together, Maggie was dealing with a completely different set of emotions.

She paced around Natasha's suite in the hotel, crossing the room at intervals to stare impatiently out the window. At last she saw Natasha and Carla coming up the street with Moira and Robin.

Robin trailed behind with Carla. The smaller girl clutched her teddy bear in one hand and a messy clump of wildflowers in the other. Moira walked at Natasha's side, deep in conversation with the movie star about something.

From time to time, Natasha threw back her head and laughed merrily.

Maggie watched their approach with a sinking heart, hoping she wouldn't be forced to make conversation with all of them. She needed to speak with Natasha alone. If Carla and the children came upstairs as well, Maggie would have to go down the hall and wait in her room until they were gone.

But, as luck would have it, only one pair of feet ascended the stairs after the group entered the hotel lobby. Listening tensely by the door, Maggie could hear the laughter of the two small girls down in the kitchen, along with Carla's musical voice.

"Hello, darling!" Natasha said breezily, appearing in the doorway. "How did your real-estate deal go?"

"Doug's in Austin this afternoon, checking on land prices." Feeling stiff and awkward, almost on the verge of tears, Maggie went back across the room and sat by the window.

Natasha followed, removing the silk scarf she'd wrapped around her head and face to protect skin that was still tender after the surgery.

"That carousel is the most wonderful creation!" She sat down gracefully in the opposite chair. "It wasn't here back when we made the movie. I had no idea they'd acquired such a lovely thing."

Maggie looked thoughtfully at her employer.

Natasha Dunne was truly an exquisite woman. Her beauty and appeal went beyond the perfection of her features and the loveliness of her body. She was one of those people who come along rarely in each generation, a woman so dazzling that she was able to capture and hold the dreams of an entire population.

But Maggie had always believed her employer was, at core, a warm and generous person. Now it appeared she'd been wrong.

Natasha was a cold, manipulative liar, and always had been.

The realization was still too shattering and painful for Maggie to grasp.

"Honey?" Natasha leaned forward to look at her in concern, then put a hand on her arm. "Maggie, what's the matter? Is there—"

"Don't touch me," Maggie said, pulling away. She knew it was a childish reaction, but she could hardly bear to be in the same room with this woman.

Natasha looked hurt and bewildered. "Sweetie, I don't know what…"

"Read this." Maggie took the note from her pocket and handed it over, staring at the older woman. "Then tell me what it means."

Natasha read the note and seemed to crumple before Maggie's eyes. In an instant, her face aged by decades. She looked drawn and terrified.

"Where did you…" Her voice broke. "Oh, God, how could he possibly betray me like that?"

"Jeb Carlson had nothing to do with it," Maggie said coldly. "He doesn't even know I have this. It was stored behind the frame on a portrait of you that he keeps in his living room. I found it when Jeb and Doug were in another room talking about real estate."

Natasha looked at the note again. Her hands were shaking so badly that she dropped it. Maggie got up to retrieve the piece of paper, folded it carefully and put it back in her pocket.

"I was so young," Natasha whispered, still looking ravaged. "And Jeb was…oh, God, how I adored that man. I'd never met anybody like him."

"You were married!" Maggie said furiously. "To your only true love. But I suppose it was just too hard for you to get along without a man during those few months that Jeremy Calder had to be away, fighting and dying for his country?"

Tears began to roll down Natasha's cheeks. Maggie watched her for a moment. Then, still automatically protective, she got up and went over to lock the door so nobody would see her employer's messy grief.

Natasha murmured something inaudible.

"I can't hear what you're saying." Maggie stood above the other woman with her arms folded. "But I can tell you, Natasha, that I despise you."

"Why?" Natasha looked up piteously. "Because I made a mistake when I was twenty-two years old? Because I fell in love?"

"You were married!" Maggie struggled to control her anger. "To your one true love. And I got involved in this whole maudlin quest of yours to return to the place where you lost him." Maggie stared down at Natasha's bright head. "I had to endure a lot of anger and resentment in this town, and all because I believed you were truly following your heart, trying to make peace with the loss and pain you suffered when Jeremy died."

She was silent for a moment, staring at the window as she thought about Doug's sweet caresses, and then the disapproval she'd seen so often on his face.

But the memory hurt too much. She shook her head and turned back to Natasha.

"I gave up a lot because of this job you sent me here to do, Natasha. But I did it because I'm such a stupidly loyal person. And because I truly believed in you."

The other woman was still weeping, her body shaken by occasional deep shudders.

"And now," Maggie said, "I discover it was all a huge lie. There was no deep love for your husband at all. You were cheating on him with another man, actually carrying somebody else's baby when Jeremy died. You're just contemptible, Natasha. I'm leaving today, as soon as I can pack my things."

MARGOT DALTON 271

Natasha looked up, her face smeared with mascara, her eyes wild. "No, Maggie, you mustn't leave me! Listen, let me tell you—"

"Tell me what?" Maggie said coldly when her employer hesitated.

"The truth," Natasha whispered.

"Well, that should be a nice change." Maggie hated the sarcasm in her own voice, but she couldn't forgive the woman who sat there crying.

Because of Natasha's lies and her own belief in them, Maggie had driven Doug Evans away, lost the man she could have truly loved.

"There was no marriage," Natasha said tonelessly. "Not really. It was all a sham that the studio arranged for publicity."

"Between you and Jeremy Calder?" Maggie said.

"He was homosexual, Maggie." Natasha gazed at her earnestly, beginning to calm down a little. "Jeremy was living with a young man he called his butler. The studio couldn't afford to have the public find out. They'd invested millions to build Jeremy's image. And this was still the sixties, when that sort of thing wasn't at all acceptable."

Maggie began to feel a glimmer of understanding. "So the studio arranged a phony marriage between Jeremy and you to hide the truth about him?"

Natasha nodded miserably. "It was more successful than anybody could have dreamed. Public opinion soared, for both of us, and our box-office sales went sky-high. And when he was sent to Vietnam, fans went crazy. They couldn't get enough of us. But in the meantime, I'd never even..." Natasha's face colored with emotion. "I was every man's sexual fantasy, Maggie, but in real life I was still a virgin. At least, until I met Jeb Carlson when I was here in Crystal Creek, working on that movie.''

''And then you got pregnant.''

Natasha stared at the window, her eyes wide and faraway. ''I was just so terrified,'' she whispered. ''I had no idea what to do. Jeb and I were both frantic. When I finally confessed the truth to the director, he almost killed me.''

''I guess the studio wasn't too thrilled, either.''

''They went into an emergency huddle and proposed all kinds of things,'' Natasha said. ''Like a publicity release saying Jeremy had taken a secret leave and come home for a weekend, and I'd become pregnant at that time. But all the men in his unit would have known it was a lie. Jeremy had been with those men every day and every night for months on end.''

Maggie listened in silence, realizing that Natasha was deep in the past now, barely aware of her.

''I was only two months along at the time,'' Natasha said. ''Finally they went into negotiations with the army, trying to arrange that somebody would fly Jeremy home for a weekend. Later they could say that stress made the baby come early. But before they could work it out...'' Her voice broke.

''Jeremy was killed,'' Maggie concluded the statement for her. ''And then you were really in a pickle.''

''Oh yes, I was really in a pickle,'' Natasha agreed with a bleak smile. ''So their final solution was for me to go into mourning and not emerge for almost a year. By then, of course, the baby was born and taken away from me. I had time to pull myself together, get my figure back and develop this cover story. In the meantime, my agent came to terms with the studio.''

"What were their terms?" Maggie asked, though she already had a fairly good idea what Natasha must have agreed to.

"I was never to see Jeb again, and never to mention to anybody that the baby had ever existed. If I gave away my secret or their part in it at any time in the future, the studio could fine me the equivalent, adjusted for inflation, of twenty million dollars. God knows how much it amounts to by now," Natasha said bitterly. "Probably enough to pay off the national debt.''

"You mean the terms of that contract are still in force?" Maggie asked in disbelief.

"If they weren't," Natasha said simply, "I'd be with Jeb Carlson this instant. As it is," she added with a sad smile, "I have to be content with owning his house. It's the only part of him I'll ever have.''

"But, Natasha..." Maggie looked at her employer in disbelief. "Why are you still letting money stand in the way of your happiness? You already gave up the man's baby for money. Why don't you do the decent thing for once in your life? Go out there right now, tell him how you feel and damn the consequences. Obviously he still loves you, or he wouldn't have kept your picture all these years.''

Natasha covered her face with her hands and began to cry again. "I can't," she said in a muffled voice. "He hates me. I told him I never wanted anything to do with him, and I'm sure he believed me.''

"But it wasn't true." Maggie said sadly.

"You have no idea how much power those studio executives had over my life, Maggie. They owned me, and I was terrified of them. And I was so ashamed to have people know what I'd done..."

Her voice trailed off into a ragged whisper while Maggie stood watching her.

"I had no idea Jeb would ever come back to this town," Natasha said. "If I'd known, I never, never would have done this. I couldn't bear to see him, Maggie. Not after what I did."

Again, Maggie looked down at the huddled form in the chair. "So many lies, so much pain, and all because of the damn money."

"You don't understand," Natasha pleaded. "There are still...other facts I can't ever tell you. But one thing wasn't a lie, Maggie."

"Really? What's that?"

"I wanted to come back to this town and make it my own because Crystal Creek was the only place where I've ever known true love. That's the truth, and nothing will ever change it."

"One thing has changed," Maggie said grimly. "I'm not going to stay with you and help you buy this town, Natasha."

Her voice broke. On the verge of tears, Maggie rushed from the room and headed downstairs to her car before she could encounter any of the other hotel residents.

FOR A LONG TIME she drove aimlessly over the country roads surrounding Crystal Creek, too upset to be aware of where she was going.

Late in the afternoon when the sun began to dip below the hills, Maggie saw a flare of gold in the distance and realized it was the fading daylight that glinted off the tall windows of Jeb Carlson's house.

Without thinking any further, she pulled over and parked in the circular driveway outside his front door, then went up and rang the doorbell, shivering as she waited in the coolness of the afternoon breeze.

Jeb answered the door after a few seconds, carrying a small gardening trowel in his hand. On one tanned cheek was a smear of dirt that made him look even more appealing than she remembered.

"Maggie," he said, looking over her shoulder in obvious surprise. "I didn't expect you and Doug back here until—"

"I'm alone," she said abruptly. "As far as I know, Doug's still in Austin."

"Come in." He put the trowel down beside the front steps, then held the door open for her.

Maggie followed him into the tiled entry, still in the grip of almost uncontrollable emotion.

Jeb caught a glimpse of himself in a mirrored console and wiped the dirt from his cheek, then gave her a questioning glance.

"I stole something from you," she said curtly, "and I want to return it."

"You stole something from me?"

Wordlessly she reached into her pocket, took out the folded slip of paper and handed it to him.

Jeb looked at the paper and gave her a searching glance, then took her arm and led her to the living room. She sank into one of the leather chairs, gripping a cushion nervously in her lap. He sat opposite her, waiting.

"I confronted Natasha with that," Maggie said, gesturing at the paper in his hand. "She broke down and told me everything."

"Everything?" he asked.

"How her marriage to Jeremy Calder was all for publicity, and how she fell in love with you and got pregnant while she was here filming her movie."

Jeb leaned forward in the chair, still watching Maggie closely. "What else did she tell you?"

"What else is there?" Maggie said grimly. "She told me how they sent her into seclusion for a year, took her baby away when it was born and made her promise she'd never tell anybody a word of what happened. If she did, she'd have to pay an enormous fine."

"And now you're very angry with her," Jeb said quietly.

"Damn right I'm angry!" Maggie felt tears begin to sting in her eyes. "Rather than pay a fine, she lied to everybody all these years. She cheated you, and the public as well. And she…"

Jeb waited while she struggled to compose herself. At one point he reached over and patted her arm. The gentle sympathy of his touch was almost more than she could bear.

"I believed her," Maggie said at last, forcing herself to continue. "I went along with her silly plan to buy this whole town like a piece of jewelry because I felt sorry for Natasha and her sad story about her lost love. And all the time, it was just a pack of lies."

"Not entirely," Jeb said. "It's true that Natasha

fell deeply in love while she was here in Crystal Creek." He smiled sadly. "I was a witness, Maggie."

"But that didn't give her the right to..."

Again Maggie floundered, unable to find words.

"I'm going away," she said at last. "I told Natasha I was going to pack my bags and leave her, and I fully intend to. This is only a job, after all, and it's time for me to quit."

"Please don't make threats like that," he said with sudden intensity. "If you leave Natasha over this, it will kill her."

"I doubt it. She's not nearly as tender and sentimental as she pretends," Maggie said bitterly. "If she were, she could never have told all those lies to everybody."

"Tell me why you're so upset," Jeb said after a moment. "Is it because Doug Evans disapproves of what you're doing, and Natasha's plans have caused so much conflict between you?"

Maggie gulped and nodded, wondering again how this stranger with the soft voice could be so insightful and easy to talk to.

"I feel completely betrayed and cheated by Natasha," she murmured. "And it was all because of money."

"Without her money," Jeb said quietly, "Natasha Dunne wouldn't be able to do all the charitable work that's so important to her. If she lost her fortune, she couldn't continue to help people like you and your brother."

"But who wants help when it's all based on lies? Natasha should have asserted her independence years ago, and told the studio what to do with their damn secret contract!''

''She could never do that. You don't know the rest of this story, Maggie.''

''There's more?''

''The studio made other threats to her,'' Jeb said. ''Ones that mattered far more to Natasha than the threat of an exorbitant fine.''

Maggie looked at him, bewildered. ''How do you know that?''

He held up the tear-stained note. ''This wasn't the only letter I got from Natasha after she left Crystal Creek. She wasn't supposed to contact me, but she still sent two more letters. One came three months after this one, to tell me the terms the studio had forced her to accept. And the last one arrived about fifteen years ago while I was working in Houston.''

''Two other letters?'' Maggie said, dazed.

''I destroyed both of them for her safety, but I could never bring myself to part with this one.'' He smoothed the bit of notepaper in his hand, then touched it briefly to his cheek.

''Jeb…how can you still love her so much after all she's done?''

''I told you, she had no choice. They made threats to her, Maggie.''

''What kind of threats?''

''They told Natasha,'' Jeb said, ''that if word of our relationship or the illegitimate baby ever leaked out to the press, they'd expose our child and tell the whole world who she was. For Natasha, it was the worst thing that could possibly have happened. The baby was growing up safe and happy, in complete privacy. Natasha knew the media would have a field day. She couldn't bear the thought of our child growing up in the public eye."

Maggie's head began to spin. "You mean, Natasha didn't do this for the money at all? She kept the secret to protect her baby?"

"Both of us did."

"But…did she know where her child was?" Maggie asked in confusion.

"She's always known It was the only condition she insisted on with the studio. Natasha agreed to everything, as long as she could be allowed to know where her baby was and that it was happy and well cared for."

"I never knew any of this," Maggie whispered. "So, has Natasha…have either of you ever seen your child? After the baby grew up, I mean?"

Jeb leaned back in his chair, staring out the window at the rich glow of the river far below. The setting sun cast soft ripples of pink and gold across the surface of the water, and glistened on the wings of the pelicans.

"Our baby was born in Switzerland," he said at last, "and taken away from Natasha within hours. The next day she wrote me this letter." He held up the sad little note with its telltale splashes of tears.

"How awful it must have been," Maggie whispered, her anger gone. "Poor Natasha."

"The baby was smuggled back to America in great secrecy. At first Natasha wasn't told much, except that it had been sent to a hospital in Cincinnati and adopted by a nice young farming couple who'd been wanting a child for years. After a while Natasha was allowed to know their names and given some pictures of the baby.''

Maggie stared at him, thunderstruck, her jaw dropping.

''The child was never told the truth, of course, and neither were the adoptive parents.'' Jeb gazed out the window again. ''They believed this baby had been born to a very young high-school student whose family wanted to hide the facts of the birth. But through the years, Natasha found ways to keep in touch. And when the adoptive mother died of cancer...''

''She gave us money,'' Maggie whispered, still dazed. ''She sent money through her charity. And then after my father was killed...''

''Natasha took you in, along with your brother. Nothing in the world could ever have made her happier, even though she wasn't able to tell you the truth.'' Jeb smiled in fond reminiscence. ''That was when I got the final letter from her. It followed me halfway across North America before it finally reached me.''

Another realization dawned in Maggie's stunned mind, just as incredible as the things he'd already been telling her.

''You're my father,'' she said.

''Yes.'' He drew Maggie to her feet, then folded her in his arms. ''I'm your father.''

''Your eyes,'' she whispered against his shirtfront. ''They always reminded me of somebody, but I couldn't think who it was.''

Jeb hugged her and laughed aloud, breaking the tension in the big room.

''We look a lot alike, you and I, Maggie. That was

one of the things your mother told me, back when you were fifteen.''

"But…'' She drew away from him and moved around the room, picking things up aimlessly and setting them down, staring at the smiling portrait of Natasha.

"We have to do something," she said. "There can't be any more lies. Now that I know the truth…''

"The truth is our own business," Jeb said. "And your privacy still needs to be protected. But I agree, now that you know the whole truth, Natasha can't be threatened anymore.''

Maggie smiled wistfully. "If they fine her millions of dollars and reduce her to bankruptcy, will you look after her?''

"I always would have," he said quietly. "Even though she couldn't believe it. Natasha's never been secure about other people's love for her.''

"But you're right, the money wasn't what really mattered to her," Maggie said. "She cared about me being allowed to grow up in peace and security. That's why she kept her secret all those years.''

"Yes, I believe that's true.''

"My God," Maggie whispered, staring at the portrait of the beautiful woman who'd been the center of her life for so many years. "Natasha is my mother!''

"And she loves you, Maggie," he said. "Nobody has ever loved you more, right from the moment you were born.''

"I have to go and…'' Maggie turned blindly toward the door.

"Go and talk to her." Jeb finished her statement, following Maggie through the foyer.

Maggie turned back to give him another hug. "Thank you," she said, feeling shy and misty. "Thanks so much for everything."

"I love you, Maggie," he said. "You've grown into such a fine woman."

"What should I say to her?" Maggie asked, drawing away to look up at him.

"Tell her you know the truth. Tell her how you feel," Jeb said. "And after you've done that..."

He paused and stepped back, looking at Maggie intently.

"Yes?" she said. "After all that, what should I do next?"

"Give her a hug, and then bring her here," Jeb said, his face lighting with sudden, boyish happiness. "Bring Natasha to me."

CHAPTER NINETEEN

MAGGIE DROVE BACK to town through deepening twilight. The sky in the west was a deep purple banded by a fiery rim of orange, and the wind was fresh. Above the horizon, a couple of stars twinkled, looking cold and impossibly distant.

Her head began to ache and she rubbed her forehead automatically, hardly aware of what she was doing.

Oddly enough, she wasn't even thinking very much about the incredible revelations Jeb had just made. On a deep level, far below her conscious mind, she must have sensed the truth about her relationship with Natasha long ago. That was why she wasn't utterly shocked and paralyzed by what Jeb had told her.

Now, through the tumult of Maggie's thoughts, only one thing was certain.

At this moment, she wanted Doug Evans more than she'd ever wanted anything in her life.

"I love him," Maggie whispered aloud. The words astonished her, but saying them felt so good that she did it again. "I really, truly love him."

But what if it was too late? she thought in anguish. What if he'd already formed such a negative opinion of her that nothing would change his mind?

She should never have agreed to Natasha's scheme.

When she reached the hotel, Maggie wasn't able to face anybody. She slipped through the lobby amid a gust of merriment from the pub, and hurried up the stairs to her room.

Doug was back, she realized when she went over to look out the window. His car was parked behind the hotel, and Dundee was gone.

Maggie bent to touch the folded quilt by the radiator where the big cat liked to sleep, and felt like crying again.

It was the ultimate, silent rejection.

You can't even look after my cat, Doug seemed to be saying in the distance. I won't trust you with anything that matters to me.

"Oh, hell," Maggie murmured in despair, flinging herself onto the bed.

She buried her face in the pillow for a moment, then rolled over to hug her arms and stare at the ceiling.

At that moment Maggie would have given anything to feel the big tabby cat lying warmly on her stomach, purring like a dynamo and licking her hand with a rough, comforting tongue.

"No more tears," she muttered to herself. "I've cried enough tears. It's time to get back in character. Time to leave Crystal Creek and figure out some way to get on with my life."

She climbed off the bed, went into the bathroom to splash some water on her face and comb her hair, and was about to venture down the hall to Natasha's suite when a timid knock sounded at the door.

"Darling," a voice called. "Are you in here?"

Maggie felt a moment of utter panic, then realized it was better this way. They might as well get the confrontation over with in this room, away from possible onlookers.

"Come in, Natasha," she said. "It's unlocked."

The door opened and Natasha slipped inside, her face still ravaged with grief.

"I was afraid you'd left already." She lowered herself heavily to sit on the edge of the bed. "But Doug came in here about an hour ago to get the cat, and he said your things were still here. Then I was afraid...something might have happened to you. Doug was worried, too."

"Was he?" Maggie said.

She took a chair and pulled it closer to the bed, sitting down so she and Natasha were almost touching.

"When I left, I went out to Jeb Carlson's place," Maggie said, her voice husky with emotion. "Nat, he told me everything."

Natasha jerked her head erect as if she'd been struck. "What do you mean?"

"I mean everything. The whole story, Natasha, from beginning to end. I know who I am now."

Natasha gasped and covered her mouth with both hands.

Maggie moved onto the bed and took the older woman's slender body in her arms. All her angry pain vanished in a flood of tenderness and sympathy.

"How awful it must have been for you," she whispered against Natasha's perfumed hair.

"I loved him," Natasha sobbed in her arms. "I'd

never known a love like that. Jeb used to come up here and visit me late at night, after the rest of the crew was asleep. He'd climb onto the shed roof, and then through the window.''

"That very window? In this room?" Maggie looked around, enchanted.

"You were...you were conceived in this room, darling.''

Maggie shook her head, still lost in the wonder of it all.

"And I loved you so much," Natasha said brokenly. "When they showed you to me, you were only a few hours old, but you looked like a sweet little flower, so tiny and precious. And then they..."

Numbly, Maggie patted her mother's back.

"I wanted you so much," Natasha whispered. "But there was no way I could stand up to them back in those days. They were all such powerful men, and so terrifying, and I was just a girl.''

"You did the best you could," Maggie soothed her. "And I had a wonderful childhood. You don't have to feel guilty about me. The one who's suffered the most in all this," she said, "is Jeb.''

"I can't believe he...kept a picture of me," Natasha said softly. "I thought he'd never want any reminders of me, after the way I treated him.''

"He's at his house right now, waiting to see you," Maggie said.

Natasha sat back and stared, her eyes widening in astonishment. "When?''

"He told me to give you a hug, and then bring you out to see him.''

"But I..." Natasha got up and moved away in

distracted fashion, then gripped the windowsill tensely and stared out into the darkness. "I can't go and see him!" she said in panic. "Look at me, I've been crying all day. I'm just a wreck."

Maggie chuckled, welcoming the laughter after all the wrenching emotion of the past hours and days.

"Listen to you," she scoffed fondly. "Widely recognized as the most beautiful woman in the whole world, and you're still as insecure as a teenager. Go wash your face, put on some makeup and meet me down at my car in ten minutes."

"Shouldn't we wait until..." Natasha wrung her hands anxiously.

But Maggie shook her head. "He's already waited thirty years, Natasha, and I think that's just about long enough. You be downstairs in ten minutes, or I'm coming up to get you."

BY NOW, Maggie felt as if she'd been driving back and forth between the Crystal Creek Hotel and Jeb Carlson's house for most of her life.

But this time Natasha huddled beside her, silent and strained, her hands gripped tightly in her lap. It was fully dark by now, but Maggie could see the other woman's face in the dim flare of light from the dashboard.

Despite her obvious fear, Natasha had never been more lovely or more vulnerable. And when she glanced over at Maggie with a look of desperate appeal, she seemed pitiably young, practically the same age she'd been when Jeb Carlson first saw her.

"How could he possibly care about me, after what I did to him?" Natasha muttered.

"That's the spirit," Maggie said with forced cheerfulness as she drove up in front of the big house, now ablaze with lights. "You just keep on reinforcing those positive thoughts, Nat."

Natasha crouched in the car, refusing to get out. "Please," she whispered, "let's just go back to the hotel. Maggie, this is a mistake. He doesn't—"

But the door opened at that moment. Jeb Carlson stood there, waving to them.

"Come on." Maggie tugged at the woman in the car. "I told you, the poor man's waited a whole lifetime for this. Don't make him wait any longer. Go in there and talk to him."

"What about you?" Natasha climbed out reluctantly, then turned to Maggie in panic. "You aren't leaving? I don't want you dealing with this all alone, dear. I need to help you."

Maggie smiled and caressed her mother's smooth cheek. "You're still thinking about me, even at a time like this," she said.

"I've been thinking about you for your entire life," Natasha said simply. "Every single moment."

"If you keep that up, we'll both start crying and you'll ruin your makeup again," Maggie said briskly. "Now go!"

"But what about you?" Natasha lingered nervously by the car.

"I'm going for a walk," Maggie said. "I want to stroll out on that path by the…"

Pain washed over her suddenly, making her voice tremble a little.

"I think I'll just sit and look down at the river for a while," she whispered.

But for once Natasha wasn't aware of Maggie's emotion. Instead, she turned to walk hesitantly toward the big house, and the man who waited for her in the lighted doorway.

Maggie shrank back into the shadows, watching as Natasha approached the lover she hadn't seen for thirty years.

The man and woman faced each other, neither speaking for a long, tense moment. Then Natasha reached out a trembling hand and placed it against Jeb's shirtfront. He covered it with his own, and touched Natasha's cheek with a tenderness that took Maggie's breath away.

At last Jeb folded the slim woman into his arms and buried his face against her hair. Maggie stood with a lump in her throat, watching their embrace.

Those are my parents, she thought, knowing the wonder of this truth was going to take a long, long time to comprehend.

The door closed behind them and the light vanished. Maggie gazed at the looming bulk of the big house, feeling lonely and excluded even though she knew this moment was theirs, and theirs alone.

At last she turned and made her way along the moonlit path to the little hollow overlooking the river, the same place where, just a few days earlier, she'd lain naked in Doug's arms under a blue Texas sky.

FOR WHAT SEEMED like hours, Maggie sat hugging her knees under a canopy of stars, looking down at the silvered river flowing through the valley.

The wind lifted and stirred in her hair, and cooled her hot cheeks.

She looked around vaguely, trying to understand her place in this new and astounding world she'd just discovered.

All her life, Maggie had felt much like one of those stars in the black void overhead, utterly remote and unconnected to anything or anyone. Now, with mind-boggling abruptness, she'd become more akin to one of the flowers growing at her side, tied to a place and time, rooted somewhere in the world.

In the past she'd assumed that making this discovery would fill all the empty places in her soul and make her happy.

Only now did Maggie realize how wrong she'd been. Where you came from was important, but it didn't matter nearly as much as where you were going.

And most important of all, Maggie thought, burying her face against her knees, was who made the journey with you.

She thought of her birth parents, finally together back there in the big house, and the years of happiness they'd wasted.

Now that Jeb and Natasha were alone behind those closed doors, the problems that had kept them apart so long seemed senseless and trivial.

But at the same time, a whole world seemed to separate Maggie and Doug, and she had no idea how to bridge the chasm. Even more, she knew that if she couldn't find some way to his side, she'd be lonely for the rest of her life.

Suddenly Maggie jumped and gasped in alarm as

a tall figure came looming out of the darkness and settled next to her.

"I brought a blanket," Doug said, "but this time you'd better use it to keep warm instead of sitting on it."

He draped the blanket around her shoulders and settled next to her, looking out across the river valley.

Maggie stole a cautious glance at him, feeling weak with tenderness and desire. The moonlight glimmered softly in his hair and edged his fine profile with a thin line of silver.

"Where did you come from?" she said at last. "How did you find me?"

"Jeb called me out to the house to discuss business. After a while, Natasha got worried about you and sent me to find you."

"Did they...tell you anything?" she ventured, afraid to look at him.

"Yes, I've heard the whole remarkable story," he said, rolling his r's in the way she loved.

"Remarkable," Maggie echoed hollowly. "God, that's an understatement, isn't it?"

"You know," he said, reaching out to pull the blanket a little higher around her shoulders, "I half suspected something like this."

"Oh, come on, Doug. How could you possibly have suspected?"

"We Celts have the second sight, you know," he said placidly.

She shook her head, trying to smile. "Sorry, but I doubt if I've ever met a man less mystical than you, Douglas Evans."

"Actually, Jeb hinted to me once about a child born out of wedlock that he'd never seen. When you talked about being adopted, and I saw how much your eyes were like his…well, I sort of wondered, just for a second or two, if it could actually be possible."

Maggie studied his profile. "Is that why you brought me out here to see his house?"

Doug smiled and stretched his legs, gazing down at the brilliant sheen of the river. "Of course not. I wanted to make a big juicy real estate deal."

Again she shook her head, then remembered what he'd said. "You just told me Jeb called you out here to talk business. Surely Natasha isn't still going ahead with this…"

Maggie hesitated, at a loss for words.

His eyes crinkled with amusement. "This daft plan?" he suggested.

"Yes," Maggie agreed. "This daft plan of hers."

"Not anymore," Doug said. "She's going to sell her other houses and move in with Jeb. But you'll all have to be prepared for the consequences, and Jeb and Natasha are certainly bracing for a backlash."

"So she really believes the studio will still fine her all those millions?"

"There's a good chance," Doug said. "People have long memories where money is involved. Especially huge amounts like that. But Natasha has a great plan, and a very generous one."

"I accused her today of not caring for anything but money," Maggie told him, her voice shaking. "How could I have been so wrong?"

He patted her shoulder in a comforting fashion.

"Natasha understands you, Maggie, and she adores you. Now that you know the truth, she's much more free to follow her heart. What she plans to do, actually, is divest herself of a good deal of her fortune in advance, just in case the studio lawyers come after her."

"How will she do that?" Maggie asked.

But from the glow on Doug's face, she already knew the answer.

"Right away, probably this week," he said, "Natasha's going to donate twenty million dollars to a charitable trust for the town of Crystal Creek. The money will be administered by a committee of trustees and be available to offer low-interest loans to town residents. It will also generate enough revenue to lower property taxes and still allow for civic improvements, scholarships for deserving kids, help for emerging businesses, all kinds of good things."

"Oh, Doug," she whispered, smiling. "Isn't that wonderful?"

He gave her a brief hug, then seemed to remember what he was doing and dropped his arm again. When it was gone, Maggie felt chilled and lonely.

"But Natasha and Jeb are more worried about the possible other consequences of getting together," he went on.

"What's that?"

"They're afraid your identity will be revealed, and your privacy compromised."

Maggie thought about the hordes of media she'd dealt with so often during her long career with Natasha, and the relentlessness with which they pursued any whiff of scandal.

"It's a sobering thought, all right," she admitted. "Doug, I'd be lying if I said I wasn't a bit daunted by the prospect."

"Natasha and Jeb aren't willing to live together if it's going to cause you any pain."

"Oh, for goodness' sake," Maggie said impatiently. "They've already sacrificed thirty years of their lives to protect me. I can deal with a bit of media scrutiny."

"Well, I can think of a way all that media interest wouldn't be a problem," Doug said, still gazing down at the river.

"How?" she asked.

"You can stay right here in Crystal Creek. Make it your home. Media people aren't going to hang around for more than a week in this backwater, Maggie. Not for some thirty-year-old scandal. If you aren't living in New York or traveling to London and Rome, nobody's going to pay much attention to you."

Wistfully, Maggie considered his suggestion.

How wonderful to stop jetting around the world, to stay in one place and put down roots, and make neighbors of the good-hearted people in this small ranching community.

"Rose and Terry and the little girls are going to be here," Doug said, pressing his point. "Those two seem to be so much in love all of a sudden, they can't keep their hands off each other. Neither of them will be going anywhere. And Natasha and Jeb are head over heels. They're going to be living right here in that house and watching the sunset over the river every night."

"But I..." Maggie looked down at her hands, twisted nervously together. "I need a job, Doug. I can't just hang around Crystal Creek and live off my new family like some lazy teenager."

"I'll give you a job," he said placidly. "You can keep the books for my hotel." He gave her a teasing glance. "You're a pretty good bookkeeper when you force yourself to concentrate."

For the first time Maggie nerved herself to look directly at him. "You'd really do that for me?" she whispered. "After all the things I've done, you don't...hate me?"

"Come on, Maggie, this is no way to conduct a job interview. You need to show a little more confidence."

"But I can't believe you still want me around, after all the things I said, and the way I behaved..."

His arm came around her again. Maggie settled gratefully into its warmth.

"When I was in Austin today," he murmured huskily in her ear, "I bought a gift for you."

Her heart began to pound. "What kind of gift?"

"It's a bonny wee basket for Dundee, all padded with tartan," he whispered. "I'm giving it to you, sweetheart, to keep wherever you please."

"But...what are you saying, Doug?"

"I'm saying you can have my cat."

She laughed, and wasn't aware of the tears flowing down her cheeks until he reached out to brush them away.

"Do you really mean it?" she asked.

"You already have my heart, Maggie," he murmured against her hair. "So you might as well take my cat, as well."

"Oh, Doug, I love you. I fell in love with you the first time I saw you, carrying Robin into the hotel lobby and setting her down so gently on the couch."

"Ah, but I loved you long before then," he said. "I loved you the first time I saw you driving around Crystal Creek, plotting to ruin my life."

She found his lips and kissed him, marveling at the sweetness of his mouth.

Now that all the problems were gone and the obstacles miraculously removed, kissing this man seemed like the most natural thing on earth. Maggie couldn't bring herself to draw away from him.

"You know, I was just thinking," she murmured against his lips, "that I always used to feel like one of those stars up there, cold and alone, a million miles away from everything. I had no roots, no basis for my existence. And now, suddenly, I have...everything. It's so hard to fathom."

"I know, dear," he murmured.

Maggie realized in the comforting warmth of his embrace that he fully understood the magnitude of what had happened to her on this amazing afternoon.

In fact, this man would always understand, as long as they lived.

"Now I feel more like one of these flowers," she whispered, "rooted in good soil, growing under a wide sky. And you're my sunshine, Doug."

"No way," he protested. "Nothing that far away. I'm growing right beside you, darling. And soon," he added with a touch of his irrepressible humor, "there could be some cross-pollination going on."

"Ye really, truly think so?" she teased, imitating his brogue.

"Aye, lassie." He gathered her into his arms, chuckling. "Flowers are like that. But," he added, lowering his voice to the husky burr she loved, "flower seeds are carried on the wind. I have a better way."

"Do you, now?"

Soon their laughter stilled and passion flared and sang between them. He kissed her with rising hunger, holding her tightly in his arms while the distant stars sang above them in the endless, eternal music of the spheres.

HARLEQUIN®
SUPERROMANCE®

You are now entering

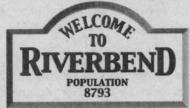

WELCOME TO
RIVERBEND
POPULATION
8793

Riverbend...the kind of place where everyone knows
your name—and your business. Riverbend...home of
the River Rats—a group of small-town sons and
daughters who've been friends since high school.

The Rats are all grown up now. Living their lives and
learning that some days are good and some days
aren't—and that you can get through anything
as long as you have your friends.

Starting in July 2000, Harlequin Superromance brings
you Riverbend—six books about the River Rats and
the Midwest town they live in.

BIRTHRIGHT by Judith Arnold (July 2000)
THAT SUMMER THING by Pamela Bauer (August 2000)
HOMECOMING by Laura Abbot (September 2000)
LAST-MINUTE MARRIAGE by Marisa Carroll (October 2000)
A CHRISTMAS LEGACY by Kathryn Shay (November 2000)

Available wherever Harlequin books are sold.

HARLEQUIN®
Makes any time special ™

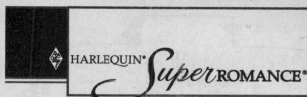

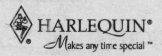

**Don't miss
an exciting opportunity
to save on the purchase of
Harlequin and *Silhouette* books!**

Buy any two Harlequin or
Silhouette books and save
$10.00 off future Harlequin
and Silhouette purchases

OR

buy any three
Harlequin or Silhouette books
and save **$20.00 off** future
Harlequin and Silhouette purchases.

**Watch for details
coming in October 2000!**

PHQ400

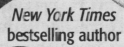